Elizabeth Andrews is a well known fae artist and author living amongst the green hills and valleys of the west country and is known for her love and knowledge of the country's folklore. It was this interest that led to her writing and illustrating her bestselling book
'Faeries and Folklore of the British Isles'
An illustrated guide to all the magical creatures that populate Britain. Following the interest this created she has since written and illustrated
'Faerie Flora'
an exploration of the myths and legends surrounding our most common flowers and plants.

First published in Great Britain 2012
A World of Magic Myth and Legend
www.magic-myth-legend.co.uk
Copyright Elizabeth Andrews 2012
The moral right of the author has been asserted
All rights reserved
No part of this publication may be reproduced, stored in a retrieval system or transmitted in any form or by any means, without the prior permission in writing of the author, nor be otherwise circulated in any form of binding or cover other than that in which it is published and without a similar condition being imposed on the subsequent purchaser.

The Lavender Witch

Elizabeth Andrews

Devon, a beautiful green county of gentle rolling hills and woodlands. Steeped in history and home to the Anglo Saxon tribe the Dumnonii from which the county reputedly gained its name. Dumnonii meaning 'deep valley dwellers'; an apt name for this beautiful countryside. Hiding scores of small villages and hamlets deep in the fertile valleys of the Blackdown Hills and reached by a maze of winding single track lanes enclosed on either side by high banks and hedges that in high summer grow together and meet overhead forming long green tunnels. Within just a few miles of the bustling towns and roads you enter a different world where the past is so close that it could be just around the next bend of the road.

The small village of Medbury, worthy of mention in the Domesday book is bounded by the river Yarty to the west and the county border of Dorset to the east, its single street winding its way along the valley and rising gently to the slopes of Castle Hill. The street peters out at the rambling buildings of Castle Farm, originally the last residence on that road but with the overgrown orchard to the side of the barn recently having been sold, a new dwelling had risen inside the old stone walls of the orchard. The builders rubble had gone, lush green turf had been laid and a new gravel drive led up to the front door. Orchard Cottage was finished, and deep in the soil something stirred

Friday

Protected by a low stone wall the orchard at Castle Farm had flourished for over a hundred years but over time neglect and disease had taken their toll. Only two gnarled and twisted trees now remained, a handful of shrivelled apples clinging to the moss covered branches.
Wasps, from a nearby nest, swarmed over the fruit sucking what little juice was left from the drying pulp.
   A stray insect flew in through the kitchen door and buzzed slowly around the room attracted by the empty tubs of the Indian food on the table. Kitty flicked it away with a tea towel and swept the debris into a carrier bag.
   'Thanks for bringing the take away.'
Gordon pushed his empty plate away and stood up, adjusting the belt over his bulging waistline. 'I drove past the Indian and thought of you.'
   'How romantic.'
   'Not really,' he said, looking at the piles of boxes in the hall, 'after coping with this all day I thought the last thing you would want to do is cook.'
   'I wasn't going to,' she confessed. 'It was going to be a sandwich and a sausage roll.'
   'What time did the removal company finish?'
Kitty sighed and pushed her greying hair back from her face.
   'I think we finished unpacking the van about five, so then they had one last cup of tea and went on after that.' She picked up the dirty plates and piled them in the sink. 'I've run out of milk as well, they drank so much tea and coffee. I was brewing up the whole time they were here.'
  'At t least they worked hard for it, moving all our junk in one trip! I'm sure they deserved all the tea they could drink for that mammoth task.'
A cool breeze blew in the door, outside dusk was falling and the last few minutes of bird song drifted over the newly landscaped garden.
   'Thank goodness it stayed dry, there's nothing worse than trying to move in the rain.'

Gordon opened the fridge. 'Yeah... We were lucky this time, is there enough milk left for a cup of tea?' he picked up the carton and shook it. 'Nope, it's dry,' he complained. 'It will have to be a black coffee.' Kitty pulled a couple of clean mugs out of a cardboard box on the table.

'I think I've got enough coffee left but we are out of tea. And by the way, there's something wrong with this door,' she indicated the back door. 'It won't stay open.'

Gordon raised his eyebrows and sighed mockingly. 'A new house and you're finding fault already.'

'I'm not finding fault, it just won't stay open. And the front door is just as bad. It kept shutting when we were trying to bring things in. I'm sure the men thought I was doing it for a joke, so Greg propped it open with your armchair. He had a look at it; he said it might be the hinges.'

Gordon rubbed a hand over his face. 'Okay, I'll look at it tomorrow; have you found the coffee yet?'

'What?'

'The coffee,' he said impatiently. 'Oh never mind, I've got it,' Gordon opened the jar. 'There's not enough here for one cup let alone two,' he looked at his watch.

'I wonder if the village shop is still open.'

Kitty looked up from the box. 'I shouldn't think so, not at this time of night.'

'Then there is nothing for it, we will have to go to the pub for a beer.'

'A beer? Well,' she hesitated. 'Yes, that would be nice, I could do with getting out of here for a while,' she looked at the dog who was pushing his now empty bowl around the floor. 'And Nero could do with a walk,' she bent down and fondled his ears. 'You've been such a good dog today, haven't you?' Kitty straightened slowly wincing. 'I'm going to ache tomorrow,' she complained, rubbing her back.

'You were supposed to leave the heavy lifting to the men.'

'I had to help Gordon; I couldn't stand back and just watch.' She turned away from him to shut the back door and noticed an elderly grey cat sitting in the doorway.

'Hey, we've got a visitor, our first one. Hello puss.' She put out a tentative hand and gently tickled it behind its ear. 'Now, who do you belong to?'

Gordon came back in from the hall, he had taken off his jacket and tie and had pulled on a thick jumper.

'Who are you talking to?'

'A cat,' she turned back to the door. 'Oh, it's gone already.'
'It's probably from the farm or a stray.'
'Too plump to be a stray.'
'Then it's from the village or the farm, and no... we are not taking it in,' he warned her.
'I wasn't thinking of that,' she muttered. 'Anyway Nero wouldn't like it, would you boy?'
She patted his head, stepped over him to shut the door then caught sight of her hands covered in the black ink from the newspapers.
'I had better wash my hands first, they are filthy from unpacking this lot,' she looked at the box of crockery. 'I should have got rid of all this china before we moved, who uses cups and saucers these days anyway?' she said, moving the box off the table. 'We've got far too much now.'
'Didn't you wash them before we ate?'
'Nope,' she grimaced. 'I forgot, I was too hungry, never mind,' she rinsed them quickly under the tap. 'A bit of ink won't kill me.'
Gordon waited impatiently as Kitty dried her hands and got the dog lead from the utility room.
'Are you ready now?'
'Yes,' she replied calmly. 'Where's my handbag?'
Gordon was walking to the front door and called back over his shoulder 'You don't need it, I've got some money. Will you come on, Kitty!'
Gordon pulled the door shut behind him and followed his wife down the drive. He glanced back at the house.
'Once we sort out the front garden the place will look as though it has always been here.'
Kitty stopped and turned round, she smiled contentedly. 'It blends in nicely with the old farm buildings, doesn't it? And it feels like home already.'
Gordon put his arm around her shoulder and gave her a hug as they walked out into the lane. 'We need to plant some more apple trees in the back garden; we can't call it Orchard Cottage if it hasn't got an orchard.'
'Perhaps we ought to grow some of the older types of apple, I wonder if Mr Beamish can remember what varieties the original trees were.'
'Maybe, it's a shame we couldn't keep a few more but I think most of the old trees were past saving.'

They turned right and followed the old stone wall of the orchard past the farm and walked down the lane into the village, the dog running a few paces in front of them

A bat swooped over their heads and disappeared into the farm buildings.

'What a lovely evening.'

The lights were still on in the small village shop as the couple walked past.

'It looks open,' said Kitty. 'Shall I try the door?'

An elderly woman stood behind the counter reading a newspaper, she looked up sensing she was being watched and smiled when she saw Kitty peering in through the window.

Kitty opened the door making the bell over the door tinkle madly.

'Are you still open?' she asked.

'Yes dear,' she looked at her wrist watch. 'Oh goodness! Is that the time? I didn't realise it was so late,' she shook her head and folded the newspaper.

'We've run out of milk, tea and coffee, all the necessities,' said Kitty with a smile.

'Are you usually open this late?'

'No, I just lost track of time, I don't usually work on Friday night but my nephew had an appointment so I volunteered.' The woman watched as Kitty wandered around the shop picking up what she needed, she also picked up a crusty loaf of bread. 'Freshly baked this morning, dear.'

'It smells lovely; I'll take one of these as well.' Kitty placed it all on the counter. 'Do you have any eggs?' she asked looking around the shelves.

'Over there by the newspapers. They're free range; they come from a local farm.'

Kitty placed a half a dozen next her other purchases on the counter. 'I'm afraid I didn't bring a bag, we weren't expecting the shop to be open.'

The woman pulled a carrier out from under the counter and started packing Kitty's groceries.

'How's the move going?' she asked suddenly. 'William's a good friend, he's been keeping me informed,' she smiled at Kitty's surprised face. 'It's a small village dear, you'll get used to it.'

Kitty smiled back at her. 'It's lovely here, it feels like home already.'

'I'm sure it does,' the woman said quietly. She passed Kitty's shopping over. 'That will be six pounds fifty please.'

Kitty opened Gordon's wallet and handed over a ten pound note. The women's hand closed over the money and Kitty's hand.

   'Sybil,' she said.

   'Sorry?'

   'Sybil Leavenham, my name,' she explained. 'I know you're going to be happy here Kitty, and if you need help with anything,' she shook Kitty's hand as if to emphasis the point. 'Anything at all just ask.'

   Kitty smiled hesitantly. 'Thank you, that's very kind of you.'
Sybil smiled and released her hand; she nodded towards Gordon standing outside.

   'He's getting impatient and he wants his beer.'
Kitty glanced around; her husband was gently tapping on the window and gesturing at her to her to hurry up.

   'I'd better go,' she gathered up the bag and her change. 'Thanks, see you again.'

   'Oh you will. Goodnight.'
Kitty smiled and pulled the shop door closed behind her. Gordon looked at the carrier bag in her hand and smiled ruefully.

   'I thought it was just milk and coffee you were getting?'

   'I needed a few things for breakfast as well.' Kitty handed back his wallet and looked up, Sybil was standing in the window calmly watching the couple outside.
Kitty waved and she smiled slightly in response.

   'She seemed very nice; she's a friend of Mr Beamish. She knew all about us.'

   'The village spy network.'

   'She even knew I was called Kitty.'
Gordon looked puzzled for a minute. He started to say something but behind them the shop lights suddenly turned off leaving them standing in the dark street.

   'Time to go I think,' as he said this, he turned and glanced back into the darkened interior of the shop. Just on the other side of the window a dim figure stood, arms folded watching them through the glass. Gordon shrugged off the strange feeling of unease and took Kitty's hand. 'Come on; let's get off to the pub, Kitty.'

   The street was deserted, pools of light shone out of the cottage windows lighting their way down to the public house. They crossed the narrow lane leading to Castle Hill and walked the few yards to the traditional square red brick building, which had a brand new sign hanging over the front door.

'The Witch and Broomstick. They've changed the name. It used to be The Red Lion,' said Gordon.

'I don't remember coming here before,' said Kitty glancing at Gordon in the dim light. She stared up at the lurid painted sign; it depicted a fearsome looking witch riding across the night sky on a broomstick.

'What a strange thing to call a pub.'

'Remind you of anybody?' Gordon asked, raising an eyebrow.
Kitty looked puzzled. 'Not really.'

'No? I thought it was quite a good likeness of your mother.' He laughed at her indignant face and pushed open the door to the public bar and reminded her, 'I used to play darts here many years ago with the Young Farmers Club.'

'Of course... Your wild, misspent youth.'

'Really wild, half a pint of cider and a bag of chips on the way home,' Gordon grinned at her and shrugged.

'Yes and I expect you still had change from a shilling or was it a farthing?'

'Half a pig actually, so who's buying, you or me?'

'You are, I left my bag at home, remember?'

'Oh darn,' he said ruefully.

Inside it was deserted except for the landlord who was wiping down the bar. It was a traditional pub with horse brasses hanging from the old beams with a few unusual additions to the decor.
Gordon bumped his head on one as he approached the bar.

'Good evening, what can I get you?'

'Evening, nice and quiet in here,' said Gordon, looking around the small room. 'Well, now let's see... what local beers have you got?'
The landlord smiled. 'It's a bit early for the regulars yet, they'll be in later. Now,' he said, turning to the pumps. 'We have Plymouth Pilgrim, Hunters Gold, or there's Palmers IPA, and I've just put on a fresh barrel of Otter.'

'I'll try a pint of the Otter thanks, what will you have Kitty?'

'I think I'll have the same but just a half.'
Kitty stared at the toy witches hanging from the beams.

'Why witches? Are you getting ready for Halloween already?'

'They are up there because of our famous local witch, The Witch of Medbury.'

'Who? I've never heard of her,' said Kitty, puzzled.

'You can't be local then if you've never heard of Hannah.'

'My family are local, from Axmouth. They used to run The Ship Inn,' said Kitty.

'Indeed? Here you are sir,' he answered and placed a foaming beer glass in front of Gordon who took a mouthful.
'That's a good brew,' he said appreciatively. 'That doesn't sound like a Devon accent, where are you from?'
'My partner and I are from Woking in Surrey. We think it's important to keep the local traditions alive. It's surprising that so few people around here know about her.'
'Really,' Gordon said drily.
'Rumour has it that she was an evil old woman who terrorised the village, it's even said that she killed several people. She was snatched away by old Nick himself at the end.'
'Where did you find out about all this? It sounds like nonsense to me,' said Gordon, disparagingly.
'Sheena is very interested in the occult, she has been researching the witch and thought it would be great to try and bring local history alive. She was even thinking of having a séance here.'
'A séance?' said Kitty.
'Perhaps you'd be interested in attending?'
'I don't think so,' replied Gordon hurriedly and pushed Kitty towards a small table near the fireplace. 'I don't think we want to get involved in anything like that.'
Nero, following closely and their heels plodded over to the smouldering fire and sat down on the hearth with his nose just inches from the burning embers. Kitty hooked a finger through his collar and pulled him away from the fire.
'Move you silly dog, you'll burn,' she said, pushing him under the table. 'Now sit there, I hope they don't mind the dog coming in but the landlord didn't say anything did he?'
Gordon placed the glasses down on the table and sat down.
'The dog is fine Kitty, stop fussing.' He put a glass in front of her. 'There you are.'
'Thanks.' She picked up one of the beer mat from the table and peered at the crude cartoon. 'Look, the witch is on here as well.'
Kitty handed it to Gordon for him to read and while he searched for his glasses in his coat pocket she took the opportunity to gaze around the pub. Her examination of the profusion of horse brasses hanging around the fireplace was cut short by the sound of Gordon laughing as he read out the text on the mat. '"*The Witch of Medbury*
In the early 1800's at Castle Hill near the village of Medbury lived a witch called Hannah, who was reputed to possess great powers. She was the most famous witch in East Devon and could change into a

hare, bewitch animals and it is said her powers caused the death of several residents of the village. Hannah died a horrible death dragged out of her cottage on Castle Hill by the Devil and left hanging in a tree." For God's sake where did they dig this nonsense up from?'

'Perhaps they're going to turn this into a theme pub with a hologram of a hags head coming out of the wall.'

'They could hire your mother to sit in the corner of the bar, an authentic witch. Can she cackle?

'Oh how cruel!' she laughed. 'Anyway she would scare all the trade away.'

'Very true....well, here's to the first day in our new home.' Gordon raised his glass to his wife. 'Here's to our new home, at last!' And settled back in his chair; closing his eyes he sighed, 'I've been looking forward to this for months, no maintenance, no painting windows, no worrying about guttering or dodgy drains, great!'

'The old house wasn't that bad.'

'I was tired of having to continually patch things up and we don't need all that space, not now.'

Kitty looked a bit glum. 'Will we have room for all the children at Christmas?'

He stared at her over the top of his glass. 'They're not children anymore; they have all got their own homes and families. We can go to them for Christmas; let the kids wait on us for a change.'

'The grandchildren will still be able to come and stay if they want, we'll be able to squeeze two or three into the spare room, that would be nice,' she said hopefully.

Gordon took a few mouthfuls of beer and sighed contentedly. 'They don't need to stay; they only live a few miles away. I'm looking forward to a nice peaceful retirement, no kids, no decorating, just fishing!'

Kitty shook her head. 'I'm sure you don't mean that and anyway you're not retired yet.'

She sipped her beer slowly and stared at her husband.

Gordon put down his glass. 'Just one more year and that will be it.'

The landlord came over and gave the smouldering fire a vigorous poke and then placed a fresh log on the rekindled flames.

'It's a bit early for a fire but it gives the place a welcoming feel, don't you think?' he asked, addressing Kitty.

'Yes, a fire is always nice,' she agreed. 'And it's getting chillier in the evenings now; I think our Indian summer is over.'

He nodded in agreement. 'Are you here on holiday?'

'No, we've just moved into Orchard Cottage, at the top of the village.'

The landlord looked blank. 'I don't think I know that property.'

'It's the new house at Castle Farm,' explained Kitty. 'We bought the orchard from Mr Beamish.'

'Of course, Castle Farm, I know the one you mean. We walked up the lane a few weeks ago; it's those lovely old buildings at the top isn't it?'

'That's right,' said Kitty.

'We haven't seen Mr Beamish in the pub yet.'

Kitty looked at him in amusement. 'I don't think you will; he is rather elderly.'

'Did you say you were from Axmouth?' he went on, 'That's a busy little village isn't it? Right on the holiday route. There is a nice pub there; I can't remember what it's called.'

'The Ship,' put in Kitty.

'No, no, I'm sure it was The Admiral. We stayed there while we were viewing different properties. Very busy little pub and it is a nice area. W e didn't realise how quiet this village was when we leased this pub.'

'Medbury *is* off the beaten track,' agreed Kitty.

'Yes, but,' he brightened, 'We do have plans, we're going to concentrate on food and try and get a regular clientele and give it a bit of atmosphere. Sheena is working on the menu this morning. She's going to experiment with a Caribbean theme; she wants to get away from the usual pub grub. Gastro pub I think she calls it.'

'Good food will attract customers, even out here,' said Kitty. 'We'll look forward to seeing how you get on.'

'We'll be launching the new menu in a few weeks, I hope you will be able to come and join us?'

Kitty glanced at Gordon uncertainly. 'Yes I'm sure we will be able to make it, won't we?'

'Wonderful, I'll be able to tell Sheena that we have had positive feedback already.'

Kitty nodded and smiled faintly at him as he hurried back to the bar. 'Caribbean?'

'Hmm... He's going to have a table reserved for you now.'

'Oh well, it might be okay, I'm not sure how that is going to go down with the locals though, I'm sure they would rather have good pub grub.' Kitty yawned and rubbed the back of her neck. 'I'm so tired and stiff, everything is aching and I'm really looking forward to a long soak in the tub tonight. It seems a long time since the removal van came this morning.' She hesitated. 'It's a shame you couldn't get the day off to help, it would have made it a bit easier.'

'That's why I hired that removal company, so they could do the work, not you.'

'Yes but even so...'

'I told you that we are really busy at the moment and I couldn't spare the time Kitty. Now would you like another drink?'

'No. Thanks.'

'Okay, let's get on back then as you're tired. We can have an early night and finish unpacking in the morning.'

Gordon picked up the empty glasses and took them back to the bar.

'Thanks,' he said, ducking his head to avoid the witches.

'Thank you, hope to see you again,' called the landlord from behind the bar.

'I'm sure we will be back and we'll give your regards to the witch if we see her on the way home.'

****

Outside it was already dark and there was an autumnal nip in the air. They walked slowly back up the hill towards the cottage, a few cars speeding past on their way home from the coast.

Just outside the farmhouse Mr Beamish was talking to the elderly lady from the shop.

'Hello,' he called across. 'Been for a walk? Mrs Leavenham said she saw you earlier.'

'We needed groceries and some fresh air, so we abandoned everything and retreated to the pub,' said Kitty, smiling at the pair.

Mrs Leavenham said comfortably, 'It always takes a few days to get sorted and settle in.'

Mr Beamish smiled, his pale blue eyes disappearing into the wrinkles around his eyes. 'It's a lovely evening for a stroll, and this weather is supposed to last a few more days.'

It was difficult to tell how old he was, his face was quite careworn and rugged and he had the peculiarity of farmers his age that while the lower part of his face was ruddy and weathered the forehead was soft, white and unlined from spending the most part of his life wearing a cap.

He ran his hand through his thinning hair. 'It's nice to have you moved in at last, though I have enjoyed watching the house go up. It's amazing how quickly they can build a house these days.'

'All this activity going on in William's orchard has kept him entertained for weeks you know,' Mrs Leavenham looked at the old man sympathetically. 'He's going to miss talking to those builders of yours.'

Mr Beamish started laughing. 'If it hadn't been for me I'm sure your house would have been built in half the time.'

'You must come in and have a coffee when you're passing and have a look around now it's finished.'

'I'll take you up on that.'

****

'Did that cat come through here?' asked Kitty, hurrying into the kitchen.

'What cat?'

'The grey one I saw earlier, from the farm.'

Gordon looked up from his newspaper and stared at her over his glasses; he finished a mouthful of sandwich and shook his head. 'I didn't see a cat.'

'I was coming down the stairs and it was sat in the hall.'

'Look in the front room then.'

'It couldn't have gone in there, the door's shut.' She peered around the kitchen and under the table. 'Are you sure it didn't come in here?'

'You must have been seeing things, Kitty.'

'Oh for goodness sake, that's your answer for everything isn't it?' she said sarcastically. 'Kitty's seeing things!'

'Okay, calm down,' he answered irritably. 'If there is a cat in here somewhere it will pop out soon enough. Open a tin of Tuna or something, the smell will bring it out from where ever it's hiding.'

Kitty snorted and went back into the hall; she stared around the small space wondering how she could have missed it.

'What's all this on the doormat?'

'Not cat poo I hope,' he said drily.

'No... It's dried up twigs or something,' Kitty bent and picked up a piece. 'It's lavender! How strange, where did that come from?'

She stared down at the fragrant stalks in her hand and shook her head.

'You must have tracked it in from the garden, or the dog did.'

'There isn't any lavender in the garden. There is nothing left alive out there, apart from the two apple trees, the diggers saw to that.'

'I expect there is, somewhere,' said Gordon, turning back to his newspaper.
Kitty straightened and sighed rubbing her head, she looked at the scattered seeds and twigs on the mat.

'I can't be bothered to clean this up now; I have had enough for today. I'll do it in the morning.'
Gordon yawned and pushed his plate away from him.

'Yeah it can wait, let's have an early night and we'll finish unpacking in the morning.

****

Kitty pulled back the duvet and climbed thankfully into bed, she lay back against the soft pillows and closed her eyes, hoping the nagging headache she'd had all evening would go.
The sound of Gordon rattling about in the bathroom receded. As she began to doze soft footsteps approached across the bedroom carpet. Her side of the bed dipped slightly and a cool hand began to gently stroke the hair away from her forehead.

'Night,' Kitty mumbled, not even bothering to open her eyes, her bedside light clicked off leaving that side of the room in darkness and Kitty was just aware of a figure walking slowly across the room and out onto the landing.

Saturday

'I thought you had cleaned this up?'
'What?' Kitty called from the utility room.
'All this mess on the front door mat.'
'I did it earlier with the vacuum cleaner.'
'It's still here, Kitty,' he said impatiently, shaking his head.
He hefted the pile of books to one arm and bent down to pick up the mat, meaning to shake it outside. The books started to slip from his grasp as he did so and spilled onto the floor. 'Dammit!'
'What's the matter?' asked Kitty, coming into the hall.
'I'm trying to do two things at once and failing miserably,' he snapped. 'Look at this mess.'
Kitty looked at the lavender scattered over the floor.
'I'm sure I did that,' she said puzzled.
'Well you couldn't have, you probably meant to and went on and did something else and forgot about it. I know what you're like.'
Gordon took a firm grip on the pile of books and walked off into the sitting room leaving Kitty staring blankly at the mat.
I'm sure I did it. Didn't I? she thought to herself.
 Shaking her head she headed back into the kitchen to fetch a broom. Nero's tail was gently thumping on the side of his bed and he was staring intently at the back door.
Kitty opened the back door for him.
'Did you want to go out Nero?'
He clambered out of his bed and stared out into the garden wagging his tail, Kitty followed his gaze.
Sat just outside on the path was the grey cat.
'Hello puss,' Kitty said softly.
She looked down and held out her hand, as she did so she saw their new neighbour Mr Beamish standing at the end of the garden and staring intently over the wall towards her. Kitty raised her hand and waved at the old man before looking down at the cat again.
The cat didn't move, it just fixed her with a calm gaze from its strange pale eyes then stood up, stretched and sauntered past her into the kitchen.
'Oh come in, please,' she said, smiling in amusement. 'And Nero behave yourself,' she told him firmly.

The cat rubbed itself against Kitty's legs purring gently.

'You are friendly, aren't you?' she said, bending down and gently tickling the cat behind its ear. 'Would you like something to eat? How about some Tuna? That's all I've got, I'm afraid.'

The cat followed Kitty around the kitchen purring gently while she found a saucer and a tin of fish in the cupboard.

'Talking to yourself again?' inquired Gordon, from the hall. He came to the door and peered into the kitchen holding a box in his arms.

'The cat is here again, so I'm going to feed it,' said Kitty, opening the tin of Tuna.

'It has obviously taken a fancy to you Kitty, or it knows you're a soft touch.'

'Who, me?' she grinned.

Kitty turned back to the cat, saucer in hand but it had disappeared from the kitchen.

She glanced out into the garden but there was no sign of it outside the house either.

'My! That cat moves fast, it's disappeared again.' She looked at the saucer full of fish she had prepared for it. 'Oh well, never mind, I'll put it outside the door and hopefully the cat will find it.'

'If Nero doesn't find it first.'

'He's not going to touch it, and anyway I'll shut the door so he can't get it.'

'We're not adopting a cat, you know I don't like cats,' he said firmly.

'That's why it ran away,' she said, pointing an accusing finger at him.

'Yeah, my fault again.'

Kitty looked at the box he was holding. 'What's in there?'

'Photographs, I think some of them are framed so you'll have to sort through them and decide which ones you want up. We haven't got room for all of them on the walls.' Gordon walked back into the hall. 'I'll put the box in the sitting room for now,' he called over his shoulder.

'Okay, I'm just coming.' Kitty placed the saucer of food outside and looked towards the end of the garden where the apple trees were. Mr Beamish was still leaning on the wall staring across at the house, she waved uncertainly at him and quickly shooed Nero back into the kitchen. 'Go on in Nero,' she said quietly. 'And no, you're not having it,' she said, shutting the door firmly.

Nero sighed and followed her sulkily into the sitting room.

'Where's the box?' she inquired.

'Over there.' He gestured to the oak bookshelf behind the sofa; the box was sitting on the top shelf.
She started sorting through the box pulling out different photographs of the children in various poses.

'Look at this one of Eve and Roger at the zoo, that's a nice photo and there's this one of all of us on holiday in Scotland. That's a nice one as well.' Kitty put the two pictures to one side and continued pulling out different framed prints. 'Our wedding, that will have to go up and this one of your parents...'

'Not too many Kitty, I don't want you cluttering up the place like the last house.'

'It wasn't cluttered,' she said indignantly. 'It was homely.'

'Let's try being homely without so much clutter.'

'You're such a grump Gordon. We've got some lovely pictures of the children and I want to display them,' she said firmly.

'Just choose the more recent ones then,' he suggested.

'In that case I'll leave out your parents' picture,' she replied tartly.

'Suits me.'

Kitty turned her back on him and rummaged further into the box. Right at the bottom was an old album full of faded sepia photographs. I'd forgotten I had this, she thought to herself turning the thick brown pages. 'I've found mother's old photo album,' she said to Gordon.

'Hmm?'

She looked closely at the groups posing stiffly in their best clothes.

'I'm not sure who all these people are,' she said, slowly turning to the last page. 'Oh... I recognise this group,' Kitty said, pleased to able to recognise the faces. 'This is great-granny's family.' She looked closely at the group. 'It must have been a wedding, they all look very grand and some of the men are wearing buttonholes. I wonder whose wedding it was? It doesn't say...'

'Ask your mum, she's bound to know,' Gordon said absently, untangling some wires that he had found in the box. 'I was so careful to coil these up neatly and now look at them. Right, now this is the one I wanted, and I'm sure I put it in the box with the television,' he grumbled.

'Do you need a hand with that?'

'Nope, I'll have all these wires plugged in next to no time now I have found everything. I could do with a cup of tea though.'

She closed the album and placed it back in the box, picked up the framed prints she had chosen and placed them on the coffee table.

'Here are the pictures I'd like up, Gordon.'

He glanced at the pile. 'How many have you got there?'

'It's only a few, there are some more in another box upstairs. There's that lovely picture of Emily somewhere.'

'Oh yes, that will have to go up.'

'Now that's sorted I will go and make some tea.' Kitty walked out into the hall, Nero following closely at her heels. 'I suppose you're waiting for your tea as well,' she said, looking down at the dog but he had stopped and was staring up at the top of the stairs. He started to whine gently, and Kitty quickly looked up to the landing almost expecting to see the cat but there was nothing there.

'What are you looking at you silly dog?' But Nero continued to stare his ears pricked; his tail was gently wagging and banging against Kitty's leg. She looked again at the empty space at the top of the stairs and then at the dog. 'What is it?'

Nero looked at her then at the stairs, still wagging his tail. 'You're a silly dog, come on.' She coaxed him into the kitchen and picked his food bowl up off of the floor. He followed Kitty reluctantly, still staring towards the hall then soon lost interest when he heard the dog biscuits being poured into the bowl.

Kitty made the tea and leant against the worktop thoughtfully watching as he finished off the last few biscuits. He pushed the bowl around the kitchen floor hopefully searching for any that he had missed, and then climbed into his bed. Nero wagged his tail at Kitty and settled down with his head between his paws.

'The dog's seeing things,' she said, walking back in to the sitting room with the tray of tea.

'Seeing what?'

'I don't know; something in the hall.'

'That dog is as daft as you are.'

Gordon was kneeling in front of the television trying to sort out the wires for the DVD player.

'You are such a charmer Gordon, and here's your tea.'

Kitty put the tray down on the coffee table and leant against the old oak mantelpiece watching as he pulled the television out from the corner of the room.

'This has worm,' she said, looking closely at the fireplace. Kitty ran her hand along the pitted wood and yawned. 'And there are holes all along the top.' She rested her head against it and yawned again.

'It was treated at the reclamation yard before it was delivered.' He stood up and came over to Kitty. He ran his hand lovingly over the old wood. 'It's beautiful isn't it? Look at these marks, years of wear. I wonder what this fireplace has seen, eh?'

Kitty looked at it doubtfully. 'It is nice but don't you think it's a bit big? It dominates the room. I think something smaller would have been better.'

'No, no, it's perfect, it's just what I wanted for this room, it gives it character,' Gordon said firmly.

'I guess I'll get used to it; as long as the wood worm doesn't spread.' She rested her head against the wood again and yawned. 'Oh boy, I'm tired.'

Kitty stood watching her husband as he pushed the television back into the corner. She closed her eyes for what just seemed a second, the noises in the room slowly receded and her mind began to drift.

'*Kitty*'

'Mmm?' she murmured, her eyes flickering open.

'What?' asked Gordon vaguely.

'Did you say something to me? '

He didn't answer; Gordon was staring in frustration at the instruction manual. 'These inscrutable Japanese, I can't understand a word of this!'

Kitty straightened and rubbed the small of her back. 'I'm dozing off, I had better move before I fall asleep altogether. I'll go and find some cake, would you like a piece to go with your tea?'

Gordon didn't answer, but she knew from experience that he never turned down cake so she walked slowly out into the hall and glanced through the window as she went past.

'There's Mr Beamish,' she called through to him. 'He's been hanging around outside all afternoon. Shall I invite him in for tea?'

He stood at the end of the drive leaning on a stick and staring intently at the house, his cap pulled low over his eyes.

Gordon followed her out into the hall, wires in one hand and instruction manual in the other. He peered over his wife's shoulder. 'He's admiring the house I expect,' and tucking the manual under his arm, tapped on the window and waved.

With one last long look Mr Beamish turned and walked slowly away down the lane to the farmhouse.

'I thought he would like to come in. He looked a bit grim, don't you think?' Kitty looked at Gordon in surprise.

'Perhaps he's having a bad day.'

Kitty suddenly felt worried. 'You don't think he's regretting selling us the orchard do you?'

'Kitty, for goodness sake why should he? You heard him yesterday he's been enjoying watching the house go up. And anyway we gave him a good price for the land; he's laughing all the way to the bank.'

'He didn't look as though he was laughing,' Kitty for some strange reason shivered.

Gordon looked at her. 'Some cake would be nice.'

'Okay, okay, I'm going!'

She opened the cupboard to get a couple of plates and as she shut the door a slight scent of lavender wafted around her head. Slightly puzzled she stepped back looking around the kitchen.

There was a yelp from behind her. 'Oh Nero! You made me jump. Sorry, did I step on your toes?' Kitty patted the dog's head and picked up the cake tin.

She heard footsteps approaching along the tiled hall floor and out of the corner of her eye caught a flicker of movement in the doorway.

'I'm just coming,' Kitty said turning around.

The doorway was empty.

'What was that?' Gordon called through from the sitting room.

Kitty blinked in surprise, she was just going to answer him when she heard the same footsteps run lightly up the stairs.

Kitty hurried out into the hall and stared up the stairs. 'Gordon, was that you?' she called.

'Was what me?'

Kitty spun around in surprise, Gordon was still kneeling in front of the television, tuning in the channels.

'I heard somebody run upstairs, I thought it was you.'

He looked up from the control box and peered over his spectacles. 'Perhaps it was the dog.'

'No,' she said impatiently. 'He was in the kitchen with me.' Kitty looked nervously up the stairs and then glanced into the front room at her husband. 'Do you think you ought to go and look?'

'I would have noticed if somebody had come in the front door.' He continued flicking through the different channels and then looked up as Kitty remained hovering nervously in the doorway. 'Kitty,' he said impatiently. 'You just heard a few creaks and groans that's all, perhaps it was the wind outside or something. Are you going to stand there all afternoon?'

She looked uncertainly up the stairs. 'But I heard somebody go up there, I'm sure it was footsteps, Gordon.'

Kitty walked to the bottom of the staircase and peered up, the light was fading and the area above was in shadow.

'There is nobody in the house except us,' he stated, his attention back on the television. Gordon glanced towards her still hovering in the hall and said impatiently, 'Well go and check then if it will make you feel better.'

She stepped back hesitantly and moved into the front room. 'I don't suppose it was anything, like you said it was probably the wind.'

Sunday

'I think I'll explore that footpath as you are going fishing.' Kitty stared out the kitchen window into the garden. A light breeze was blowing across the tops of the trees, and the sky was clear and bright apart from a few clouds scudding across the horizon. 'It's too nice to stay indoors.'

'It's a lovely morning, that's why I thought I would make the most of it before I go back to the grind tomorrow.'

'What time are you going?' she asked, finishing the washing up and stacking it in the drainer.

'Why don't you use the dishwasher?' he asked impatiently.

'It's only a few cups and plates; it's quicker to do it like this.' She picked up a tea towel and started to dry the plates.

'What you mean is that you haven't worked out how to use it yet.'

'I didn't want one, you're the one who insisted on having the silly thing,' she said calmly, before pushing past him to pack the china away in the cupboards

Gordon sighed and started to put a few things into a lunch box. 'I just thought it would make your life easier, that's all.'

'But there's just the two of us now Gordon, I could have done with one when the children were living at home, that would have been really useful.'

Kitty picked up the thermos she had prepared for him and handed it to him.

'There you are, it's coffee, is that alright or would you prefer tea?'

'You didn't have to do that, I'm quite capable of making it for myself,' he said, taking it from her and pushing it into the corner of his bag.

Kitty didn't answer, she busied herself wiping around the new granite worktops and watched him packing the rest of his food into the rucksack.

'What's the weather forecast?' he asked.

'Fine all day and rain coming in tonight.'

'That sounds okay, so I won't get wet while I'm out. I'll be off as soon as I've found everything.'

Kitty folded her arms and leant back against the sink watching as he rummaged through the boxes in the utility room looking for his fishing reels.

'Looks like you'll be going next week then.'

'Ha, ha,' he said drily.

Kitty shifted and pushed herself away from the worktop. 'I think I'll get ready and go now, it looks so lovely out there and Nero needs his walk.'

The dog looked up when he heard his name and wagged his tail.

'Which footpath?' enquired Gordon.

'I'm going to try the path up the lane; I think it leads towards the hill.'

'Isn't that Castle Hill?'

'I'm not too sure, but I'll find out when I get there.' Kitty put her boots and raincoat next to the front door. 'Right, my things are ready, how about you Gordon?'

He was pulling out different rods and examining them. 'I think I will take this one today. Right,' he said. 'I have got everything I need so I'm going and I'll see you later.' With that he kissed Kitty on the top of her head and walked out of the front door.

'Good luck dear,' she called after him.' Bring back a big one!'

****

Kitty walked briskly up the narrow lane, it was little used and a ridge of grass had grown up in the middle of the road which was full of pot holes.

Nero trotted along in front pushing his nose in to all the interesting smells along the way, finding all the rabbit holes that were hidden deep in the hedges. By the time they had reached the stile his fur was covered in dirt and grass seeds

'You're in a state already Nero and we haven't got to the hill yet.' Kitty said, panting from the steep climb up the lane.

The signpost pointing to the hill was lying half in the hedge almost covered by a tangle of flowering bindweed, the lettering faded and illegible. She found the stile buried deep in nettles and brambles. It didn't look as though it had seen much use recently, the wood was rotten and the whole thing looked extremely rickety.

Kitty tentatively pushed the prickly branches out of the way, careful not to get snagged then clambered over while Nero scrabbled underneath.

It was difficult to see where the footpath led but Kitty headed for the hedge that ran up to the top of the hill. It was the remains of an old moss covered wall from which over many years trees had sprouted and grown twisted and shrunken, their roots reaching from the wall like bony fingers.

She reached the top of the hedge and paused, turning to look at the view, giving herself time to catch her breath. She pulled down the zip of her coat and let the cool morning breeze blow around her. The hillside was bright with the morning sunshine and below her the river snaked its way through the green fields to the harbour at Seaton. The tide was out and the muddy flats stretched out on either side of the narrow channel of the river.

Cormorants and ducks waded about in the mud and Kitty caught sight of a white egret, a recent immigrant to the area.

On the horizon grey storm clouds were gathering, it looked as though the predicted evening's rain was going to arrive early.

At the top of the hedge another stile led into a small rutted track that snaked around the side of the hill. Kitty followed it as it led upwards to the top which was crowned in a small coppice of hazel.

Underneath the trees the air was cool and green dappled, she walked slowly following the dog snuffling along in the long grass. The path ended abruptly in a thick tangle of bramble, not deterred Nero pushed his way through regardless of the thorns.

'Nero, where are you going? You silly dog.' Kitty pushed through after him, tearing her coat on the thorns and stubbing her foot on a pile of old bricks hidden in the tangled undergrowth. 'Damn,' she grumbled, surprised to see the remains of an old building on the hill. Although there wasn't much left of the structure, just four crumbling walls surrounding a stone slab floor. There was evidence of an old garden behind the cottage walls, overgrown but a few robust rose bushes still struggled to bloom in the tangle.

Kitty caught the fragrance from some straggling lavender bushes lining a path that trailed off in front of her. The grass was surprisingly short in the clearing but then Kitty caught a glimpse of a small white tail disappearing quickly under the brambles. Nero bounded after the rabbit in hot pursuit, but it ran beneath the tangled stems and disappeared down its burrow. The stems of the bramble bushes were too thick for the dog to push his way through and he whined in frustration and started scrabbling in the sandy soil trying to dig the rabbit out of its hole.

Sunlight shone through the trees making the clearing bright and cheerful; bees buzzed around the lavender creating such a feeling of peace that Kitty perched for a moment on part of the wall.

Closing her eyes she lifted her smiling face to the sun enjoying the warmth. She lost all track of time sitting in the sun but gradually became aware of the sound of footstep approaching up the stony lane and the regular thump of a stick on the ground. Kitty's eyes flicked open; the sunlight had faded and a chill wind sprang up and blew across the clearing making the dried stems of the lavender rustle. Kitty shivered, suddenly aware how quiet and remote the ruined cottage was. Nero came trotting up to her, his tail down and ears drooping. He pushed his head into Kitty's lap and whined.

'Come on let's go,' she said quietly, and stood up. The footsteps came closer and she fancied she could hear the sound of breathing behind the tangle of brambles.

She walked quickly off down the path; outside the confines of the garden it seemed darker as though the storm clouds had already arrived. For a moment Kitty was reluctant to leave the warmth and light of the garden but a few stones rattled behind her, and calling the dog hurried off through the old garden gate that was still hanging from its wooden post. A narrow path led off down the hillside and Kitty followed it, half running, eager to get off the hill and away from whatever or whoever was behind her.

The path widened as she got farther down but it became increasingly rough with stones and potholes, gullies that had been gouged out by rain water and then filled with silky mud and sand. Kitty scrambled on worried that she would sprain an ankle; the thought of being stuck there with an injury made her slow down and take more care. Glancing behind Kitty could see nothing but the feeling persisted that she was being followed.

Nero's ears were still down and every now and then he would stop, look back up the path and growl.

'Nero come on,' she called impatiently. She had spotted a gate, and on the other side of that was a narrow road. 'There's a road, hurry up.'

Nero had stopped completely and was staring back up the path, his hackles were up and he was trembling. He started growling at the dark shadows under the trees as more stones rattled down the path after them.

The unexpected sound of a car driving down the narrow lane made her start; Nero barked defiantly one last time at the shadows and came running over to her side.

'Come on.'

Kitty hurried down the hill hopping over the potholes and reached the gate. She leant on it for a few minutes getting her breath and stared back up towards the hill; she still had a strange prickling feeling of being watched by unfriendly eyes. Kitty opened the gate and stepped out into the road, in the distance were a few buildings and she could just see the church tower. She followed the road downhill hoping to get to the village quickly and plodded on, her legs aching from the unaccustomed exercise but very relieved to be off the hill. Kitty only glanced behind her once as she walked into the village, just to her left was the public house The Witch and Broomstick and even though it was still quite early there were already people sitting outside with drinks.

Kitty waved and called, 'good morning' in relief. Turning right she headed back up the road to the cottage with Nero tucked in close to her side.

There was low rumble of thunder and the sun disappeared behind the dark clouds that Kitty had seen earlier. A gust of wind blew up the hill and whipped her hair into her eyes.

'Looks like we timed this well, Nero.'

A few spots of rain spattered on the road. Her legs were too tired to hurry but they still managed to make it back to the house before the rain started to fall too heavily.

Kitty unlocked the back door and pushed it open.

'Come on inside before we get wet.'

Nero collapsed into his basket near the radiator with a sigh, his tail giving a few brief thumps.

'Tired?' she bent and gave the panting dog a reassuring pat. 'That was an interesting walk wasn't it!' Kitty laughed nervously to herself. 'I don't think I'll be going up there on my own again.' On that thought Kitty locked the back door. 'There! Now I'll put the kettle on and calm down.'

Kitty had just finished making herself a sandwich when she heard a car on the gravel drive, a door clunked shut and there was her husband coming in the front door laden down with bags of tackle and fishing rods.

'I didn't expect to see you for a while.'

'I gave up, I was all fingers and thumbs today and nothing was biting. And the weather wasn't looking too good so I decided to come home.'

'Would you like a sandwich? I'm just making myself one.'

'Please, I ate my lunch in the first hour, I was so bored.' Gordon put his bag down on the table and gave her a quick kiss. 'How was your walk?'
Kitty buttered some bread and started slicing some cheese.

'I found a cottage up there, it was in ruins though and an old garden with roses and lavender, it was lovely. Except somebody else was up there and I got a bit spooked. Silly really but I didn't hang around so I followed the lane down and came out near the pub.'
Gordon filled the kettle, turned it on and took a mug from the cupboard.

'Isn't the witch's cottage up there, on Castle Hill?'

'Perhaps it was her,' she joked.

'No, it was probably some farmer wondering what a middle aged woman was doing trespassing on his land,' he sounded a bit short.

'It was a footpath,' Kitty said defiantly.

'Well you don't know who could be wandering around up there, you should be more careful.'

'I had the dog with me,' she protested.

They both turned to look at Nero who was lying on his back, legs in the air and tongue lolling out of his mouth. His legs were twitching and he was making whimpering noises as he dreamed of rabbits.
They both laughed.

'Here's your sandwich.'

'Thanks, but stay off that hill Kitty.'

'I'll take you up there next time and show you the cottage.'
There was crack of thunder overhead and they both jumped; the kitchen grew dark as the rain clouds massed over their house.

'Oh, here it comes,' said Gordon, just as he spoke the heavens opened and the rain fell from the sky in a hissing torrent.

****

It rained nonstop for the rest of the day but by the evening the skies had cleared and the first few stars had appeared.
Gordon took the opportunity to put the car away in the garage.

'What a beautiful evening.' He stood on the drive with his hands on his hips and stared up at the clear night sky. 'It smells wonderful out here.'
Kitty glanced at him through the open door on her way to the sitting room, outside the shadows lengthened along the drive and she shivered.

'Are you coming in Gordon? It's getting cold in here.'

'Just coming.' He looked around to the end of the drive where he heard a noise.

'Evening,' he called, and raised a hand in greeting.

'Who was that?'

'Not too sure, there was somebody there, just passing I suppose.' He pushed the front door shut and entered the sitting room.

Kitty was sat in front of the empty fireplace. 'I wonder who used to live there?' she pondered.

'What are you talking about? Who used to live where?'

'On the hill, it's lovely spot but quite a lonely place to live.'

'Ask Mr Beamish, he's bound to know.'

'Do you think that really was the witch's cottage?

'It's just a story Kitty.' Gordon sat down in the armchair on the opposite side of the fireplace, stretched his legs out and sighed. Yawning, he glanced around the room.

'That air freshener is nice.'

'There isn't one in here; I still haven't found the ones I bought in the supermarket.'

'There's a nice smell coming from somewhere, it must be you, dear.' He rubbed his neck and arms. 'I'm really out of practice casting, my arm and shoulders are killing me,' he said ruefully, then paused and cocked his head on one side.

Outside there was the sound of hurrying footsteps on the gravel drive followed by a sudden crash on the front door, making the glass panels rattle.

They both jumped and the dog started barking in the kitchen.

'What was that?' Kitty gasped.

Gordon leapt to his feet, rushed into the hall and yanked the door open.

'What is it?' Kitty followed him out into the hall.

'Nothing, there's nothing here.' He stepped outside and gazed around the outside of the house. 'Put the outside light on.'

Kitty clicked it on and the light flooded the drive.

'I can't see anything,' he said.

Kitty folded her arms tightly around her and shivered, it was very quiet and the pool of light made the shadows seem even darker.

'Perhaps it was an animal, a rabbit or something.'

'A rabbit? It sounded more like a rhino charging the door!' he exclaimed, examining the door. 'Well there aren't any marks on it...' He walked a few paces down the drive and peered into the dark shadows at the end of the drive. 'There's something moving down there,' he exclaimed, quickly crunched down the gravel and stood looking up and down the road, it was very quiet and one of the resident bats skimmed low over his head, but there was no injured animal lying in the road that he could see.

Kitty watched him from the doorway. She could just see his white shirt in the darkness and as she stood there it seemed that the shadows started to lengthen and the circle of light cast by their lamp grew smaller.

'Gordon,' she called.

He didn't answer and moved away following the road down into the village, she watched his figure disappear into the gloom and listened to his footsteps on the road. With a start she realised that the footsteps had changed, it was the same heavy tread and measured thump of a walking stick on the tarmac that she had heard that afternoon on the hillside. A feeling of chill and dread crept over her again. Kitty stepped back into the hall and slammed and locked the door, while chiding herself for being silly. Nero pushed his nose against her leg making her jump; she was surprised to see the dog still in the house.

'Why didn't you go with dad?' Nero usually followed Gordon everywhere and never turned down the chance of a last minute walk. 'Are you a scaredy-cat as well?'

He started to whine gently which slowly turned to a growl, he put his nose to the crack under the door, the hairs standing up on the ridge of his back.

'It's alright, there's nothing there,' said Kitty, trying to sound calm but she wasn't too sure whether she was trying to convince herself or the dog.

The back door banged open making them both jump.

'Gordon! Where did you go? I was getting worried here on my own.' He came in and closed the door, looking at her in surprise. 'Why?' he questioned. 'I wasn't gone that long, I walked to the entrance to the farm, and I thought I saw something disappearing down the lane but I couldn't catch it so I suppose it couldn't have been injured.'

'What was it, a rabbit?'

'No it was too big to be a rabbit, and anyway I couldn't see it properly.'

Gordon put the kettle on and pulled out the biscuit tin from the cupboard, Kitty stayed in the hall looking into the kitchen.

'Have you locked the back door?' she asked nervously.

'Why are you so jittery?' But he turned and locked the door. 'There! Happy now?'

'I'm not jittery; I was just worried that's all.' Kitty shivered. 'I think I'll go and have a bath.' She walked out into the hall. 'Do you think we should leave the outside light on?'

'What for?'

'Well just in case, in case it comes back.'

'No, turn it off. It's a waste of electricity.'

Kitty switched the light off and made sure the front door was locked. Gordon watched her in amusement from the kitchen

'Making sure the bogey man doesn't get in?'

'Very funny.'

She walked slowly up the stairs and was half way up when a slight fragrance reached her.

'Kitty'

She felt a slight touch on her shoulder and yelped in shock, Kitty swung round to see who was behind, lost her footing and sat down with a bump on the stair.

'What is it now?' Gordon came out from the kitchen holding a biscuit. 'I thought you were going for a bath? Did you trip?'

'There was somebody behind me on the stairs, there's somebody here!' Her white face peered at him through the banister.

'Don't be daft, there's nobody here. It's just your imagination working overtime again.'

'I wasn't imagining it,' she snapped. 'Somebody said my name and touched my shoulder.'

Gordon laughed at his wife's upset face. 'You'll be saying the house is haunted next.'

'Well perhaps it is.'

'How can a new house be haunted,' Gordon said impatiently.

'Perhaps it's the orchard, maybe something awful happened here years ago and the ghosts have invaded the house, like building on Indian burial grounds or something. Remember the film Poltergeist?'

He looked at his wife in disbelief. 'That was just a stupid film, this is real life Katherine, things like that do not happen,' he said firmly.

'Strange things do happen Gordon, just because you don't believe in them doesn't make them untrue.'

'You're absolutely right..., perhaps there is a local tradition of burying young virgins under apple trees so tomorrow you had better go out into the garden and start digging under the trees. The spade is in the garage.'

'This isn't a joke Gordon.'

'Oh for goodness sake go and have your bath and stop being so daft!'

'You can be such a git sometimes Gordon,' Kitty snapped at him.

She stormed upstairs to the bathroom and slammed the door after her. Kitty angrily locked the door checking in the shower cubicle just in case. She was just lying back in the hot scented water when there was loud bang on the door. Kitty lurched up sending water and bubbles sloshing out onto the bathroom floor

'Are you alright in there? Do you want your back washed or is your invisible friend going to do it for you?'

Kitty lay back in the bath and shouted at the closed door. 'Shut up Gordon.' She could hear him laughing outside the bathroom door. 'That's not funny!'

Monday

'You look terrible this morning.'
Kitty looked at her husband in disgust. 'Thank you, you say the nicest things.'
 She cupped a hot cup of coffee in her hands and pulled her thick dressing gown closer around her, she shivered and pulled a tissue out of the pocket and blew her nose.
   'Aren't you feeling well?'
   'No, I was coughing all night. So I didn't keep you awake?'
   'No.' Gordon carried on eating his breakfast.
She stared at him over the cup. 'That's good, wouldn't want you to lose any sleep,' she remarked blandly.
Kitty stood up from the table and started rummaging in one of the kitchen cupboards looking for the first aid box.
   'What are you scrabbling about for now?'
   'I can't remember if we've got any cold capsules, perhaps I can get some at the shop.'
Gordon stood up and carried his plate and cup over to the sink. 'I can pick up some later for you on the way back from work.'
Kitty nodded at him. 'Leave that,' she said curtly. 'I'll do it in a minute.'
Gordon planted a kiss on the top of her head. 'Okay, I'd better get going or I'll be late, ring me if you do want me to pick anything up.'

   Kitty sat at the table with a cup of cooling coffee; outside the sun was shining and it made the events of last night seem unreal but while she tried to dismiss it Kitty could still feel the touch of those fingers on her shoulder and she shivered.
She stared out the window into the garden, the apple trees still had one or two shrivelled little apples clinging to their branches. The leaves were falling fast now and were blowing around the garden in the slight breeze.
Perhaps I'll have a bonfire later, she thought. And clear all those up.
Kitty pushed the chair back and sneezed. 'Oh blast! I think I will walk down to the shop and see if I can get something for this cold.'
Although it was a lovely morning there was a nip to the air and Kitty was glad that she had wrapped up in a thick coat. Nero was on a lead this morning as there were a few cars about, probably on their way to work.

A few late sprigs of honeysuckle were still growing in the hedge and Kitty picked one and tucked it into a buttonhole.

Apart from the cars Kitty had the lane to herself and she enjoyed the walk to the shop, the fresh air was helping to clear her headache and by the time she had reached the bottom of the hill it had all but disappeared.

Kitty pushed open the shop door, leaving Nero tied up outside. The dog whined and pulled at his lead.

'Oh shush… I won't be long,' she reassured him.

'Good morning.' Mrs Leavenham was stood behind the counter unpacking some boxes; she looked up and smiled when Kitty opened the door. 'Isn't it a lovely morning after all that rain?'

'What a storm!'

'I hope you didn't get wet yesterday, I saw you walk past the shop.'

'I made it back home just in time, I walked to the top of the hill; it's quite a view from up there.'

'It certainly is, now what can I get you?'

'Have you got any cold remedies? I was coughing and sneezing all night and I can't bear having a cold.'

'Well now, I've got the usual, throat lozenges or there's this, it's called Honey Linctus. It's locally made, wonderful stuff, I always use it.' Mrs Leavenham handed over a bottle filled with a thick brown liquid.

'It looks disgusting,' Kitty picked up the bottle and peered at its contents doubtfully.

'I know, it tastes disgusting as well so be warned.' She smiled. 'But we all use it. Last year when we had that flu I ran out and couldn't get any for weeks.'

'Who makes it?'

'Oh, it's a local chap, he has a pharmacy in Seaton, everybody has the recipe but he makes it up for us.' Mrs Leavenham wrapped the bottle in a paper bag. 'I'll wrap it as the bottle is a bit sticky, this will help, I promise.'

'In that case I will give it a go, how much is it?'

'Two pounds, fifty, dear. It's been used for years around here. The recipe came originally from a woman in the village; she was the local midwife and was very good with herbs and suchlike. Here's your change, now, how are you settling in?'

Mrs Leavenham looked at her intently, head on one side.

'Oh, okay I think, I suppose it will take time to get used to being in a new place,' Kitty hesitated. 'I keep hearing strange noises in the house.'

She suddenly felt very silly admitting to it and wished she had said nothing.

'Don't worry my dear; my daughter had the same thing when she moved into a new house in Axminster. She was convinced that the house was haunted.' Mrs Leavenham laughed. 'It was just the house settling, I expect that's what you can hear.'

'Perhaps that's it,' Kitty said doubtfully, she hesitated but decided to let the subject drop. 'Well thanks for this,' she raised the bottle. 'I'd better be going, still loads to do.'

She closed the door and untied the dog. 'Come on let's go home.'

Kitty waved through the shop window at the old woman who was watching her with a slight frown on her face. She smiled briefly in response before turning back to the boxes.

Kitty spent the rest of the morning unpacking the cardboard boxes in the utility room, most of it went in the garage as it was the contents of Gordon's shed from their previous home. She squashed the empty boxes flat and piled them on the grass at the end of the garden meaning to have a bonfire.

She was just heading off to find the rake in the garage when she became aware of a figure on the other side of the wall. Kitty turned.

'Good morning Mr Beamish.'

He was leaning against the wall staring at her, his work hardened hands clenched over the rough stones.

'How are you?' she asked. 'I was just going to have a bonfire, get rid of these boxes and all the leaves need clearing.'

He didn't answer and Kitty was suddenly worried.

'This isn't going to annoy you is it? If I have a fire?'

He remained silent and Kitty was surprised by the strange intensity of his stare. Feeling very uncomfortable under his scrutiny and unsure of what to say next she turned and walked down the path to the house.

'Well... I'll get on then, Mr Beamish, nice to see you'

Kitty opened the side door to the garage and glanced back up the garden, but he had disappeared and she felt strangely relieved.

The rake was in a clutter of tools at the back, she pulled it out, reluctant to go back outside. She hesitated and peeped out the half open door.

'For goodness sake what is wrong with you, you daft old woman,' Kitty chided herself.

She spent the next hour steadily raking the grass and by the time she had finished had piled a huge pile of twigs and leaves on top of the cardboard. Kitty kept her head lowered as she worked unwilling to look up in case Mr Beamish had returned.

'Now I need some matches,' she said to herself, walking to the house. Opening the back door warm scented air met her as she entered the kitchen. 'There you are dog, didn't you want to help me in the garden?' She reached down and patted Nero's head; he looked up, wagged his tail and yawned. 'Lazy dog.' She yawned as well. 'Oh dear, now you are setting me off. I'll have a cup of tea and sit down for a minute before I light the bonfire'

Kitty put the kettle on, pulled out a chair and sat down with a sigh. She suddenly felt very tired and yawned again.

'Maybe I will leave the bonfire until later. What do you think dog?' she asked, fondling his ears. Nero just yawned and snuggled his head down into the dog box.

It was beginning to get dark and Kitty felt quite chilled sitting at the table even with a hot cup of tea. She sneezed again and decided it was time to change into something warmer. After finding a pair of thick cords and a warm jumper from one of the boxes she hobbled stiffly back down the stairs, passing the front room door Kitty had a sudden urge to light the fire. The fireplace hadn't been used yet and Gordon was looking forward to the weather getting colder so that they would have an excuse

to use it. As Kitty was still feeling chilled she decided it would be a good opportunity to try it out. The prospect of sitting in front of an open fire would be rather welcome.

Gordon had the kindling all ready piled up next to the grate and the log basket was full.

Kitty crumpled up several sheets of newspaper and put in on the grate, she was just putting on the kindling when the phone rang. Easing herself up as her knees were stiff from her afternoon in the garden she hobbled into the hall hoping to get to the phone before it stopped ringing.

'Hello?'

'Hi, it's me, just checking to see if you still want some shopping.'

'No thanks, I bought some local potion from Mrs Leavenham, she swears by it. God knows what it's in it though. It tastes disgusting.'

'Bat's blood and eye of newt. Who knows? I will be home in about 10 minutes, Kitty? Are you still there? Kitty!'

She didn't answer; she had taken the phone away from her ear and was staring back into the living room.

Kitty lifted the phone again. 'Gordon, the fire's lit.'

'That's a good idea; you can sit in front of it and warm your toes.'

'No, I didn't light it; I was just laying the fire when you rang.'

'You probably did it without realising; you know what your memory is like.'

'I didn't light it, Gordon! There aren't any matches in there so I couldn't have!' Her voice rose.

'Kitty, calm down, I'll be home in ten minutes.'

There was a click as Gordon put the phone down; there was a constant buzzing as Kitty stood in the hall with the phone still held to her ear. In the living room the fire blazed, the kindling, popping and crackling, was burning down quickly. The fire needed feeding but Kitty hesitated before entering the room. As she stood frozen in the hall she became aware of movement in Gordon's chair near the fireplace.

The phone clattered to the floor.

The chair had been pulled up in front of the fire, the back facing the door. Unable to see the occupant of the chair she edged into the room grasping the door frame to stop herself from shaking. From the chair an arm stretched out, grasped a log and placed it into the flames. Kitty drew a strangled breath and backed slowly out of the room into the hall. The fire irons clattered on the hearth, the noise spurring her into action and she dashed into the kitchen and slammed the door behind her. Leaning against it she gazed wildly around the room and lit on the block of kitchen knives sitting on the worktop. Kitty leapt forward and pulled the largest carving knife out of the slot, with her other hand she dragged one of the kitchen chairs over to the door and jammed it under the handle and sat on it.

Kitty gripped the knife tightly trying to stop her hands shaking; her knuckles began to ache where she was holding it so tight. She forced herself to let go of the knife and balance it on her knees while she shakily massaged her hands. Outside in the hall it was quiet but she could still hear the fire popping as the kindling burnt, no other sound came from the living room and Kitty's breathing was just getting beginning to slow when she heard the sound of the hearth being swept. Kitty jumped, the clatter of the knife falling to the floor made Nero start, he rested his head on the side of the dog box and looked at her sleepily.

'You're a rotten guard dog, Nero!' she whispered frantically.

The kitchen clock ticked on slowly as she watched the hands creeping around the face. Kitty strained to hear the car pulling into the drive and for an awful minute thought that perhaps he had stopped at the supermarket. She was just considering running out the back door when she heard Gordon's car. The front door banged open.

'Kitty, Kitty where are you?'

She dragged the chair away from the door and opened it. 'Gordon! Why were you so long?'

Kitty rushed towards him forgetting that she was still holding the carving knife. Gordon jumped back.

'Wow! What are you doing with that?'

'There's somebody in the living room Gordon.'

He stared at her in amazement. 'What are you talking about?' He walked into the room. 'There's nobody here,' he swung around and pulled her into the room. 'Look, it's empty.'

Kitty stared around the room nervously. 'But I didn't light the fire and I saw somebody in here.'

'Well, the fire is going a treat now,' he said wearily.

The fire was burning well, several logs had been piled on and a few lumps of coal had been placed on the flames. The room was already warm, the smell of wood smoke mingling with the fragrance of lavender.

'I've been shut in the kitchen since you rang; I was too frightened to come back in here.'

'You must have done it. I don't know what's wrong you at the moment. Perhaps you should go and see the doctor. Maybe it's the stress from the move, or something?'

He looked worried, running his hand over his hair.

'It's not stress.' Her voice trembled as she stared blankly around the empty room.

Gordon took the knife from her hand and walked into the kitchen, throwing it onto the table.

'Calm down Kitty, I'm sure there is a logical explanation.'

'What? I've just told you there was somebody in the house and you're treating me as though I was nuts.'

'For God's sake Katherine!' he shouted. 'I've had a hard day at work and now I have to come home to this!' He shoved the chair back under the table scraping it along the tiled floor. 'I think you should make an appointment tomorrow and get something for your nerves.'

'There's nothing wrong with my nerves,' she shouted at him.

Gordon pushed past her, not bothering to answer and headed for the stairs. Kitty slumped down in a chair and rested her head in her hands. Upstairs, drawers were being dragged open and banged shut as Gordon changed out of his suit. It was strange how Kitty could always tell how annoyed Gordon was by the way he opened the drawers in the bedroom.

Kitty pulled off a piece of kitchen roll and blew her nose. There was a movement at the door, she jumped and looked up. Gordon was standing in the doorway looking apologetic.

'Are you alright?'

'I'm okay,' she said gruffly, and sneezed. 'Oh bother.'

'Did you say you had some medicine?' he asked, trying to sound normal.

Kitty looked at him for a moment. 'I walked down to the shop this morning.'

She glanced away from him and stared at her clasped hands on the table.

Gordon sighed and pulled out one of the chairs and sat down. 'Shall I make tea tonight? I could make one of my curries.'

'If you like,' she said quietly.

He reached out and stroked her hand. 'Everything's okay Kitty, there's nothing wrong with the house or the orchard. You're just letting things get on top of you.'

'I'm fine, Gordon.'

He pushed the chair back and stood up. 'Why don't you go and have a soak while I make tea.'

'No,' she said quickly. 'No, I'll stay here.' Kitty glanced nervously into the hall; Nero was laying full stretch on the hall floor, fast asleep. 'Why isn't it bothering Nero?'

Gordon had his back turned while he was rummaging through the shelves in the freezer. He turned to face his wife. 'What about the dog?'

'Every time I see or hear something in this house he hasn't been worried at all.'

'Because there's nothing to be worried about, that's why.' He put a pan on the hob and started to chop onions 'What have you been doing today? Have you been busy?'

'I was clearing up the garden, I was going to have a bonfire and I saw Mr Beamish, he was acting very strangely. I thought perhaps he was annoyed because I was going to have a fire but he didn't answer when I asked him. He was really odd.'

'Oh dear, poor old Mr Beamish is going to get the Kitty treatment, now is he?'

'That's not funny.'

'Sorry.' He looked at Kitty; she was slumped in the chair looking tired and dejected. 'I'm sure you'll laugh about it in the morning.'

'I doubt it.'

Gordon filled a pan at the sink and put it on the hob before throwing some chopped peppers into the frying onions.

'Prawn curry okay?' he asked.

She nodded. 'Yes, there's a curry sauce in the cupboard if you want it, on the second shelf.' She half rose from her chair. 'Shall I get it for you?'

'No, no, sit still, I'll get it.'

Gordon opened the sauce and poured it over the frying vegetables then threw the prawns on top of the mix, stirring it all together. The rice was gently bubbling on the hob and was nearly cooked.

'Can you set the table?'

'Yeah I'll do that.' She pushed herself up from the table and sneezed again. 'Damn.'

'Bless you dear, the local magic potion doesn't seem to be working.'

Kitty blew her nose. 'Well, my throat isn't so sore now so it must be working a bit.' She put out the place mats and the knives and forks. 'I think there is some red wine left if you'd like some.'

'It should be lager with curry really but red wine will do.'

Gordon set out the plates on the table.

'That smells delicious,' she said.

He brought over the dish of rice and curry. 'Help yourself; I just hope I have cooked enough rice.'

****

They were halfway through their meal when a strange drumming started on the roof.

'It's raining again; sounds like a hard storm,' said Gordon, staring at the window.

'That's really loud!' She paused with a forkful of food half way to her mouth. Kitty turned to look out the window but by now it was already dark and she couldn't see a thing. The drumming got louder and louder until they were almost deafened.

Kitty said alarmed, 'That sounds like hail but surely it's not cold enough for that?'

The ferocious downpour continued, drumming on the roof and pinging off the windows of the kitchen, they sat in silence, their food forgotten. The lights in the kitchen flickered and Gordon glanced towards the hall in alarm.

'Where did we put the torch?'

'You don't think we're going to have a power cut, do you?' asked Kitty worried, as she spoke, the lights flickered again. 'I think it's in the garage but there are some candles in the living room.'

'I'm sure we're not going to need them Kitty, so don't worry.' Gordon reached across and patted her hand reassuringly. 'It's just the storm messing with the power lines, that's all.'

Nero whined and climbed out of his dog box; he pushed his way through their legs to get under the table and sat next to Kitty's legs whining gently. She groped underneath the table to find his head and gave it a gentle reassuring pat.

'I'm glad I'm not out in this,' Gordon had to raise his voice so that Kitty could hear him over the drumming noise.

Kitty leant towards him over the table. 'Do you remember that news report of hail stones in America that were the size of golf balls?'

Gordon nodded. 'Sounds like we have hail the size of boulders, but I don't think I'll go out just yet for a look.'

The sound slowly abated until within a few minutes there was just occasional ping of the hail stones on the window.

'It's stopping; thank goodness,' he said, rising from his chair. Gordon opened the back door. 'Let's look at the icebergs,' he joked and switched on the outside light.

It shone out brightly lighting up the path and illuminating half of the garden, the apple trees just beyond the pool of light were dark fingered shapes casting shadows onto the farm buildings behind the stone wall.

The path was bone dry, no hail or rain had fallen outside.

He stared outside perplexed.

'What the... Look at this, there's nothing out here Kitty. It's dry, nothing has fallen at all!'

Kitty came to the door and peered over his shoulder.

'What was it then? Perhaps a branch fell on the roof or something.'

'That wasn't a branch, it sounded like hail but where is it?' Gordon stepped out onto the back step and looked left and right. 'How strange,' he said and walked down the side of the house.

'Gordon, don't go too far,' she said in a panic, peering out of the door after him.

'I'm just here Kitty.'

'You have to admit that this is strange.'

He looked at her impatiently. 'I'm sure there is a logical explanation.'

'Well what is it then?'

'What?'

'The explanation.'

He thought for a minute. 'I'll let you know when I think of one.'

'Good evening.' A voice came from the dark lane making Kitty jump. She could just make out the figure of Mr Beamish waving an arm in greeting as he walked down the lane.

'Evening,' Gordon called out, turned and caught sight of the expression on his wife's face 'He's just a harmless old man,' he said in exasperation.

'But he's always around when something strange happens; perhaps he's trying to scare us off his land.'

She watched the old man disappear down the lane.

'Now why would he want to do that?'

Gordon pushed her back into the warm kitchen and shut the door.

'Perhaps it's because we're not locals.'

'Of course we are. Your family come from Axmouth, mine from just over the hill. If we were any more local as you put it, we would have been born in his farmyard!'

'Perhaps he just doesn't like us then.'

'He's a very nice old man, he's always friendly.'

'He wasn't friendly when I was going to have my bonfire.'

'Why, what did he say?'

'Well nothing, he didn't say anything, he just looked, well you know...weird.'

'Weird! Perhaps he thinks you're weird, perhaps he's heard that you're seeing ghosts. That's weird.'

'But he was being very strange,' huffed Kitty.

'You're imagining things again Kitty, come on,' he said calmly. 'Let's just get on with our meal before it gets too cold.'

'What was that programme called from years ago, the spooky one?'

'The Twilight Zone.'

'That's it! We're living in the Twilight Zone!

****

'It's still a clear night out there,' he said, pulling the bedroom curtains closed. 'No more hail or boulders falling.'

'It wasn't hail.'

Kitty padded through from the bathroom.

'You have left all the lights on,' Gordon complained.

'I'm going to leave them on.'

'Don't be ridiculous, I have to pay enough for the electricity as it is!' Gordon strode past her to the bathroom and turned out the light then turned off the one on the landing, leaving the hall in darkness except for the light flooding out of the bedroom. As he did so he heard the sound of footsteps in the hall below and glanced down the stairs expecting to see Nero moving about.

He leant on the banister and called down, 'Back in your bed, Nero!'

Down in the dark well of the hall a pale faced figure stood looking up at him.

Gordon uttered a muffled yelp and staggered back from the top of the stairs. He stared in horrified amazement, frozen to the spot as the grey clad figure stared intently up at him, keeping her pale eyes fixed on his she gathered her long skirt in one hand and slowly lifted one foot and placed it on the first step.

'What is it?'

His gaze just for a minute flicked away from the strange apparition as Kitty called from the bedroom, when he looked back the figure had vanished.

'There's somebody down there,' he called through to her.

There was a thump as Kitty jumped out of the bed and ran out to the landing.

Gordon was peering intently down into the hall.

'Turn the light on. Quickly!'

Kitty clicked on all the switches, flooding the stair and the downstairs with light.

'There was somebody stood there at the bottom of the stairs, I could just see her in the dark staring at me.' He ran a shaky hand over his chin and shook his head in disbelief.

'It was a woman?'

Gordon nodded and started slowly down the stairs.

'You're not going down are you?' Kitty pulled at his arm in panic. Gordon shrugged her off. 'Damn right I am! If somebody is in my house I want to know who it is.'

He carried on closely followed by Kitty who kept a firm grip on his arm.

Nero came out from the kitchen and wagged his tail.

'Why isn't he barking?' Gordon looked puzzled; he turned the lights on in the living room and stared around the empty room, even peering behind the door.

'You didn't check behind the sofa.'

'The front door is locked so she didn't get out this way,' he said, checking the bolt on the door.

There was nobody in the study and the kitchen was empty except for the dog that had climbed back into his bed and was watching them curiously.

'And this door is locked.'

Kitty shivered. 'Now who's imagining things?'

'I didn't! She was there. I could describe to you in detail what the woman was wearing and what she looked like and if I could, I would draw a portrait of her for you!' He ran a hand over his hair and rubbed the back of his neck. 'This is ridiculous! This is a new house, new houses don't have ghosts.'

'Perhaps she climbed out one of the windows.'

'They're all locked,' he said. 'And I would have heard her opening one. I don't understand this at all Kitty.'

She folded her arms tightly around her body and shivered.

'So I wasn't being hysterical then! There is something in this house.' Kitty pulled at her bottom lip. 'What are we going to do?'

Gordon sighed and looked around. 'I think we had better go back to bed, come on,' he put an arm around her shoulder and gave her a hug. 'Sorry I didn't believe you,' he said apologetically. 'I think we'll leave all the lights on, just for tonight, otherwise we'll be jumping at all the shadows.'

Kitty pulled the quilt up and watched Gordon sitting thoughtfully on the edge of the bed.

'What?' she asked. 'What are you thinking about?'

'Nothing.' He got up and looked out of the window.

'What is it?'

'Nothing, go to sleep.'

Gordon pulled the curtains closed and climbed into bed. He pulled the pillows up behind his head and picked up his book, perched his glasses on his nose and began to read.

'Are you going to read?' she asked incredulously.

'Yep, this is a good book and I want to finish it.'

Kitty curled up in a ball close to his side, the quilt wrapped up around her head. His hand came down and started to gently stroke her head.

'Go to sleep Kitty.'

She didn't think for a moment that she would but a strange feeling of calm swept over her and she felt herself slowly relaxing and drift off into a deep dreamless sleep.

Tuesday

The next thing she heard was the incessant beeping of the alarm, Gordon didn't stir; he was still propped up on his pillows, glasses awry on his nose and the book open in his hand.
Kitty reached across him and switched it off. She brought him a cup of tea a few minutes later but he was still asleep.

'Gordon, Gordon.' She poked him on the arm. 'Wake up.'
'Hmm...'
'You'll be late for work.'
He opened his eyes and yawned. 'What time is it?'
'Half seven.'
'Didn't hear the alarm,' he mumbled, rubbing his head.
'You were out cold, what time did you read to?'
'Don't know; it was a good book.'
She picked up the book and looked at it. 'It doesn't look like you read much, you haven't finished it.' She dropped the book back onto the bed next to him and headed for the door. 'Hurry up, and I'll make some breakfast.'

****

Kitty put a plate of toast on the table just as Gordon shambled in yawning.
'Oh darn, my back is stiff.'
'Sleeping like that I'm not surprised.' She looked at the clock on the kitchen wall. 'You had better hurry or you'll be late for work.'
'I think I will have the day off, I've got some hours owing to me. I know it's short notice but I'm sure the office can manage without me.'
'What?' she said jokingly. 'They'll go into meltdown if you're not there.'
'They'll manage,' he repeated, sitting at the table and buttering some toast.
Kitty sat down in the chair opposite and stared in disbelief. Gordon never had time off except for holidays and was never ill.
'Why?' she asked.
'I was thinking last night, about all this, trying to make sense of it.'
'And?'

'I couldn't to be honest, I'm completely baffled. But I do know what I saw and there was somebody or something stood at the bottom of the stairs.'
She said nothing, staring at her husband who for once looked a bit rattled. He usually sailed through life completely calm and in control. Kitty found this to be the most alarming thing of all.

Gordon checked all the windows after breakfast, trying all the locks.

'All the windows are locked tight, I was going to check them again last night but I didn't want to wake you.'

'How long did you stay awake?'

'Most of the night, I was just thinking, I finally dropped off after four. Every noise made me jump.'

'It's strange to see you so spooked.'

'Is that because I'm a thick skinned male?' he joked.

'Yes,' Kitty replied, wandering back into the kitchen. Nero looked up hopefully.

'Nero, it's walkie time, isn't it?' she said, patting him on the head. 'I'll just get ready and then we'll be off"

'What? Who are you talking to?' Gordon quickly followed her into the kitchen.

'I'm just talking to the dog; he's waiting for his walk.'

'We'll go together,' Gordon said firmly.

'But you don't like walking with me, I'm too slow, remember,'

'Then we'll have a slow walk. Go on then, go and get your coat.'

'Where shall we go?' asked Kitty, closing the front door behind them.

'We'll walk up the hill and see that cottage.'

'The cottage? Really?'

'Yes really, the cottage.' Gordon slipped his arm through his wife's. 'Come on.'

Kitty led the way up the narrow lane to the stile.

'Here's the footpath I used, the sign is broken though.'

Gordon pushed a few brambles out of the way and picked up the remains of the rotten sign.

'What does it say?'

'Castle Hill, I think,' he said, rubbing the moss off the wood.

They followed the same route up the hill that Kitty had used on Sunday and up to the copse at the top.

'Through here,' Kitty said, pointing to the dense bushes. She was feeling a bit nervous after the previous visit but Gordon calmly pushed his way through the brambles to the clearing beyond. There were still a few ragged blooms on the rose bushes even after all the heavy rain and the smell of lavender still hung over the garden.

'What a beautiful spot,' he said, turning full circle. 'Take those trees out of the way and what a view it would be.'

'It's quite lonely though, up here.'

'But nice and peaceful,' said a voice from behind them.

The couple started and turned round.

'Sorry, we didn't see you there,' said Gordon.

It was Mrs Leavenham from the shop, sitting on the remains of the wall, she was well wrapped up against the early morning chill, with a thick coat and a scarf wound around her neck. A small brown cairn terrier sat at her feet.

'It is lovely up here but it's becoming quite a struggle to get up that hill,' she said ruefully.

'We came up to look at the cottage,' said Gordon.

'I found it the other day,' explained Kitty, moving over the rough ground towards her.

'There's nothing much left of it now, William cleared it all out several years ago, beams, floorboards, the lot. I couldn't see that it was worth much but he said he got a good price from a chap near Ilminster.'

'What the reclamation yard?' exclaimed Gordon.

'That's the one.'

'Do you know if there was big wooden fireplace, an old oak one, really big?'

'I believe,' she hesitated, 'there was one and there was a small cast iron one in the bedroom.'

'It's the oak fireplace I'm interested in,' said Gordon in excitement.

'That was in the kitchen, they say that was where she made most of her medicines, potions and suchlike.'

'Medicines? I thought she was supposed to be a witch,' Kitty said surprised.

'Oh that's nonsense,' said Mrs Leavenham in disgust, curling her lip. 'I remember my grandmother telling me she used to come up here all the time, especially when one of the children were ill. There was no chemist to pop into then. She helped Hannah to pick all the herbs.'

'Herbs? What, from the garden?'

'Ay, it was her husband's pride and joy, so my gran said. Spent hours out here he did, now look at it. Still,' Mrs Leavenham sighed, 'It was a long time ago.'

'I didn't realise she was married,' Kitty said in amazement, and perched on the wall next to the old woman. 'She couldn't have been that horrible then.'

'No of course she wasn't, although she changed after Samuel was killed; she was a good woman but just very unhappy and lonely,' Mrs Leavenham said sadly.

'What happened to him?' she asked curiously.

'I was told Samuel was a cripple and couldn't work much but he used to help his brother with odd jobs on the farm from time to time. They were working on the river bank in one of the lower fields when Samuel slipped into the river and drowned. They found his body in the harbour a few days later.'

'How dreadful! Couldn't his brother help him?' asked Kitty.

'It was said that Robert couldn't reach him in time.'

'Robert who?'

'Why Beamish, of course.'

'What our Mr Beamish's family?' asked Kitty in surprise.

'That's right, Robert was William's grandfather. And then, as Hannah and Samuel had no living children, when she died the cottage returned to Robert Beamish.'

'What do you mean, Mrs Leavenham?' asked Kitty looking confused.

'Their father, oh I forget his name, my memory!' She tapped her forehead in irritation. 'Well never mind... their father gave the cottage to Samuel when he married Hannah. Gran always said there was no love lost between the two brothers, and Robert was furious when he found out. He didn't want the property split up; he said the land was his.'

'Well, well, Mrs Leavenham, you are a mine of information,' said Gordon.

'My husband always said I was a gossip and I suppose I am.' She laughed. 'But I have lived here all my life and I know most things about the families around here, the stories I could write! Well...' She pulled her coat around her and stood up. 'I must be going; I have to help in the shop this morning.'

'We had better be going as well,' said Gordon

Kitty shivered and stood up. 'I suppose so and I'm getting chilly. Where's the dog?'

Nero hadn't gone far; he had forced himself under the bramble bushes and was trying to dig out one of the rabbit holes. 'Nero, stop that!'

The old woman walked slowly across the garden to the path that Kitty had used.

'Well goodbye for now,' she said, looking at Kitty. 'I'm sure we'll bump into each other soon.' She nodded at the couple and started to walk carefully down the rough path.

'Come on then, let's get going.' Gordon pushed his way back through the bramble bushes. 'We'll go back the same way.'

Kitty quickly followed, not wanting to be left alone.

'As soon as we get home I'm going to ring the yard and see if he can remember anything about the fireplace,' said Gordon.

'Do you think it's the same one?'

'Maybe, it's a start anyway and it might explain why she is in our house.'

'So the witch is haunting our fireplace, isn't that a bit ridiculous?' Kitty half laughed.

'Of course it is, this whole thing is ridiculous, but let's just keep an open mind, shall we?'

'It sounds like Mr Beamish is struggling for money.' Kitty climbed over the stile and paused to get her breath. 'He has a rather interesting family history but I don't see what that has to do with us.'

Gordon walked on quickly down the field to the stile. 'Maybe we will find out. Come on.'

'What happened to the slow walk?'

'I want to phone the reclamation yard so hurry up.'

Gordon wasn't on the phone long but Kitty couldn't catch much of the conversation as he had shut the kitchen door, after straining to hear for a while she gave up, shrugged her shoulders and started to make some tea.

The door opened and he came in looking very pleased with himself.

'Well I was right! The fireplace did come from Hannah's cottage and you'll never guess what else they found!'

'A dead body?'

'No!' he said impatiently. 'There was a dried bull's heart up the chimney, stuck all over with nails.'

Kitty looked blankly at him. 'What?'

She put two mugs of tea on the table and pulled out a chair.

'It's quite common to find things like that stuck in chimneys, under floorboards. Old bottles filled with pins, skulls, old shoes.'

'What are you talking about, Gordon?'

He picked up a mug. 'It's all to do with witchcraft.' Gordon walked over to the sink, stared out of the window into the garden and sipped thoughtfully at the tea.

'So she was a witch then?' queried Kitty.

'No. I don't think so. These sort of things were used a protection against evil spirits and witchcraft.'

'But she was supposed to have been taken by the Devil; perhaps she was trying to protect herself against Old Nick.'

Kitty wrapped her hands around the hot mug of tea and watched Gordon staring thoughtfully outside.

'Shall we take the fireplace out?'

'No way,' he said crossly. 'I'll get to the bottom of this. Let me get my laptop and we'll see what we can find out about Hannah.'

'How?'

'Newspaper reports or local records. If she's as famous as the chap from the pub made out there's bound to be some information on her.' Gordon brought in his computer and opened it. 'Now let's see what we can find, I'll just Google her name first and see if anything comes up.' He tapped away for a few minutes. 'Here we are.'

Kitty pulled her chair around the table next to Gordon and started to read.

"Transactions of the Devonshire Association

About one hundred and ten years ago at a place called Medbury there lived a witch called Hannah Beamish. She was reputed to possess great powers and could turn herself into a hare when desired and the Cotley Harriers were often supposed to have hunted her across the county.

At that time a well to do Farmer Mr........... lived at Medbury, his family was prosperous and well thought of in the local area.

Hannah would often visit the farm of Mr .... begging for food and sometimes for money. For a while she was given what she asked for but then Mr......... protested that it became too much and she was refused. A young girl of eleven who was in the service of Mr.........was often a visitor to Hannah's cottage and became great friends with the witch. She would often take Hannah food even though the master forbade it.

The farmer complained bitterly that this was the beginning of his trouble. The milk would not set, the butter could not be made, bread put to bake only ran about the oven. His livestock suffered as well, sheep died of a strange sickness sometimes as many as ten in a day. A horse that Mr............ was going to sell was strangely blinded in one eye and so could not be sold.

Mr.......... said that with one thing and another he was nigh to being ruined. So he brought in a white witch from Chard. This man stayed for a month in the farmhouse while he worked to bring down the witch who was the strongest and 'runkest' he ever knew.

A large crock of water into which he had put a large quantity of barley was kept boiling all the time he was in the house. He also ordered six bullocks hearts to be hung in the fireplace, these were stuck all over with pins and nails. They slowly melted in the flames and it was believed that the witch's heart would to be melted too.

The white witch was sure that this would have broken Hannah's powers and at four in the morning went towards her cottage. This was Good Friday morning. He found the window broken and looking about he saw high above him in a tree lying on a branch the witch wound in a sheet. There she was left for the village folk and the servants to see. The tree was cut down as she was too high to be got at and as the tree fell the witch fell into a gully. Hannah's flesh was much torn and a great round bruise was found on the side of her temple, it was said in the shape of a cloven hoof.

Inside the cottage there was blood smeared about and broken glass on the floor. This was caused, so they said, by Hannah struggling with the devil who pulled her through the window.

The corpse was visited by scores of people from all parts and then buried at a crossroads between Medbury and Axminster. It was said that no horse could pass the spot without shying.

The white witch was paid one hundred pounds for his work.

The inquest on the death of Hannah was held at Axminster on April 12th 1841, the verdict was returned of 'water on the brain'. An impassioned plea by the servant girl that Hannah had been murdered was ignored by the Coroner Mr Edmund Foulstone, due to the youth and emotional state of the young girl. She declared that she had witnessed Mr........threatening to kill Hannah and that she knew Hannah to be no witch. This evidence was struck from the records. Hannah Beamish became the most famous witch in East Devon. The manner of her death suggests that the devil must have been extremely angered that she had been bested by the white witch"

Gordon and Kitty sat silent and stunned.

'Well,' said Gordon slowly. 'I can't believe this. After finding blood and glass in the cottage, the body hanging in a tree and it's put down as water on the brain.'

'What is water on the brain?'

'No idea, but whatever it is, it certainly wouldn't account for her death like this,'

'How could a death like that be anything but murder?'

'A hundred pounds was lot of money then, enough to risk murdering somebody for it,' Gordon said thoughtfully, rereading the article.

'I wonder who the servant girl was.' Kitty said.

'Let's see if we can find out, I'll just save this and I can print it out later.'

He rummaged in his laptop bag for a memory stick.

'Hey! I've just had a thought,' Kitty said excitedly. 'You don't suppose that the servant girl was Mrs Leavenham's grandmother?'

'I wonder?' He looked at her thoughtfully and smiled. 'You know you can be quite bright sometimes.'

'Thanks dear, you're too kind.' She grinned at him. 'Can we ask her? She would know if it was her grandmother. I bet she would know who the farmer was as well, Mrs Leavenham seems to know everything about this village.'

Gordon started tapping on his keys again.

'Let's see what else we can find first. I will put in newspaper reports and her name and we'll see what comes up.' He tapped away for few minutes and suddenly pointed at the screen. 'Hey look at this; we're really hitting the jackpot today! It's a newspaper report about Samuel's death.'

"*The Seaton Chronicle*

14th March 1840

The tragic death of Samuel John Beamish second son of Joseph Beamish of Castle Farm, Medbury, Devon occurred on the 14th day of March 1840. The late Samuel Beamish was drowned after falling into the River Axe. Samuel had been working with his brother Robert Beamish making repairs to the fence bordering the river and had slipped while working and had fallen into the water. His brother Robert had been unable to reach him and Samuel was swept away. His body was found on the 16th of

March, in the harbour at Seaton by Mr Abraham Tulley, Harbour Master.

The remains of Samuel Beamish were laid to rest at the church of St John the Baptist, Medbury.

The Coroner Mr Edward Foulstone recorded death by misadventure at the Inquest held at Axminster 20th April 1840."

Gordon stared pensively at the wall. 'I think I will go and see if Mr Beamish is about and see what he can tell us about Hannah.'

Kitty stood up from the table, 'I'm coming as well,' she said firmly.

'You don't have to; you can stay here as you don't like him.'

'I'm not staying here on my own and anyway I want to hear what he has to say, and you won't tell me everything.'

'Just because I don't repeat every single word of a conversation, I'll distil it and give you the essence.'

'But you always miss out the interesting bits,' she complained.
Gordon stared at her and hesitated, 'I don't know though, perhaps it would be better to go and see Mrs Leavenham first, see if we can find out the name of the servant girl and the farmer.'

Gordon slipped the lead over Nero's head and pulled him to the side of the lane as a car drove slowly up the hill, the vehicle turned into the farmyard before it reached them. A young woman who had a striking resemblance to Mrs Leavenham raised her hand in greeting to the couple as she pulled off the road.

A fine drizzle started to fall wetting the tarmac. Kitty pulled up the hood on her coat and zipped it up against the rain and hurried down the lane after Gordon.

The village was deserted, their footsteps echoing off the walls of the cottages as they walked through the narrow street to the shop. It was closed, the sign on the door declared that it was half day closing.

'Damn,' said Gordon. 'She must live in the village, if we see anybody we could ask.'

'Or we could look in the phone book and ring.'

Gordon stared moodily at the locked door for a moment. 'Oh well,' he said and turned pulling the dog to heel. 'That's a shame; I really wanted to talk to her.'

Kitty walked out into the middle of the street and looked up and down.

'There's nobody about today and it's no good asking in the pub, they wouldn't know.'

'Perhaps she is in there having a pint.'

'I can't see her perched on a bar stool, can you?'

They walked back through the village and up the hill, the rain had become heavier and little rivulets of water ran down the side of the lane carrying the fast falling leaves of autumn.

A horse and rider appeared out of the farm entrance, they recognised her as the young woman from earlier. She waved, turned left and rode up the lane past their house, the hoof beats quickening into a trot.

'Perhaps he's not in,' Kitty said, as they walked into the farmyard.

'He's in.' Gordon pointed to the house where he could see Mr Beamish opening one of the lower floor windows.

'Hello there,' he called. 'Everything okay?'

'Fine Mr Beamish, we just thought we'd pop in and say hello.'

'Well that's nice, I've been meaning to come over and see how you have settled in. Come on in and I will put the kettle on.'

'Is it alright if we bring the dog in? He's a bit wet,' said Kitty, glancing down at Nero. His fur was soaked; the mud from the lane had splashed up around his legs and stomach and was slowly dripping off in wet muddy rivulets onto the doorstep.

'Of course, I'm used to wet and muddy dogs, he can sit in front of the Rayburn and dry off.'

Gordon opened the front door and stepped into the stone flagged hallway, Kitty carefully wiped her feet on the doormat before following him inside. Mr Beamish stood in the open doorway of the kitchen, a smile of welcome on his face.

'Come on in you two, the kettle has just boiled.'

Nero sat down with a sigh and stretched out on the rug in front of the glowing stove.

'It's lovely and warm in here, Mr Beamish.' Kitty held her cold hands over the range. 'I would have liked one of these in our kitchen but there wasn't enough room as we had the gas oven as well.'

'This has a back boiler so I get hot water from it as well, nice in the winter but it gets a bit warm in here in the summer,' he said ruefully.

'I prefer something a bit more up to date,' said Gordon. He looked at the ageing range. 'I remember having to clean out my parents Aga every weekend and I swore then I would never have one of the damn things.'

Mr Beamish shrugged and put the teapot on the table. 'I suppose I'm used to it, there's many a cold night that I've spent in front of it with a sick lamb so it has had a lot of use over the years.'

They sat down at the kitchen table with their mugs of tea.

'Hope you don't mind sitting in the kitchen but I spend most of my time in here as it's the warmest room in the house, and to be honest...' He smiled slightly and looked embarrassed. 'I find it more comfortable.'

'Not at all.... We walked up to the cottage on Castle hill this morning, I didn't realise that land belonged to you. It must have been a lovely place to live, what a view,' said Gordon.

Mr Beamish stirred his tea. 'It's alright in nice weather, but there's no electricity, water or drainage. I thought about renovating it and renting it out for holiday lets but the costs of getting all the amenities up there was just too much. So in the end I just took everything out of the cottage and sold it off.'

'There's not much of the building left now.'

'I know, it seems a shame to let the cottage fall down but getting up there on foot is difficult enough, I would have had to put a road in and that would have been really expensive.'

'We saw Mrs Leavenham up there walking her dog.' Kitty leaned forward and looked at him keenly.

'Is she still managing to walk up there? She ought to be careful, she's getting on a bit now and if she should fall...'

'Mrs Leavenham did say she found it a struggle to get up the hill these days,' Kitty said, stirring her tea. 'She was telling us all about Hannah and Samuel.'

'Oh yes, I believe her grandmother was very fond of Hannah.'

'The strange thing is...' began Gordon. 'That the fireplace that I bought from the
reclamation yard is Hannah's, from the cottage.'

'Really?' Mr Beamish looked surprised. 'I sold all that off several years ago.'

'It's quite a coincidence isn't it? I checked with the owner of the yard and it is definitely the same one.'

'Well I never! So it's come home to roost.'

'Do you know why she was known as a witch? From what Mrs Leavenham has said she was no such thing,' asked Kitty.

'Oh, that was just some rumour that started, it was a long time ago and I don't think anybody really knows what went on then.'

'We first heard about it in the pub.'

'Really? I don't go in there now; it's changed hands, hasn't it?' Gordon stared thoughtfully at the old man over the table. 'Did you know your grandfather, Robert Beamish?'

'Not really, why?'

'Mrs Leavenham was talking to us about him.'

'Was she? Well, I just remember a very old man, although my father always said he was a very difficult man to live with.'

'Difficult?' inquired Gordon.

'That was just my father saying that, he was always a bit tight lipped about his dad.
They didn't get on. Gran said that father was more like granddad's brother Samuel. He was a kind soul, when he married Hannah they moved up to the cottage on the hill.'

'Yes we heard about that, it was a shame that he drowned.'

'Drowned? Where did you hear that?' Mr Beamish asked rather sharply.

'Mrs Leavenham told us, she said that he fell into the river near your lower fields.'

'I don't why Sybil would have said that.... not that I know much about his death.'

'We found a newspaper report about it,' said Gordon firmly.

Kitty looked at Mr Beamish in concern, his face had become very still and he was staring blankly at his hands clasped around the mug of tea.

'The report said that Samuel had slipped while helping Robert with some fencing and had fallen into the river and drowned,' continued Gordon.

'Drowned... I hadn't heard that before,' he said quietly.

'It must have been dreadful for Hannah,' said Kitty.

Mr Beamish ignored her and continued, 'Nobody ever spoke about Samuel's death. I don't see how he could have drowned there. Where our fields run down to the river it runs wide and shallow. I have fallen in enough times myself and the water only reached my knees. It's strange the report said he drowned, my father never mentioned anything about it.'

'What was he like?' asked Gordon.

'Who?'

'Robert Beamish.'

'Oh... As I said he and father didn't get on, he liked his gardening and books and grandfather despised anything like that. I don't think anybody was sorry when he died. The first thing that father did after the funeral was drag out all of grandfather's things into the orchard and burn the lot. I remember watching him, I still remember it as though it was yesterday the look on his face, especially when he burned grandfather's walking stick.' His face became vacant as he stared back in time. 'I do know he had an awful temper,' Mr Beamish continued quietly. 'He beat one of the farm dogs to death. Dad could do anything with those dogs but it was different with granddad. All the dogs would slink off and hide when they heard him walking into the yard. The dog wouldn't come when it was called so he caught it and beat it with that stick...' he paused and went on sadly, 'broke the poor thing's back. He wouldn't stop even when father went for him. He said it was as though the old man had the devil in him.'

Gordon and Kitty sat at the table, the tea forgotten and cold.

'How did he get on with Hannah?' asked Kitty quietly, staring across the table at him feeling guilty that they had stirred so many painful memories up for the old man.

'I have no idea; it was a long time ago.'

'It's just that we read an article on Hannah and one interesting part was that a local farmer paid a white witch to get rid of her because he thought she was causing all his bad luck. Do you know anything about that?' asked Gordon.

'We went to ask Mrs Leavenham but the shop was closed,' interrupted Kitty.

The old man looked at her and blinked, he seemed very confused.

'Well, it's half day closing, Sybil will be at home,' he said slowly. 'Why are you so interested in Hannah and Samuel?'

Kitty started to answer but Gordon put a hand on her arm.

'I suppose it's because we have Hannah's fireplace that we have become interested in the history of it, and Mrs Leavenham seems to know so much about the families of the village.'

Mr Beamish smiled slightly.

'Sybil is related to most of the people here. She was the youngest of ten children; her mother came from a large family as well. They all lived in the village at one time or another so I suppose she would know all about the families here.'

'Do you have children, Mr Beamish?' asked Kitty.

He brightened. 'Oh yes, I have two boys, well, not boys now, of course. Edwin lives in New Zealand, he had a sheep farm out there; his son has taken that on now he's retired. My eldest son Derek lives in Poole, he was an accountant.'

'So he won't be taking on the farm?'

'No, he has no interest in farming or his children and I can't imagine Sharon, his wife, moving to the country.'

'How do you manage on your own?' Kitty glanced around the untidy kitchen.

'I don't farm the land now; I rent out the fields to Mr Squires. He has the farm just past the village.'

'Do you miss it?'

'Not the work,' he laughed. 'I don't miss that at all but I do miss having the animals about. Sybil's granddaughter stables her horse here so I have Jester to talk to.'

'We saw her coming out of the yard, it's a lovely horse,' Kitty carried on. 'I used to ride years ago before the children were born.'

'Jester is getting on a bit now; I think Debbie said he was about fourteen. He's the only animal left on the farm now.'

'Isn't that grey cat yours?'

William looked surprised. 'It turned up at the weekend so I assumed it was yours.'

'Maybe it's a stray or from the village then, it's sneaked into the house several times already,' said Kitty.

'Really? It didn't seem too friendly. It hissed and spat when it saw me yesterday.'

'Oh dear,' laughed Kitty. 'Then it definitely isn't mine, I disown it.'

'Where does Mrs Leavenham live?' interrupted Gordon, determined not to be sidetracked by the talk of horses and cats.

'Priddy Cottage, it's the little cottage near the church.'

'Is she in the phone book?'

Mr Beamish put his hands on the table and pushed himself up. 'I'll get her phone number for you.' He rummaged about in the piles of paper and books on the dresser and pulled out a small address book. 'Ah, here it is.' he copied it out onto a piece of torn off newspaper and handed it to Gordon.

'Thanks Mr Beamish, I'll call her later. I'm sure she won't mind.'

'I doubt it, she loves talking about the village and what goes on here. Well... she just loves talking; it's harder trying to get her to stop.'

Gordon stood up and took his empty cup over to the sink. There was a pile of dirty crockery in the sink.

'Oh leave that,' Mr Beamish waved his hand in the general direction of the sink. 'I will get round to it later.'

'Thanks for the tea,' Kitty stood up and tucked the chair under the table. 'You must come over for coffee,' she reminded him.

'I will indeed, I would have been over before but I have had a bit of a cold and haven't been out much.'

'I hope you're feeling better?'

'I'm fine now, Sybil brought up a bottle of that foul mixture she sells; the miracle cure.'

'I have had some of that, it tasted disgusting.'

'She forces me to take it and then tells me I'm feeling better whether I do or not!'

Mr Beamish stood in the doorway and looked out into the yard. 'It's a good job you haven't got far to go.' The rain was coming down heavily and it had become quite murky outside. 'Debbie won't be out long in this,' he said, looking out into the falling rain.

'Now you must come over and see the house sometime,' said Kitty firmly.

'I certainly will,' he replied, patting Kitty on the arm.

She smiled at him, she felt quite a fool for thinking him capable of any ill feeling towards them. A flicker caught her eye. 'Oh, there's the bat,' she exclaimed.

'They're in the feed store.' He gestured to the stone building on the right, a flight of stone stairs led up to a plank door. 'There is quite a colony in there; nobody goes in there now so they don't get disturbed.'

'Doesn't Debbie keep the horse feed in there?'

'It's in the stable next to Jester. I haven't been in there for years.'

'It's a shame to see it so quiet here.'

'I know, this isn't how a farm should be,' he said sadly, looking around the empty yard. 'I had hoped that one of the boys would take it on but they weren't interested. This farm has been in our family for five generations, still... what they do with it after I'm gone is up to them.'

'Well they won't have to worry about that for a while Mr Beamish,' she said, smiling up at him.

He looked at her and grinned. 'I am ninety four; I'm not going to go on forever although I have told Sybil that I want my telegram from the Queen.'

'You don't look ninety four,' said Kitty, looking surprised.

'I don't feel it but I'll be very disappointed if I don't get one.' He looked over at Gordon who was walking out the gate with the dog in tow. 'You had better hurry; your husband is leaving without you.'

Kitty sighed and watched as Gordon disappeared through the gate into the lane.

'I suppose I had better go and catch him up.'

Mr Beamish turned back to the front door. 'I hope this rain soon eases up, it makes my bones ache.'

'Perhaps Sybil has a cure,' Kitty joked.

'Oh no, don't mention it to her. I dread to think what she would find for that.'

He stood in the doorway and watched as Kitty walked across the yard, as she got to the gate she turned, meaning to wave but a flicker of movement in an upstairs window caught her eye. She paused, staring up at the window

'I hope you're not looking at the peeling paint.' He smiled ruefully at her. 'It's a lovely house isn't it? It's a grade II listed building but it's sadly needs a bit of TLC now.'

'No, of course not William, it's just that..,' she answered, still staring at the dark second floor window, then jumped slightly on hearing footsteps behind her.

A hand tugged at her arm.

'Come on Kitty, stop chatting. I'm getting wet.'

They waved to Mr Beamish and watched as he went inside and shut the door. Without the light flooding from the open door the yard seemed very dark and quiet. Gordon slipped his arm through Kitty's.

'Come on, let's get going.'

They walked quickly back along the lane to their front drive, as they rounded the corner they could see a small blue car in the drive.

'Who's that?'

'It's Eve's car.' As he spoke their daughter opened the car door and got out.

'There you are. I've been so worried; I've been ringing since this morning, where have you been?' she called.

'Why, what's wrong?' Kitty hurried forward; she could see a small hand waving from the child seat in the back. 'Is everybody okay?'

'We're fine; it's you I've was worried about.'

Gordon gave his daughter a hug. 'We're fine,' he reassured her.

'I popped into your office this morning and you weren't there. Your secretary said you called in early and told her you weren't going to come in. I've been ringing all morning!'

'There's nothing wrong, I decided to stay home today. We had a few things to sort out that's all.'

Kitty looked at him worried that he was going to tell Eve. He caught the look and shook his head.

'But you never have time off,' Eve persisted.

'Well I am today,' he said firmly. 'Come on. Let's get out of the rain.' He pushed them towards the house and then opened the back door of the car. 'I'll get Emily, go on in.' Gordon unbuckled the seat and lifted out the little girl. 'Hello my little poppet, have you come to see gramps then?'

'Dad, can you bring in the pink bag as well?' called Eve, from the front door.

'Okay.' He slung the strap over his shoulder, pulled Emily's hood up and hurried into the house. Kitty closed the door after him and locked it.

'Not a word mind!' he warned her quietly.

'I wasn't going to say anything.'

Eve was taking off her coat in the kitchen and didn't hear them whispering in the hall.

'Your neighbour's not very friendly, is he?' she called to them.

'Who?'

'The old guy, you know. He was glaring at us from the lane. I was going to talk to him but he looked so fierce that I didn't bother.'

'When was this?' asked Gordon.

'Just before you came back. I hope you're not going to have problems with him.'

'That wasn't Mr Beamish; we were just talking to him in the farmhouse.'

'Well it looked like him. I have met him before, remember?' Eve said indignantly.

Emily was wriggling in Gordon's arms, she had spotted Nero.

'Go on then, down you go'

She pottered over to the dog. 'Nero's wet.'

'Yes, he is a wet doggie,' agreed Kitty. 'Let's go and dry him off.' She took Emily's hand and led her into the kitchen. 'Come on Nero.'

Gordon followed and put the bag down on the table. Eve unzipped it and pulled out a handful of letters.

'Mrs Walker gave them to me this morning, that's why I went into your office.'

'Why didn't she just redirect them?' he said, picking them up.

'She was going to but then she saw me so I said I would drop them off.'

Gordon leafed through them quickly. 'It's nothing important, just junk mail.'

'It gave me an excuse to come round.'

'You don't need an excuse Eve.'

'I was going to come over yesterday but it was my mother-in-law's birthday so we went out for a meal.' She looked around the kitchen. 'This looks really nice. It's quite different from the last time I was here.'

'Once the windows were in, the builder really cracked on with it all and he finished on schedule.'

'That's a first, isn't it!' Eve looked at her mother kneeling in front of Emily taking off the little girl's coat. 'Are you happy with it, mum?'

Kitty looked up and hesitated. 'Yes of course'

Gordon looked at Kitty and smiled. 'Mum hasn't got used to it being so quiet yet.'

Kitty pulled herself up. 'I'll get used to it.'

'Have you done anything to the garden yet?' Eve leaned on the edge of the sink and stared out of the kitchen window. 'What's that?'

'Just some rubbish I was going to burn.'

'Why don't you take it to the dump?'

'Are you staying long?' interrupted Gordon.

She laughed. 'I've only just got here and you are trying to get rid of me already.'

'Dad didn't mean that,' Kitty glanced warningly at him. 'It's just that it's a horrible night for driving.'

'I'll be fine, stop fussing mum.'

'Well okay then, I'll put the kettle on.' Kitty stared out of the window as she was filling the kettle and could just see the figure of Mr Beamish walking out of the farmyard. 'I wonder what he's doing out in this weather?' she said in surprise. 'That's not going to do his aches and pains any good.'

Gordon stood up from the table and looked over her shoulder.

'Shut the blind as it such a horrible night, Kitty,' he said abruptly. 'Why don't we take the tea into the front room and I'll light the fire,' He picked up Emily and carried her out into the hall. 'Make sure the back door is locked,' he called back.

'I'll do it. Yep, it's locked, bolted and drawbridge up,' Eve looked across the kitchen at her mother who was fussing nervously with the cups. 'I didn't think there was any crime in the country.'

'It doesn't shut properly so we have to lock it,' Kitty looked away from her daughter as she answered and concentrated on making the tea.

Eve stared at her mother. 'Are you sure you two are alright?'

'Of course, we're fine.' Kitty smiled reassuringly at her daughter. 'Bring the biscuit tin, it's in that cupboard,' she nodded to the cupboard near the door. 'Let's see if dad has got the fire going yet.' Emily was standing in front of the fireplace watching the first few flames licking around the kindling. She turned to her mother and pointed at the flames.

'Look what gramp's done.'

Eve pulled her back. 'Not too close Emily.'

'She's fine,' said Gordon. 'I'm here to watch her.'

'I think she ought to come out of the way Gordon; that kindling spits.'

'Okay, okay,' he stood up and picked up Emily and put her into his chair. 'There now you can sit in gramp's chair and watch the fire or those two won't give me any peace.'

Eve passed him a cup of tea before flopping onto the sofa. 'Poor old granddad,' she mocked and curled her legs up on the cushions.

'Are you going to stay to tea?'

'No, I had better get back soon or Rob will wonder where I am.' Eve stared at the fire watching the flames licking round the logs. 'I love the fireplace.'

'Haven't you seen it before?'

'No, dad told me about it but it hadn't been delivered the last time I was here.'

'Mum was worried it was too big for the room,' he said, dunking a biscuit in his tea.

'No, it's fine. Where did it come from?'

'Well...'

'Near Ilminster,' interrupted Gordon. 'It's been treated for worm and I think it looks great,' he added firmly.

'I do as well,' Kitty stared at him. 'It's just that I was worried it was too big but I've got used to the size now.'

Over the crackling of the logs Kitty could hear footsteps approaching up the gravel drive. She stiffened and stared warily at the window. Gordon followed her gaze; he had also heard the footsteps.

'I'll just see who that is,' he said, keeping calm. He pulled back the curtains and stared out into the darkness. There was a muffled crunch and a car alarm started its insistent beeping.

'My car!' Eve leapt to her feet and ran towards the front door.

'Wait a minute,' Gordon darted forward and caught her by the arm. 'Stay here and I will go and look. You need to watch Emily with the fire.'

'Mum can do that,' she said impatiently and pulled open the door. Kitty picked up Emily from the chair and held her close.

'Wassat?'

'Nothing Emily,' she brushed off the biscuit crumbs from her sticky little face and smoothed back the wispy hair. 'Gramps will see to it.'

'Mumma's gone,' she said, pointing to the door.

'No, she's just outside with gramps, look,' Kitty carried her over to the window and pulled back the curtains, she pointed to the two figures outside. 'There's mummy.'

They were bent over examining the side of Eve's car. She let the curtains drop back and walked back to the chair near the fireplace.

A few minutes later the front door slammed open and Eve burst in, flushed with annoyance.

'Oh dear, what's happened?' Kitty asked her daughter.

'Something's hit my car,' Eve said indignantly. 'The door looks as though it's been kicked!'

'What?'

'There's nobody out there but we heard footsteps on the gravel.'

'Yes, yes I did as well,' she said faintly. 'Where's dad?'

'He's gone to look in the lane and see if he can see anybody. Who would do that!' she exploded. 'Are you having problems with your neighbour?' she rounded on her mother. 'Is that what's going on?'

'No, not really, it's a bit more complicated than that,' said Kitty hesitantly. She pulled her daughter further into the hall and shut the door. 'Dad's not going to be happy I told you, but the house is haunted.'

Eve stared at her mother.

'Oh for God's sake mum! Somebody has just put their size tens into my car door and you're babbling about ghosts!'

'I'm not babbling, Eve,' she said crossly. 'Strange things have been happening and even dad has seen her.'

'Dad has seen what?' he asked, opening the front door and coming in.

'Your ghost,' Eve snapped.

'I didn't want mum to tell you,' he sounded annoyed.

'You mean she's serious?'

'Yes, it seems we have acquired a ghost but I'm going to solve the whys and the wherefores so there is no reason to worry.'

'And you are telling me that a ghost has just damaged my car?'

'I'm not sure that a ghost can do that but I am not going to discount anything just yet.'

She stared from one to another.

'How am I going to claim that on my Insurance, "I was hit by a runaway ghost"?'

'This is no joking matter Eve; mum has been getting really upset over it.'

He took Emily from Kitty's arms.

'This is a new house... so where did it come from?' asked Eve incredulously.

'Let's go and sit down and I'll try to explain. I will tell you what we have found out so far,' he led the way back into the front room. 'Our fireplace used to belong to a woman who lived on Castle Hill. She was rumoured to be a witch. Now hang on....' he held up a hand as Eve tried to interrupt. 'Our neighbours disagree with that but she did die in a very strange way and I think she was murdered. I also think it was her ghost that I saw inside the house last night.'

Eve stared at her father open mouthed. 'Are you serious? You actually saw a ghost? You? Mister Cynical?'

'Yes.'

'What... oh this just gets better. Why would she damage my car?'

'I don't know.' He shrugged and stared at his daughter. 'But I think you should go before anything else happens.'

'But you can't stay here, if you seriously think that.'

Gordon hesitated. 'I would like you to take mum with you,' he glanced across at his wife.

'I'm not going if you're not.' Kitty stood up from the sofa and glared at him. 'I'm the one that she spoke to, remember.'

'I know,' he said, trying to be patient. 'That's why I think you should go with Eve. Spend the night there and I will pick you up in the morning.'

'No, if you are staying then so am I.'

'I think you have both gone mad, ghosts can't kick holes in cars.'

'Since when have you become an expert?' he asked sarcastically. 'I don't know what she's capable of and I'd rather not find out but I think we haven't seen the last of her yet.'

'Mrs Leavenham knows a lot about Hannah and we want to see her to see if she can help in any way.'

'Who is Hannah? And who is Mrs Leavenham?'

Kitty looked at her blankly. 'Oh, of course, sorry dear. Let's start from the beginning. Hannah who was supposed to be a witch but wasn't of course, lived at Castle Hill with her husband Samuel who was our Mr Beamish 's grandfather's brother and......'

Eve put her head in her hands and groaned. 'Oh God no, Dad, you explain please!'

'Gordon, *stop* laughing!'

'It's simple, Hannah was accused of being a witch by a local farmer, he paid a white witch to get rid of her and she died in mysterious circumstances. Okay, with me so far?'

'Who was the farmer?'

'We don't know and that is why we want to see Mrs Leavenham who knows all there is to know about the village, plus her grandmother was friends with Hannah.'

'Show Eve what you found on the computer about Hannah,' suggested Kitty.

Gordon put Emily back into his chair and strode off into the study to find his laptop.

'Right, move up you two so I can sit in the middle,' he opened the laptop and plugged in the memory stick. 'Now here we are. This is what I found earlier, read it'

Eve read it and then read it again, a puzzled expression on her face.

'This doesn't make any sense, dad.'

'No it doesn't, mum has an idea that Mrs Leavenham's grandmother was the little girl. So we think she may be able to help.'

'Why don't you try tracing Hannah through the census records?'

Gordon clapped a hand to his head. 'Damn, why didn't I think of that?'

'The 1841 Census is the earliest so start with that one,' Eve suggested, peering over his arm at the screen.

Kitty pulled Emily on to her lap and put her arms around the little girl, she was starting to grizzle and rub her eyes.

'Emily's getting tired, Eve.'

'Just give her a cuddle mum I'm sure she'll be fine,' said Eve, not looking up from the computer. She pointed at the screen. 'Dad, just put in 1841 census.'

'Can you do that? Just look up records of people?'

'You can find out anything on the internet these days mum, you should really get out more, you know,' Eve said, half sarcastically.

'Now, now, mum doesn't do technology,' said Gordon calmly. 'She has enough problems working the dishwasher.'

Kitty hugged her granddaughter and whispered in her ear, 'Aren't they a pair of meanies Emily?'

They stared intently at the screen while Gordon clicked on different sites to find the right census records.

'What's that one?'

'Family search, let's try on this site. Right, 1841 Census. This is it.' He tapped in Hannah Beamish. 'Date of birth?' he queried.

'Just put her name in and see what comes up.'

'It needs place of birth as well so if I just put in Medbury, Devon and we'll start from there.'

'But we don't know she was born here, dad.'

'Well, we'll assume it for now.'

'Hey, look at all the Beamishes in Devon, are there any in Medbury?'

'Here's one, ah... this must be Robert Beamish. Let's look at his record.' Gordon clicked onto Robert's name and the next page opened up.

'Damn! We have to pay to see any more, I'll need my card number. Kitty can you fetch my wallet? I think it's in my jacket.'

Kitty slid Emily off her lap onto the sofa and got up. 'I won't be a minute.'

She found his jacket hanging over the banister in the hall and paused, listening to the wind howling around the house and buffeting against the windows and door. Outside there was a crash as the wheelie bin was blown over and Kitty could hear the scraping noise as it was driven across the drive.

'What was that, Kitty?'

'It was the bin going over in the wind.'

The wind whined around the eaves of the house shrieking louder and louder as she listened.

'Kitty! Did you find it?'

'I'm just coming,' she answered, hurrying back into the room. 'I was listening to the wind.'

Eve looked up. 'I don't think I will be driving home in this for a while, I'll ring Rob after we have done this and warn him I'm going to be late.'

Gordon didn't answer; he was concentrating on entering all his bank details onto the site.

'This is going to cost me an arm and a leg,' he grumbled.

'If we can find out some more information about Hannah it will be worth it.'

Kitty knelt in front of the fire and gave the crumbling logs a poke. She placed a log on the dying embers, the flames quickly licking up around the dry wood. The wind moaned down the chimney driving the smoke back into the room. Kitty coughed and waved a hand in front of her face.

'Look at all this smoke; it's being blown back down the chimney.'

She turned, neither of them were listening to her, they were intent on the laptop.

'Look Kitty, we have found the census record of Robert Beamish. He was 22 years old, unmarried and his father Joseph was the head of the household, living at Castle Hill Farm, Medbury,' Gordon scanned the rest of the household. ' Able Facey, 27, born Seaton, unmarried Agricultural Labourer; Rosie Guppy 38, born Medbury, unmarried, Dairymaid; Fred Dawes, 18, born Medbury, Agricultural Labourer.'

'Are there any other Beamishs in the village?' asked Eve.
He put his finger on the screen and carefully went down the list.
'Nope, no Hannah Beamish.'
Kitty looked at them from her position in front of the fire place.
 'Well, she won't be in the census forms.'
 'Why?' Gordon peered at her over his glasses.
 'The census used to be taken in the summer and Hannah died in the spring, you don't have to be a computer genius to know that.'
 'Now you tell us, thanks mum!'
 'Well you two are supposed to be the computer whiz kids.' She put another log on the fire and grinned to herself. 'Try looking for her death,' she suggested.
Gordon clicked onto a different list and tried the name Beamish.
'Here's one, Samuel Beamish 25th April 1840.'
 'We've seen that already,' said Kitty.
 'No we haven't, this Samuel was only six weeks old when he died, must be a different family.'
Gordon sat back and rubbed his hands over his face.
 'God! This is so frustrating!'
 'So you can't find anything for Hannah? Birth or death?'
 'Nope, not a thing.'
 'How strange,' mused Kitty.
They fell silent while outside the wind screamed around the house. Another puff of smoke blew into the room.
 'Smokey room, Nana,' Emily was getting tired and she rubbed her eyes which were stinging from the smoke.
 'Shall I put Emily to bed in the spare room?'
 'I ought to be going,' Eve said uncertainly, staring at the window but the curtains were drawn against the storm outside. 'But it sounds really bad.'
 'Perhaps you had better stay,' said Gordon. 'I don't like the idea of you driving home in this.'
 'Yes,' agreed Kitty. 'Ring Rob and tell him you're going to stay at least until the storm blows over.'
They sat listening to the howling wind which seemed to be mounting in intensity every minute, in the hall the letterbox started to rattle.
 'Wassat noise,' Emily whimpered.
 'It's just the wind; it's making the letterbox rattle, that's all. It's nothing to be worried about, Emily.'
Kitty tried to soothe her but she slid off her lap, ran over to her mother and scrambled up on to her knee.

'Let's see what else we can find,' said Gordon, tapping the keys. Nero appeared in the doorway with his ears down and looking very mournful.

'Come on Nero,' Kitty called to him. He pattered over the carpet and came to sit by her legs, and laid his head in her lap. 'He doesn't like storms,' she stroked him soothingly on the head. 'Poor old dog.'

'Poor doggie,' Emily, forgetting the storm for a minute, scrambled down and came over to give him a pat on the head.

'Gently Emily,' warned Eve. The little girl's pats could be a bit hard and Nero was already looking sorry he had come in to join them.

'What else have you found, Gordon?'

'Nothing for Hannah and nothing else for Samuel. Robert Beamish is on the 1851 census as head of the household so I suppose his father must have died.'

'Perhaps he's running the farm.'

'Let's see now, yep he's running the farm, no father on the census. Oh and look at this he's married, to a Rachel, born 1814, Exeter.'

'What was that?' The noise of the wind howling around the house had grown so loud that Kitty and Eve were having difficulty in hearing him.

'Rachel,' he said loudly. 'Born 1814 Exeter, and they had two sons. Edward F. born 1841, Medbury, and William, born 1844, Medbury.'

'Hang on a minute, 1841? He wasn't married in the 1841 census. He was single,' said Eve suddenly.

Gordon looked at her surprised. 'That's right, he wasn't. Well, well, looks like they had the honeymoon before the wedding.'

Eve grinned. 'I didn't think that sort of thing went on then.'

'Hah! Don't you believe it, things haven't changed that much,' he snorted.

Kitty laughed, she was just going to speak when Nero started growling.

'Nero stop that.' For a minute she thought that the dog had lost patience with Emily's attentions and was growling at the little girl. But he was staring at the door, his hackles had risen and a low ominous growl rumbled around his stomach.

'Nero, shush,' commanded Gordon.

'Why's Nero growling, nana?'

'He's upset, it's the storm,' Kitty tried to comfort the dog but he stood up suddenly, pushing Emily out of the way and padded towards the door with his tail and ears down.

A terrific gust of wind howled around the house, the letterbox rattled frantically and in the kitchen the back door suddenly crashed open,

blowing into the room all the debris from the garden including Kitty's carefully collected pile of leaves and cardboard.
Nero started barking frantically, lunging towards the hall and then retreating back to the safety of the front room.
Amidst the wind howling, Emily shrieking and Gordon shouting at the dog to be quiet Kitty could just make out a human voice bellowing in rage.

'Can you hear that?'
She jumped as Eve grabbed her arm. 'Who is that shouting?'
'I don't know. Gordon?'
He had run into the kitchen to shut the door. 'I thought I told you to lock it, Kitty!' he shouted.
'I locked it, dad! Mum said it didn't shut properly,' Eve said indignantly and followed him into the kitchen, with Kitty hurrying after her.
Gordon had managed to push the door shut against the howling wind and push the bolt across, then dragged the table over and jammed it against the door as the lock continued to rattle ominously with the force of the wind. Gordon looked at the mess of leaves and rubbish on the floor.

'Where's the broom?' he yelled to his wife, trying to make himself heard against the shrieking outside.
The wind buffeted the door making the table slide across the tiled floor.

'Dammit, we need something heavy on the table. Kitty... Kitty!'
They stared wildly around the kitchen looking for something to jam against the shaking door.

'What about jamming a chair under the handle?' suggested Kitty, pulling forward one of the pine kitchen chairs. Gordon shook his head.

'It will just slide across the floor.'
He leant his weight against the table to keep it from sliding and looked towards the hall, the letterbox on the front door was flapping wildly and the wind shrieked louder and louder, whining and howling around the house, the rain lashing at the windows and doors.

'Check the front door, one of you,' he said quickly.
Eve ran to the door and tried the lock.

'It's okay, it is locked.' She turned as she spoke and with one howling blast the door burst open throwing her across the hall floor.

'Eve!' Kitty shrieked, and struggled along the hall to reach her, forcing herself against the wind but it was blowing so hard that she could hardly stand. 'Eve, are you okay?'

'Yeah, I think so,' she felt the back of her head and then looked at the smear of blood on her hand. 'My head's bleeding.'
Gordon struggled through from the kitchen holding onto the banisters.
   'Stay there you two; I'll see if I can get to the door.'
He was leaning into the wind almost bent double against the force of the blast, which carried with it small stinging pieces of gravel from the drive. 'Mind your eyes.'
Kitty had one arm linked around the newel post and was being pressed back against the stairs. The force of the wind pushing against her chest made it difficult to breathe and she found herself gasping in the dust laden wind.
Gordon had reached the door and was bracing himself against it trying to close it against the force of the wind shrieking into the hall.
Eve was crouched on the floor at his feet trying to protect her face against the small pieces of flying gravel. Kitty could hear her muffled crying.
   'Come on grab it and let's get it shut,' he shouted.
Kitty reached across to the door.
   'Alright, one, two, three,' and with that they both heaved and slammed the door shut. Gordon shot the bolt across. 'God, I hope this holds.'
 The door vibrated under the force of the wind hitting it, a hail of gravel was being driven against the hall window and there was an ominous crack as a large piece smashed into the glass.
   'Let's get the chest from your study and put it across the door,' Kitty suggested. She straightened wearily and wiped her face, feeling a slight stickiness on her skin she glanced down at the little smears of blood on her shaking hand. She stared blindly at it for a second before wiping her hand down her leg and turned to Eve who was struggling to stand. She was sobbing and holding her head.
   'Eve, are you okay?' Kitty knelt over her, putting a comforting arm around her shoulders. 'Get up off the floor, come on,' and helped Eve to her feet.
Gordon leant back against the door with his eyes closed, gasping for breath.
   'Kitty, let's get that chest in case the door blows open again.'
She looked up cocking her head to one side and listening.
   'I don't think we need to, listen!'
The wind had suddenly dropped.
   'It's stopped! Just like that. Can you believe it,' Gordon said amazed. He turned to the two women. 'Are you alright?'

Eve started sobbing and reached for her father.

'It's okay, it's stopped now,' he reassured her, putting an arm around her.

'My head's bleeding dad.'

'I'll get a towel,' Kitty headed to the kitchen, pulled a clean hand towel from the laundry basket and hurried back to hall. 'Here use this.' She examined the cut on the back of Eve's head. It was only small but there was large egg shaped swelling under her hair.

'It's not too bad, it's nearly stopped bleeding now,' she reassured her and pressed the towel to it. 'Hold this, and press it firmly onto the cut.'

Eve took a few shaky steps forward, wiping her eyes with one hand while holding the towel to her head and glanced into the front room.

'Where's Emily?' she suddenly said, looking wildly around the empty room.

Kitty froze, realising that she had given no thought to her granddaughter who they had left alone while they had struggled with the doors. She hurried to the door and stared into the room. 'Gordon, she's not here.'

'I'll check upstairs.'

'You don't think she went outside?' said Eve, fighting to control the trembling in her voice.

Kitty placed a comforting hand on her arm and squeezed it.

'She couldn't have, we would have seen her,' she said firmly. 'Now calm down Eve, she is in the house somewhere.'

They could hear Gordon upstairs running from room to room, opening and slamming doors. 'Emily, Emily where are you? His voice sounded increasingly strained with every second that his granddaughter was missing.

'Eve, come and sit down and then I'll go and help,' Kitty put an arm around her daughter and led her over to the sofa. 'Sit down here, we'll find her, don't worry.'

Nero was stretched out in front of the fire; he raised his head and watched them his tail thumping gently on the rug. Kitty's next few words became strangled in her throat as she gazed at the dog's fur; thin red streaks were smeared across his muzzle and down the sides of his face.

'What is that on the dog?' her voice trembled, as she peered over the edge of the sofa, for one wild second wondering what she might see.

Emily was sitting cross legged, hidden from view at the end of the sofa, the contents of Eve's handbag scattered around her.

'Emily! There you are,' she said with relief. 'What are you doing with mummy's lipstick?'

She turned and grinned at her grandmother, her gleeful little face was smeared in bright red lipstick and big globs of it covered her hands and clothes. The last little bit was being used to draw stick figures on the carpet.

Eve leapt up from the sofa where she had collapsed a few seconds earlier, and pushed her mother to one side.

'Emily, thank goodness! I was so worried.' Eve knelt down next to her and wrapped her arms around her daughter, hugging her tightly.

'I'll tell dad that she's here,' Kitty said in relief, and trotted out into the hall. 'Gordon,' she called up to him. 'It's alright; she was in the sitting room behind the sofa.'

'Oh, for the love of God, woman!' He pounded down the stairs. 'I was worried sick!'

'We all were Gordon, so calm down.'

He followed her back into the room.

'Is she alright?' he asked anxiously, looking at Emily and Eve sat in front of the fireplace.

'Emily has found Mummy's make up so she's having a great time,' Kitty smiled slightly and gestured at Emily's lipstick smeared face.

The little girl twisted round to look at him and grinned. 'Look gramps, I'm drawing.'

He sat down on the end of the sofa and reached over to ruffle her hair.

'Well at least she's okay.'

'She's here,' Kitty said suddenly.

'Who?'

'Hannah, I can smell lavender.'

Eve sniffed. 'So can I.'

Emily smiled and pointed to the stick drawings on the floor. 'Look, it's the lady.'

'What lady, sweetie?'

'She's been talking to me, she likes flowers.'

Emily opened one of her sticky little hands. 'Look,' and although crushed and bent and covered with lipstick Gordon could still make out the remains of a few sprigs of lavender. He paused for a few minutes, unable to believe his eyes. He drew a deep rasping breath and stood up quickly.

'That's it, we're going. We'll spend the night at Eve's.'

He picked up Emily and held her firmly to his chest, gesturing for Eve to get to her feet.

'Grab your things Eve; we'll use your car.'

Gordon ushered them out into the hall, casting one worried look back into the room.

'Kitty! Where are you going?'

'I was just going to get a few things.'

He pulled her off the bottom stair. 'No! We're leaving now.' His usually calm voice sounded strained and his hand grasping Kitty's arm was trembling slightly.

'Come on mum, I want to go,' Eve tugged at her arm. 'Let's just get out of here.'

'Okay, okay, but the dog has to come.'

'Just stop talking and get in the damn car,' he said and slammed the front door behind them.

'What about the lights?' Kitty looked at her husband enquiringly. 'We haven't turned them all off...Gordon?'

Nobody answered, Eve jumped into the back seat with Emily held tightly on her lap and then pulled Nero onto the seat next to her. Gordon squeezed behind the steering wheel fiddling with the seat to get more leg room.

'Are we all in? Right, lock the doors and let's get the hell out of here.' He started the car and crunched the gear stick into first. 'Sorry Eve, I'm used to an automatic,' Gordon joked, trying to sound normal. He reversed slowly avoiding the over turned bin and headed along the drive.

'Thank goodness it was collected today otherwise the rubbish would be everywhere.'

'Mum!'

Gordon flicked the headlights onto full beam and drove through the gateway, just for an instant the lights picked out a figure stood to one side.

'Gordon, it's Mr Beamish, don't you think we should tell him why we're going?'

He slowed the car almost to a halt and glanced in the rear view mirror. Without a word he put his foot on the accelerator and sped along the road, past the farm and down into the village.

'Slow down!' Kitty was clinging to the door. 'Mr Beamish will think we've gone mad.'

'That wasn't William,' he ground out.

'Of course it was, I saw him,' Kitty turned and stared at him. 'Calm down Gordon, do you want me to drive?' She looked over at him in concern, his hands were shaking on the wheel and his face was twisted in a strange expression.

'Gordon?'

'It wasn't William.'

'Are you sure?'

'Yes! Hey... look at this!' he slowed down as they drove through the middle of the village.

'Look at what?'

'The road, its bone dry, they haven't had any rain here at all.' Kitty stared out of the window and then peered through the windscreen up at the night sky.

'But it's a clear night, no rain clouds at all.'

Eve stirred restlessly on the back seat and sat forward to nudge her father's arm.

'Dad, can we go now? I want to go home.'

'Okay Eve don't worry, we're just going.'

****

They pulled into the drive of Eve's small semi and Gordon switched off the engine. The hall light clicked on flooding the driveway with light and Rob opened the front door.

'There you are,' he sounded annoyed. 'I was getting worried,' his voice changed when he saw them all in the car. 'What's wrong?'

Eve scrambled out of the back holding the sleeping Emily tightly.

'What's that on Emily?' he said, leaping down the front door step towards his wife.

'It's alright, it's just lipstick,' Kitty quickly reassured him.

Rob looked from his mother-in-law to his wife.

'Are you alright?' he asked Eve, looking in concern at her pale face and the smear of blood on her face.

'No!' she wailed. 'It was awful. I hurt my head and I thought I had lost Emily.' The rest of her explanation was lost in sobs. Rob put his arms around her and his daughter and led her to the door.

'Come on inside.' He glanced across at his in-laws. 'Thanks for bringing them home.'

'I'm afraid we're going to be staying the night, Rob,' said Kitty.

'What? Well of course,' Rob looked at her surprised but went on, 'Come on in then, although I don't know where you're going to sleep.'

'A chair by the fire will do fine, so don't worry.' She turned to Gordon who was leaning against the side of the car. 'Are you okay?'

'Yeah I'm fine,' He pushed himself upright. 'Let's get in, I need a drink.' He put an arm around her shoulder and gave her a hug. 'Sorry I didn't believe you Kitty.'

'That's okay.' She rested her head on his shoulder for a minute before taking his arm and pulling him towards the house. 'Come on let's go and see if Rob has any whiskey, I think we could all do with one.'

****

'I can't believe you're serious! This is ridiculous.' Rob looked in astonishment at his father- in- law.

'That's what I have been saying for the last few days and I still can't believe it,' said Gordon quietly.

'But it happened,' Kitty said firmly. 'And we have to find out why she is haunting us.'

'Are you sure she's not out for revenge?'

'Revenge against whom? We haven't done anything to her; we've just got her fireplace.'

Rob was fidgeting impatiently with the bottle of whiskey.

'Well, I'm sure there must be an explanation for it, it sounds like you're letting your imaginations run away with you.' He stared at his wife and shook his head.

'We weren't Rob! You weren't there; you didn't see what it was like and that voice screaming outside!' Eve shuddered. 'It was awful.' She looked at her parents. 'You can't go back there; you'll have to sell the house.'

'We're not selling, Eve. Dad and I will get to the bottom of this.' Gordon looked at his wife, his expression troubled.

'I don't know Kitty, perhaps we should sell.'

'Gordon! After all the work we have put into the house and anyway I don't feel that she means us any harm.'

'Mother!' Eve shouted at her. 'Are you mad? After tonight, how can you say that?'

'I don't know, it's just a feeling I have.'

'Well we'll see, we'll go back tomorrow and see what happens,' said Gordon slowly.

'You would get a good price for it,' added Rob.

'We're not selling,' Kitty said firmly. 'And anyway we need to see Mrs Leavenham; she might know something that will help.'

 A knock sounded on the cottage door but Hannah didn't move from her position in front of the fire. She stared drearily into the flames and wished whoever it was would go away.
The latch clicked. 'Hannah? Are you well, me dear?'
She turned slowly. 'Michael.'
He came further into the room, his cap clasped in his hand. 'Missus sent I up to see if you needed anything.'
 'Is Mary well?'
 'Aye, she's doing well, baby as well. He's a fine chap.'
 'You look after her mind, and make sure she don't do too much.'
 'Daughter can look after the house till she's up on her feet again' Michael looked at Hannah bent over the fire and then glanced at the empty crib near the wall.
 'Are you sure you're well? You could come and stay with us for a few days till you feel better. We'd make room for 'ee.'
 'Now Michael Guppy, you've enough mouths to feed in your house without inviting more people to your table.'
 'Well,' he hesitated, staring at her pale drawn face. 'Here's something for your pot tonight.' He laid a plump hare on the table. 'I've skinned and gutted it for 'ee.'
Hannah managed a faint smile. 'You're a kind man, Michael.'
A pink tinge appeared on his cheeks. 'Aw now, one good turn, as they say.'
Hannah turned to look him squarely in the face. 'I hear he's been spreading tales about me again.'
 'Ay well, nobody takes any notice of him, we'm all know them tales ain't true.
There ain't one of us in the village you haven't helped at one time or another.'
 'Their memories be short, Michael.'
 'Dunne worry Hannah, everything will blow over soon enough. He'll find somebody else to gripe about, you wait and see.'
She turned back to the fire, her shoulders slumped. 'Haven't I suffered enough and still he hounds me, he's a devil that one, curse him. He won't be happy till he sees me gone. Damn him and his family.'
 'Now, now Hannah.' Michael looked worried. 'Don't 'ee let anybody hear you'm talking like that woman, that'll just bring trouble.'

A tear rolled down her cheek. 'Well why won't he let me be? Hasn't he done enough to me already, I don't think he's going to rest easy until he has every stick and stone that be mine.'
Hannah lifted her apron and wiped her face.
Michael shifted impatiently, twisting his cap in his hands.
   'Now you'd better be going or your Missus will think you've stopped off in the Red Lion.'
   'Are you sure you won't come down to the village?'
  'No, no",' she sniffed. 'No, you get on. I'll be fine and thank 'ee for the hare Michael'

Wednesday

Eve drove slowly into the drive and stopped just inside the gateway. 'Are you sure about this?'

'We'll be fine,' reassured Kitty. 'Thanks for bringing us back.'

The house looked calm and welcoming in the early morning light, the light from the hall casting a warm glow onto the front doorstep.

'You can stay with us if you need to, we don't mind.'

'Thanks Eve, but it was a bit of a squeeze with all of us and we can stay in a hotel tonight if we need to.'

Gordon opened the car door and climbed out. 'We left the lights on.'

'I did tell you last night before we left,' reminded Kitty as she tried the front door. 'You didn't lock the front door either.'

She pushed the door open, inside the hall floor was covered in the leaves and twigs that had blown in the back door the day before and there was a fine covering of grit and sand over everything. Kitty's feet crunched as she walked across the hall towards the kitchen.

'Where did we put Mrs Leavenham's phone number?'

Gordon hovered in the doorway. 'It's in the kitchen, pinned to the fridge.'

'Come in then and shut the door, we've got some tidying up to do.'

She looked at him hesitating in the doorway; he looked very ill at ease and was glancing nervously into the front room.

'Are you okay?' she asked.

'As fine as anybody could be under the circumstances.'

Nero padded after her into the kitchen and jumped into his box by the radiator and settled down with a satisfied grunt.

'Well Nero is happy to be back.'

'Stupid dog,' grunted Gordon.

Eve stood next to her father, holding his arm and staring around the room. 'Do you want me to stay and help clear up?'

Kitty was struggling to move the kitchen table away from the door. 'Come and help me move this then I can throw all this rubbish back into the garden, I knew I should have had the bonfire and not just left it.'

Eve moved forward reluctantly into the room and took hold of the edge of the table and helped her mother drag it back into the middle of the kitchen.

'Gordon, can you get the broom?'

'Why are you bothering with all this now, let's just get hold of Mrs Leavenham.'

'You ring her while I clear this mess up,' Kitty said firmly and pulled out the broom from behind the door of the utility room. She brushed a pile of leaves out and into the middle of the kitchen and then stopped and looked at Gordon who was still hesitating in the doorway. 'Well, are you going to call her?'

He gazed blankly at her.

'Are you sure you're okay?' she asked.

'Yes, yes I'm fine Kitty, stop keeping on.' He pulled the scrap of paper off the fridge and headed back to the hall. 'I'll phone her now.'

Eve hovered in the doorway looking first at her mother calmly sweeping the floor and then at Gordon.

'Do you need me here, mum?'

'No dear, if you want to go I quite understand.'

'I can't stay here, I'm sorry, not after last night.'

Kitty propped the broom up against the table and went over to her.

'It's okay Eve,' she patted her daughter on the arm. 'We'll be fine.'

'Okay, if you're sure then,' Eve tried not to sound too relieved; she moved quickly to the front door and looked at her parents.

'You will let me know what happens, won't you?'

'We will and thanks for running us back,' said Gordon, and gave her a hug.

Kitty looked at him enquiringly.

'No answer I'm afraid.'

'I'm going dad, okay?'

'Yes go on Eve, we'll be fine so don't worry,' he said calmly for his daughter's benefit. 'There's nothing to worry about.'

Gordon shut and locked the front door after Eve had driven off and walked slowly back into the kitchen, he looked at his wife impatiently.

'Kitty, let's leave all this and go down to the village.'

'I've nearly finished Gordon, out of the way,' she pushed him to one side and finished sweeping up the last of the leaves into the dustpan. 'There, all done.'

'Now can we go?'

'Perhaps she's not home.'

'We can try; she may be at the shop already. I can't stay here and twiddle my thumbs Kitty.'

****

The Post Office door was closed; the opening hours were taped onto the glass window.

'We're too early, let's go and see if she's at home, she should be at this time of the day.'

'Morning.'

They both jumped and turned eagerly but it wasn't Mrs Leavenham standing behind them, it was a woman they had never seen before.

'Good morning,' responded Kitty politely.

'Aren't you the couple from the new house at the Castle Farm?' she asked.

'That's right.' Gordon looked at her curiously.

'I'm Sheena, from the pub. My husband said you had come in over the weekend.' She looked eagerly at Kitty. 'Malcolm said you were interested in attending a séance.'

'Oh,' began Kitty. 'I thought it sounded interesting, actually....' Kitty had a sudden thought. 'Have you held many séances?'

'Not here, it's been difficult to find people who are open minded enough to accept the spirit world in this area. Would you be interested?' she added hopefully.

'I think you may be able to help us, would you consider holding a séance in our house?'

Gordon looked at Kitty doubtfully. 'I'm not sure that's a good idea Kitty,' he interrupted.

She glanced at him impatiently and rushed on, 'It might help us and it's worth a try.'

Sheena looked at the couple and excitedly tugged at the string of beads around her neck.

'I would love to hold one for you; perhaps we could get a group together?'

'No!' they both said quickly.

'It would be better if we keep it to just us three,' Kitty added, 'We're being troubled by a spirit.'

'Really!' Sheena looked delighted. 'How exciting.'

Gordon stared at her coldly. 'No it isn't actually, it's bloody frightening.'

'Oh yes, of course. If you're not used to the presence of spirits then it would be unsettling,' she nodded at them. 'When would you like to hold it?'

'As soon as possible, like now.'

'Now? That's rather short notice. I'd have to fetch a few things and prepare myself mentally for it. Tonight would be better, in the dark.'

'It has to be dark?' queried Kitty.

'No! Definitely not in the dark,' said Gordon firmly.

Kitty looked at him. 'No, you're probably right. Could you do it in an hour or so?'

'Why! You are in a rush, we can try, there's no guarantee of course that the spirits will turn up so to speak.'

'Oh, I don't think that is going to be a problem, Sheena,' Gordon added drily. 'I'm sure you won't be disappointed.'

'This is so exciting! It's Gordon and Kitty, isn't it?'

'Yep, that's right.'

Sheena half turned.

'I'll go and fetch a few things and let my husband know, I'm sure he'll be able to manage on his own for a few hours.'

'Just come up when you're ready.'

Sheena waved a hand over her shoulder as she hurried back to the Witch and Broomstick then suddenly stopped and came back.

'Oh dear, I forgot what I came for,' she giggled, and pushed a handful of letters into the post box set into the wall of the Post Office. 'Now, I won't be long.'

'Okay,' Gordon called after her as she hurried down the narrow village street, the clacking of her heels bouncing off the stone walls of the cottages.

He turned to Kitty 'Are you sure about this?'

'Who better to help than somebody who holds séances?'

'I hope we aren't going to regret this,' he said moodily. 'Shall we still go and see if Sybil is at home?'

****

Priddy Cottage was not far from the Post Office and just a hundred yards farther on than The Witch and Broomstick. They walked past, still closed this early in the morning but coming from inside they could hear Sheena's voice raised in excitement.

The cottage was in a row of small stone built cottages just in front of the church, a steep path led up to the lichgate at the rear of the houses and behind the church was the small neatly kept graveyard.

'Quiet neighbours,' remarked Gordon.

Kitty looked at him and half smiled. 'You just couldn't resist could you?' She knocked firmly on the front door. Heavy net curtains hung at the small windows and the curtains were still half drawn. A bright pink potted pelargonium stood on the windowsill.

'She must be out.'

'Bugger the woman, what's she doing, a woman of her age should be at home.'

'She's allowed a social life Gordon, perhaps she's out visiting a neighbour.'

'Well she shouldn't be,' he answered crossly.

'Stop being so touchy.'

'I think after the last few days I am entitled to be feeling a bit touchy!'

'Let's go home and we'll try again later.' Kitty took his arm and gave it a squeeze. 'Come on.'

'Okay you're right, let's go home and get ready for the séance. Although God only knows what that will bring.' He suddenly stopped. 'Talking of God only knows I wonder if there is a vicar living in the village.'

'What for?'

'An exorcism of course.'

'Do they still do that?'

'How the hell should I know? I'm a logistics manager. I'm a bit out of my depth here.'

'Doesn't it cast the spirit into outer darkness or purgatory or something?'

'As long as it casts her out of my house, I don't care.'

'Her?'

Gordon looked at her curiously.

'Yes, her, Hannah. Who else?'

Kitty's steps slowed. 'I don't know Gordon, I don't know why but I feel that she's not trying to harm us.'

'Are you serious, after yesterday?'

'Was that Hannah? All the noise and the wind? I don't know Gordon, I really don't.'

'Well I'm at a loss, I thought I could handle this,' Gordon stopped and swung round to face his wife. "But the worst thing is that she was talking to little Emily, and Emily could see her!'

'I know Gordon I was there! Perhaps she was murdered and she's not at peace, but I don't understand what that has got to do with us.'

Kitty looked puzzled and stared up the street in the direction of Orchard Cottage.

Gordon put his arm around her shoulder.

'Come on, it looks like we'll be finding out soon.'

'I hope so and I hope Sheena knows what she is doing.' Kitty's steps slowed again as they walked past the farmyard, she glanced in but the place looked deserted. 'Do you think we should tell Mr Beamish what's happening?'

'No, definitely not. I think we should keep this to ourselves, we wouldn't want him to die of fright.'

Kitty half laughed. 'I think he's tougher than that Gordon.'

'Maybe.'

The couple reached the end of the old stone wall and stopped at the entrance of the driveway; the house looked quiet and gave no clue as to the events that had occurred over the last few days.

Gordon sighed and gave her hand a squeeze. 'Come on then, let's go in and get ready for the great event.'

'I suppose we should have asked her if she needed anything for it,' mused Kitty.

'Like what?'

'I don't know, candles maybe, sacrificial goat. I haven't done this before you know.'

'We haven't got any candles or a goat; she'll have to make do with the dog.'

'She's not having the dog! She can have you instead.'

'Seriously though, Kitty I'm not comfortable with this at all,' he hesitated as he spoke and glanced around. 'I just hope it doesn't make the situation worse.'

'Well what else can we do?' Kitty said hesitantly. 'Apart from move. But I think it's worth a try and I'm sure she'll be able to help.'

'Hannah.'

She turned and looked back down the path. 'Hello me dear, what are you doing up here this early?'

'We've been baking and I made an extra loaf for you. I smuggled it out under my pinafore.'

The young girl sounded triumphant as she pulled back the soiled white apron and showed Hannah the loaf.

'That's kind of 'ee but you mustn't bring me any more food, if he should find out what you've been doing...' her voice trailed off.

'I'll be careful Hannah, dunnee worry.'

They both started as a dog barked farther down the hill.

'That'll be him, get going child and don't let him see you.'

'Aye, I'd better,' she looked nervously over her shoulder. 'I'll come up later in the week, he's off to the market in Axminster on Thursday,' she giggled. 'I think he's going courting.'

'Now you be careful...oh quick!' Hannah grabbed her by her thin shoulders. 'Hide, he be here.'

The child ducked out of sight behind the brambles, barely breathing in the hope that he or the dog wouldn't notice her crouching in the bushes.

'Now then woman, what are you doing?'

'Nothing that's any of your business, so go on and let I be.'

'Don't you tell me what my business is, Hannah Beamish. You're a blight,' he ground out. 'A blight on this village, we all know that. With your potions and spells, who knows what demons you call up...this is a good Christian village. You should go from here and leave us in peace.'

'Demons! There's only one demon in this village and that's you. Don't you think I don't know where all this nasty tittle tattle has come from, you evil bugger.'

His face flushed with rage and he drew his teeth back in a snarl. 'Evil? You'd know all about that, you old hag!'

'If Samuel was alive you wouldn't talk to me this way.'

'That cripple's gone and good riddance to him and his brat,' he spat at her.

'Damn you!' she said in quiet fury. 'Damn you to hell.'

His face twisted and he lunged at her, raising his stick in a shaking hand.

'No! Don't you dare!'

The little girl tumbled out from behind the bramble bushes and rushed over to Hannah and stood between the two furious adults.

'Leave her be,' she shouted at him.

'You! What are you doing here? I don't pay you to dawdle about on this hill. Get on back to the farm and get on with your chores or you'll feel my stick across your back.'

Hannah reached forward and put a protective arm around the girl's thin trembling body.

'You touch this child and you'll be sorry.'

'This is all your doing leading this brat astray, encouraging her to waste my time. I'm taking it out of your wages,' he yelled at the child. 'I've a good mind to send you home, let your parents deal with you.'

Hannah held her tighter and glared at him.

'Get off my land.'

He stared at her for a second, his mouth working in fury and without another word he turned and stalked off down the path.

Hannah heaved a trembling sigh and gave the girl a little shake.

'Now get on back quick and go into the dairy and find Rosie. She won't stand no nonsense from him. Now go.' Hannah gave her a little push.

'Will you be alright up here on your own?'

'I'll be alright, now go on with you.'

The young girl nodded and picking up her heavy skirt and petticoats pushed her way through the hawthorn hedge so she could take a short cut across the fields back to the farm.

There was an enthusiastic rapping on the door shortly after they had arrived home, Gordon was busy in the front room pulling out the dining table and arranging three chairs around it.

'Kitty, she's here,' he called.

'That might not be Sheena; we've only been back fifteen minutes.' Kitty hurried through from the kitchen and cautiously opened the door and peered out.

'Oh, it is you. Hello.' She opened the door wider. 'Come on in, Sheena. Gordon is just sorting out some chairs for us.'

'Hi Katy.'

'Kitty.'

'Oh sorry, Kitty, Malcolm is so sorry that he couldn't come as well but he's expecting a delivery this morning. I've been telling him all about it and he was so jealous.'

'Well, we did want to keep it to the three of us Sheena.'

'Yes of course, but Malcolm always came to our meetings in Surrey, he's such an enthusiastic spiritualist, he has such energy, such positive vibrations, very good for the circle..,' she giggled slightly with excitement. 'I've brought all my things with me, candles, cards and my Ouija board. She bustled into the front room and gazed around curiously. 'This room has such a calm aura, a perfect choice for this meeting, well done. I'm surprised to hear you've been troubled with spirits though.' She looked at Gordon curiously. 'As it's a new property, that's quite unusual.'

'Surprised isn't the word I would have chosen Sheena, but I agree we weren't expecting this in a new home either.'

'I'll put the kettle on. What would you like Sheena, tea or coffee?' asked Kitty.

'Oh no, not for me; no caffeine while I'm working.'

'Perhaps a glass of water then?'

'That would be fine, thanks.'

'Have you done this before?' asked Gordon. 'I'm a bit uncomfortable with the idea of a séance.'

'Now don't worry Gordon.' She patted him on the arm and smiled encouragingly. 'Everything will be fine.'

Sheena placed her bag on the table and pulled out two fat candles and a pack of brightly coloured tarot cards and arranged them neatly before she pulled out one of the chairs and sat down.

'Now I will just cleanse my chakras and centre myself and then we can begin.'

Gordon stared at her then glanced across at Kitty hovering in the doorway, he raised an eyebrow.

Kitty frowned at him and shook her head slightly at him.

'I'll just fetch a glass of water for you, Gordon would you like anything?'

'I know it's early but I think I'm going to need a whiskey, make it a big one.'

'Oh no, no,' interrupted Sheena. 'No alcohol, no stimulants, it will cloud our auras, we must all keep a clear awareness during this meeting.'

'You expect me to do this sober?' he joked grimly.

Sheena's plump little face beamed at him. 'There is nothing to fear from the spirit world, as you will soon find out. Now I must prepare.' Sheena slipped off her shoes and settled her bare feet flat on the carpet. 'I need to ground myself,' she explained, to Kitty in answer to her puzzled face.

She then sat straight backed on the chair and closed her eyes beginning to breathe deeply, with her hands palm upwards on her knees.

Gordon rolled his eyes and stared grimly at Kitty, shaking his head slightly. She raised a finger to her lips and left the room quietly to fetch the water. When she returned she was carrying a glass for Sheena and a small tumbler of smoky orange liquid which she handed to Gordon.

'There you are,' she said quietly to her husband.

Sheena suddenly opened her eyes and flexed her fingers.

'Now I'm ready. 'She gestured to Kitty and Gordon. 'Come and sit down.'

They pulled out a chair each and sat down opposite her.

'Let's light the candles and we'll begin. Could you draw the curtains please?'

'No,' said Gordon flatly.

She looked surprised at the sharp reply.

'Well... it's not absolutely necessary, I suppose.' She looked slightly annoyed. 'If you're going to be more comfortable like this it will have to do.'

She settled herself back into the chair and closed her eyes again.

'We'll just ask the spirits to communicate with us,' Sheena began to breathe deeply. 'Spirits are you there? Give us a sign that you are present.' She paused. 'Spirits,' she intoned in a flat low voice. 'Draw near to us and make yourself known.' Sheena paused, and began again. 'Spirits, are you with us?'

'Obviously not,' interjected Gordon sarcastically.

'Gordon be quiet,' snapped Kitty. 'I'm so sorry Sheena.'

'Now negative energies will impede the flow of communications from the spirit world, so please Gordon, and you as well Kitty, send out positive thoughts and love to the spirits.' Sheena sat in silence for a while and then sighed. 'I'm afraid the spirits are not cooperating today; the atmosphere can't be right, too negative perhaps,' she glanced at Gordon as she said this.

'Oh dear,' Kitty sounded disappointed. 'I really hoped this would help.'

Sheena looked at the couple hopefully. 'We could try my Ouija board.' Gordon and Kitty looked at her in consternation and then at each other.

'We're not too keen on that. I've heard strange stories about Ouija boards and we definitely do not want to make matters worse.'

Kitty nodded in agreement.

Sheena sighed, 'But don't you think it would be worth trying. We have a good chance of getting a result with the board.'

They sat silently as they considered it. Kitty rubbed her hands together nervously and stared at the board that Sheena had placed on the table.

'Gordon, what shall we do?'

He groaned and rubbed his hands over face. 'Okay then, let's give it a whirl. Let's try the Ouija board. So how does it work?' he asked, leaning forward and staring at it.

'It's quite simple really, we place our fingertips on the movable indicator and the spirits will move it in response to our questions, either by pointing it to yes or no or by spelling out words from the letters at the bottom. It's easy really.'

They placed their fingertips tentatively onto the triangular shaped indicator and looked at Sheena.

'Just relax and think about the spirit that you wish to communicate with, visualise him or her in your mind.' Sheena closed her eyes and called out softly, 'Spirit, are you present? Reveal yourself to us. Make yourself known to us.'

While she was talking Kitty closed her eyes and let her mind wander when unbidden an image of the cottage on the hill popped into her head.

Then under her fingertips she felt the board jerk.

'Jesus! It's moving!' Gordon snatched his hands away and sat back in alarm.

'Gordon! We might have been getting something.'

'Oh, how exciting.' Sheena clapped her hands together excitedly. 'Let's try again.'

Gordon reluctantly placed his fingers back on the board.

'Clear your minds again and relax. Is there a spirit present who wishes to communicate? Give us a sign that you are here.'

The indicator on the board remained still.

'Spirit, are you present?' Sheena asked again.

Gordon shook his head at Kitty. 'This is ridiculous, she must have pushed it.'

'This does work Gordon,' Sheena snapped at him. 'Now let's try again and please keep quiet.' She closed her eyes again and drew a few deep breaths. 'Spirits,' she intoned. 'Are you present? Do you wish to communicate with any of us?'

The indicator remained stubbornly still.

Gordon leant forward and looked at his wife. 'Kitty, you try.'

Sheena opened her eyes and stared at her. 'Why should that work?' she snapped.

Gordon turned to her. 'She has spoken to Kitty before.'

'Really!' Sheena looked a bit annoyed. 'I wish you had told me that before that you have been in communication with the spirit.'

'Would it have made a difference?' Gordon answered sharply. 'You're supposed to be the expert.'

'Does it matter?' interjected Kitty, trying to keep the atmosphere calm. 'Let's just try again.'

Gordon reluctantly placed his fingers back onto the board. 'Come on then.'

Kitty drew a deep breath and placed her shaking fingers next to Gordon's and tried to clear her thoughts and remain calm. Sheena and Gordon however were looking increasingly annoyed with one another.

'Go on Kitty, you try now,' he said firmly.

'I am the spirit's mouthpiece so any communication should come through me,' Sheena pointed out briskly.

'Well they don't seem to want to speak to you.'

She drew her hands back from the board and sat back in her chair, her face flushing in annoyance. 'The atmosphere is not right for communicating with the spirit realm; there is too much negative energy. I can't work with negative energies around me.'

Kitty kept her hands firmly on the board. 'Let me try then.' She asked quietly, 'Do you wish to speak to me?'

The pointer juddered under her fingers and slowly slid across the board to point at the word **YES**.

There was chilled silence in the room.

Gordon and Sheena leant forward and she stretched out her hands to place them next to Kitty's.

'No, don't.' Gordon pushed her hands away. 'Go on Kitty.'

'Why are you here?' she asked.

It started to move slowly again, first sliding across to the letter **Y** then back slowly across the board to the letter **O** and then to the **U**.

'**You**,' breathed Sheena slowly.

'Why do you want to speak to me? What do you want?'

'One question at a time, Kitty.'

'What do you want to say to me?'

The pointer began to move slowly again across the board, quickly gathering speed as it spelled out the word, **A V A.**

'AVA, what's that?' asked Kitty puzzled.

'Who, it's a name.'

'Who is Ava?' asked Sheena.

'I don't know any Ava.' Kitty suddenly looked worried. 'You don't think it means Eve do you?'

'Ask the spirit to identify itself Kitty,' instructed Sheena.

'Spirit, who are you?'

The indicator lurched into movement again.

H A N A H

'Hannah Beamish? Are you Hannah Beamish?'

Y E S

'Why are you here?'

Y O U

Sheena turned to her and grasped her arm, her hand trembling.

'There is a connection somewhere, you must think.'

'I don't know any Ava's,' she answered.

'Ask her.'

'Hannah, who is Ava?'

F R E N D

'Ava was your friend?'

Y E S

Gordon sat forward suddenly. 'Ask her if Ava was Mrs Leavenham's grandmother.'

'Gordon that's far too complicated a question.' Sheena leaned towards Kitty. 'It has to be simpler.'

Kitty stared at the board thoughtfully. 'Hannah, is Ava related to Sybil?'

The pointer remained still under her fingers.

'Well, we'll take that as a no then,' sighed Gordon. 'And we are none the wiser as to why she is here.'

'It's something to do with you and somebody called Ava, is it a family member?'

'I don't know of anybody called Ava in the family, I'm sure I would have remembered a name like that.' Kitty sighed and sat back from the table, and rested her shaking hands in her lap. She looked across at her husband. 'And we didn't see any Ava in the records we have been looking at.'

'You have been researching this?' queried Sheena.

'Of course we have. You would not believe what's been happening here over the last few days,' said Gordon.

The three sat around the table each lost in their thoughts until one by one they noticed a drop in the temperature of the room.

'It's getting cold; this is usually a sign that a spirit is close.' Sheena closed her eyes. 'Spirit show yourself, make yourself known to us.'

'No!' Kitty said quickly. 'That's not Hannah.'

A wave of nausea swept over her and she suddenly retched, putting her hand up to her mouth. The faint fragrance of lavender that had lingered around the room was suddenly swamped by a strange acrid smell.

'A spirit draws near, I feel that this is a male, he is not at rest. He is seeking something.' She opened her eyes and looked at Kitty in alarm. 'He is being drawn to you; he has a very negative aura, Kitty.'

As she spoke the table began to rock backwards and forwards, the Ouija board was violently swept from the table and sent flying across the room crashing into the fireplace.

'What's happening?' said Sheena in a panic. 'Spirits aren't supposed to be aggressive like this.'

Their breaths were clearly visible in the freezing room and Kitty began to shiver.

Gordon took her arm. 'Come on let's get out of here, it's not safe.' He pulled her up from the chair and put an arm around her shoulder. Gordon looked across at the frightened psychic. 'Get your things Sheena, and come on.'

'We should stay and try to find out what this spirit wants, what it needs to be at peace, don't you think?' she asked in doubtful voice.

'You can stay if you want to but we are leaving.'

The room grew darker.

'It's so cold.' Sheena clutched her bag to her chest. 'I don't know what to do,' she confessed.

'I thought you were supposed to be the expert,' Kitty snapped.

'Let's just go.' Gordon grabbed the arms of the two women and pulled them towards the hall. 'We'll argue later.'

'Nothing like this has happened to me before; we just read tea leaves and used the Tarot cards.'

Kitty angrily pulled her arm away from Gordon's grasp and swung around to face Sheena.

'We assumed you knew what you were doing, you silly woman.'

'I'm sorry; it wasn't supposed to be like this.'

'Not now Kitty, we're going. You too, Sheena.'

Gordon hurried the two women into the hall, Nero was already there whining and scratching at the front door. It was hardly open before the dog pushed his way through and ran out barking into the driveway.

'I need my handbag, Gordon.'

'Leave it, I'll come back later and get it.'

'On your own?'

'Weren't you listening, Kitty?' Gordon looked at her amazement and shook her arm. 'Whatever or whoever is being drawn to you. Do you really think I'm going to let you back into that damn house?'

'I think Gordon is right, this spirit's aura was so evil Kitty, you shouldn't go anywhere near here.' She looked nervously at the house and edged away. 'I'm sorry I couldn't help you more but this is beyond me.'

'I was afraid this would make it worse...' he snapped, turning on her. Catching sight of Kitty's white face he swallowed the rest of his sentence and did his best to talk calmly. 'Let's walk Sheena down to the village,' he suggested and turned to Sheena. 'Could Kitty stay with you for a while? Then I can come back and get the car.'

She looked at them, hesitating for a while. 'Well...'

Kitty looked at the reluctant expression on her face and said quickly, 'It's okay, I'll go and see if I can find Sybil while I'm waiting for Gordon.'

Sheena breathed a visible sigh of relief. 'Well of course, you're more than welcome to come in and wait,' she lied.

'No really, I'll be fine.' Kitty looked at her husband. 'If she's not in then I will go and wait in the church.'

'Right. I will just walk you down there and then I'll come back.'

'We ought to ring Eve in case she tries to get hold of us again,' Kitty said, looking doubtfully into the hall.

Gordon pushed her away from the door. 'I'll do that later, don't worry.'

He pulled the front door shut and followed the women along the drive.

Sheena was walking quickly in front of them and was soon out of earshot.

'I'm guessing she'll be taking up another hobby after this,' he said drily, watching her hurry past the farm entrance.

Kitty smiled weakly. 'I don't think she will be dropping in for coffee either.'

Gordon put an arm around her shoulder. 'You're shivering; I should have picked up a coat for you.'

'It's okay. I just feel a bit sick, it was that awful smell. It was like something rotting.' She raised a trembling hand to her mouth.

'Take a few deep breaths and try to stay calm,' he said, peering at her pale face.

Kitty slowed and put a hand to steady herself against the rough stone wall of the barn. She suddenly gulped and started to retch, bending double she was violently sick against the wall.

'Kitty!' he exclaimed, supporting her with an arm around her waist as she continued to painfully retch. 'I'm so sorry, I should never have agreed to this.' He looked at her anxiously as she slowly straightened. 'How are you feeling now?'

Kitty scrabbled in her pocket for a tissue and shakily wiped her mouth. 'That's better, I think.' She blew her nose and leaned back against the wall. Closing her eyes she rubbed her fore head. 'It feels like my head is in a vice.'

'I should have picked up my phone and we could have called Eve, she would have been able to come and pick us up. What a fool!' he said in exasperation. 'Will you be alright to walk down to Sybil's?' He brushed the hair back from her face and looked at her in concern.

'Just give me a minute, my legs are shaking.' After a while the colour returned to her face and she pushed herself away from the wall, blew her nose and said, 'Okay let's go.'

Kitty looped her arm through his and he held it firmly while they walked slowly down the lane and into the village.

The shop had opened by the time they reached it but Sybil was not behind the counter. Gordon peered in the door.

'Hello,' he called through the door. 'Anybody there? Sybil? Perhaps she is out the back or something,' he said hopefully.

The door in the back of the shop opened and a young man poked his head out.

'Morning,' he called. 'Sorry to keep you.' He backed through the door holding a tray of loaves. 'We have just had a delivery and I'm up to my neck this morning.' He smiled cheerfully at the couple standing in the doorway and placed the tray onto the counter. 'Can I help you with anything?'

'Yes,' said Gordon quickly. 'We were looking for Sybil, is she here this morning?'

The young man shook his head ruefully. 'I wish she was but she doesn't work Wednesdays. She's probably at home.' He looked at them curiously. 'Do you know where she lives?'

'Yes. Yes, we do thanks. We'll go and see if she is at home.' Kitty smiled faintly at him as they moved away from the entrance to the shop.

'Okay,' he called, and started packing the loaves onto the shelf. Gordon waved his hand briefly and guided Kitty back to the street.

'Are you alright?' he asked anxiously, looking at her white face. 'You're a bit shaky still; okay to walk on a bit further?'

She nodded slightly and sniffed. 'Yeah I'm okay.' She smiled slightly as they walked past the pub. 'Fancy a pint?'

Gordon smiled slightly and hugged her. 'I don't think they would let us in, do you?'

There was no sign of Sheena, she had already disappeared into the Witch and Broomstick, the lights were off and the door was firmly closed.

Kitty looked at the door to the public bar. 'Nope, I don't think they are open for business this morning.'

****

Priddy Cottage still looked deserted, the curtains were half drawn and there were no lights on inside even though it was a murky day.

'It doesn't look like she's here, does it?' murmured Kitty, still sniffing slightly. She balled the tissue up in her hand and shoved it into her pocket.

Gordon gave a few sharp raps on the door but there was no answer. He stared up and down the street, and then glanced across at the car park in front of the hall.

'Where are you going to wait? There's a bench over there by the village hall,' he suggested.

Kitty looked across at the street. 'No. I think I'll sit in the church for a while.' She glanced about the village. 'It's so quiet; I think I would be happier waiting in there.'

'Okay, if you're sure.' Gordon handed Kitty Nero's lead and gave her a hug. 'Well, keep the dog with you and I'll be as quick as I can,' he reassured her and started to jog back up the street heading back to the cottage.

'Be careful Gordon,' she called after him.

He waved a hand in response and hurried off.

Kitty led the dog past the row of cottages to the main gate of the church, she lingered for a while reading the names on the war memorial and then climbed the steps up to the gate and followed the path along the side of the church to the entrance.

The porch was dark and cool, the various notices pinned to the board fluttering in the sharp breeze that swirled around the small space. Kitty shivered in her thin jumper and tentatively tried the door. The latch clicked and the heavy door swung open. Kitty walked in slowly, her footsteps echoing around the church.

There was an elderly woman near the pulpit arranging flowers in one of the vases. She looked around when she heard Kitty enter and smiled briefly, then recognition flickered in her face and the smile became more welcoming.

'Hello, come in and have a look round. Is this your first visit to the church?'

'Yes, we haven't been here long.'

'Oh I know who you are; you're from the new house at Castle Farm. Is your husband coming in?' she added, looking at the door.

'No, he's just gone to get the car.'

The woman suddenly noticed Nero who was tucked in behind Kitty's legs.

'We don't allow dogs in the church, dear.'

'I'm sorry,' she apologised, and turned to the door pulling Nero behind her.

The woman hesitated and then called after her, 'Don't worry, just this once won't matter; after all they are God's creatures as well.' She turned back to the flowers and carefully adjusted a few blooms. 'Do you like flower arranging, Kitty?' She looked at Kitty's surprised face. 'I've heard all about you from Sybil.'

'I see,' said Kitty. 'Do you know where Sybil is? We need to ask her about something.'

The woman snipped off a few dead leaves and inserted a spray of chrysanthemums into the vase. 'There, what do you think?'

'It looks lovely.'

'Thank you.' She looked pleased at the compliment and glanced around at Kitty.

'Sybil is staying with her daughter at the moment. I think she is planning to come home tomorrow; that's what she told me anyway.'

'Tomorrow?' said Kitty flatly.

'Yes. Are you okay dear? You look very pale.'

'I'm not feeling too well at the moment.' Kitty slumped in one of the pews and distractedly pulled at Nero's ears. 'I needed to ask Sybil something.'

'Oh?' she inquired. 'Is it anything I can help with?'

'She knows so much about the village and we need to ask her about a little girl who used to live here.'

'Really, what little girl is that?' she asked, looking curiously at Kitty.

'Do you know of her? Her name was Ava.'

'Ava? No that doesn't ring a bell I'm afraid. Where does she live?'

'No, it was some time ago, that's why we wanted Sybil. She knows everybody.'

'She certainly does.' She smiled and swept up the stray twigs and stems into a plastic bag. 'There, all finished. Would you be interested in helping with the flowers? We're always looking for volunteers.'

Kitty shook her head distractedly. 'No, I don't think so, not at the moment.'

'Well if you change your mind just mention it to Sybil.' She picked up the coat that was slung over a nearby pew and put it on. 'Quite a nip in the air this morning, I think the nights will be drawing in soon. Still can't complain, it's been a good summer,' she said comfortably, and wrapped a scarf around her neck. She paused, looking at Kitty. 'Our harvest festival is next week; perhaps you'd like to help with that?'

'Yes, that would be nice.' Kitty roused herself to appear interested. 'I'm sure I could help with something.'

The elderly woman picked up her bags and started to walk down the aisle to the door.

'Is there a vicar in the village?' Kitty suddenly called after her.

'A vicar? No dear, we have to share one with Axminster and Kilmington. We haven't had anybody in the vicarage for quite some time.' She looked closely at Kitty's face. 'Are you sure you're okay?'

'I'm fine, really.' Kitty half smiled at her.

'I could give you the phone number of the church warden, if that would help?'

'No, it was just a thought, that was all. I'll see Sybil tomorrow, I'm sure she will be able to help.'

The woman nodded at her. 'Well alright, I'd better be off now. It's nice to have met you Kitty. Perhaps we'll see you and Gordon in church on Sunday?'

'Maybe.'

She half pulled the door closed behind her then poked her head back around the door. 'Can you make sure the door is shut properly when you leave? The wind sometimes blows it open.'

'Yes of course. I'll make sure it's shut. I won't be in here long; I'm just waiting for Gordon.'

'Take your time dear.' She paused, looking around the church. 'Sometimes it's just nice to come and sit for a while, it refreshes the soul. Don't you think?' She looked intently at Kitty's pale face.

Kitty nodded in response.

The heavy door closed and Kitty slumped back into the pew and closed her eyes. Nero yawned and pushed his nose into her lap; she gently pulled on his ears and smoothed the soft fur around his nose. The dog suddenly pricked up his ears, his tail started to wag and he bounced up looking expectantly at the door.

Outside she could hear Gordon's voice; she caught snippets of the conversation as they hurried down the aisle, the door opened just as Kitty and the dog reached it.

'Are you okay? Rose was just telling me how pale you look; she seemed quite worried about you.'

'Rose? What the flower lady?'

'Flowers?'

'She was in here arranging the flowers.' She gestured to the elaborate arrangements of chrysanthemums and greenery in the vases next to the pulpit.

Gordon was carrying a thick fleece over his arm. 'Here, I brought you this.'

He held it for her while she slipped her arms in and then zipped it up.

'That's better, I was getting so cold.' She shivered and pulled the collar higher around her neck. 'Sybil is coming back tomorrow, the flower lady told me.'

'Rose,' he reminded her. 'She has invited us to church on Sunday.'

'The way I'm feeling at the moment I could happily camp in here.'

'Bit chilly though,' he said, giving her a hug. 'I've got the car outside, come on.'

'Did you pick up my handbag?'

'What is it with women and their handbags?' he joked grimly. 'If the world was going to end you'd want your handbag.'

'Well, did you remember it?'

'Yes, and I threw a few things into a bag, toothbrushes, things like that.'

'What about clothes?'

'I picked up a few things, we'll manage don't worry. What I have forgotten we can buy in Axminster.'

He led her out of the church and closed the door.

'Make sure the door is shut properly, apparently it blows open sometimes.'

'Rose?'

'Yes, the flower lady told me.'

Gordon tugged at the door. 'Yep, it's pulled through okay.'

The skies had turned a uniform grey and a few drops of rain started to fall. Kitty shivered and took a firm hold of Gordon's arm.

'What are we going to do?'

'We'll find a B&B tonight and tomorrow, well, we'll see.'

'We must ring Eve; did you pick up your mobile?'

'I'll ring her as soon as we're in the car. Come on, the rain is coming on harder now and we'll get soaked if we don't hurry.'

The rain started to fall steadily as they hurried down the path to the gate. The car was parked in front of the War Memorial; Gordon opened the passenger door and helped Kitty in.

'I'll get the heater on, that will soon warm you up.'

He ran around to the other side and got in, starting the engine and turning the heater on full blast.

Kitty shivered and held her hands over the warm blast of air. 'That's better.'

Gordon pulled his mobile out of the door pocket and dialled his daughter's number. It rang for several minutes before Eve answered.

'Hi darling, it's dad. Yes everything is okay, we're just leaving. I've decided we're going to stay in a guest house tonight...... no darling, that's very kind of you but you haven't got enough room,' he paused, listening. 'Okay we'll see you later, bye.'

'Is she okay?'

'She wants us to come round for a meal.'

'Are we going to tell her what's happened?'

Gordon hesitated and stared out of the window.

'I don't think so; she was freaked out enough yesterday.'

He put the car into gear and pulled away, driving slowly through the quiet village. Kitty glanced across at the pub as they passed. An indistinct figure was in the window staring out but as they drew level whoever it was ducked out of sight. Kitty grinned wryly to herself, she had seen enough to realise who the watcher was.

The rain started to fall heavily and she could only just see the road in front of the car, the car's wipers were flicking backwards and forwards at top speed to clear the water from windscreen.

Gordon slowed the car for the turning to the Axminster road, concentrating on navigating the corner. He didn't notice the lone figure stood to one side of the street. The hunched figure stared bleakly after the car as it drove through the rain, and disappeared up the winding road leading over the hill.

****

'We'll drive through the town and see what we can see; if not there is always Seaton. There's bound to be some vacancies at this time of year,' Gordon reassured her, as he navigated the narrow winding road through the town centre. A lorry was unloading on the yellow lines near the pedestrian crossing and causing a snarl up of the traffic. He shook his head in exasperation. 'I'll have to drive down to the roundabout and turn left, we'll see what's around there,' he said to Kitty.

She was gazing blankly out of the window. 'What?'

'Are you okay?'

'Yes.' She gave him a weak smile. 'I'm feeling better now.'

He glanced at her doubtfully, Kitty's face was pale and drawn and even though the car's heater was on full blast she was still shivering.

'What we both need is a good night's sleep.'

Kitty nodded slightly in agreement. 'You haven't had much sleep for several nights, have you?'

Gordon slowed the car as he peered through the steamed up windows at either side of the road. 'I'll survive, I'm sure there were some guest houses along here somewhere.'

'What about that one?' said Kitty, pointing to a large house set back behind a laurel hedge.

'And it has vacancies. That will do,' he said, pulling into the gravel drive and slipping into an empty space between two cars. He turned off the engine and turned to his wife who was sitting quietly and staring blankly at the house. 'Come on Kitty, this will do for tonight.' She roused herself and looked at him. 'Yes okay... I'm sure it will,' she added, more firmly.

Gordon opened his door and got out. 'I'll get the bag.' He pulled a small rucksack from the back seat.

'Is that all you brought?' asked Kitty, looking at it doubtfully.

'It's all we need for now and before you ask here's your handbag,' he said, handing over a large green leather bag.

Kitty unzipped it and started rummaging through the contents.

'What are you looking for?'

'Aspirin.'

Gordon slung the bag over his shoulder. 'Let's get a room then you can have a sleep for an hour before we go around to Eve's.'

'What about the dog? Will he be okay in the car?'

She peered in the back window at Nero stretched out on the seat, the dog wagged his tail at her and raised his head in expectation.

'No, Nero stay,' Gordon said firmly. 'He'll be fine; we can pick up some food for him and feed him at Eve's house. I wish I had put a towel down on the seat though,' he said. 'Look at the mess he's made of the leather.'

'It's only dirt, Gordon. It will wipe off.'

She followed him up the front steps of the guest house and into the hall. He rang the bell on the desk and waited but not for long, the door at the end of the corridor opened and a young woman emerged from the kitchen.

'Good Afternoon,' she said politely, smiling at the exhausted couple.

'Hi, can we have a room please, I haven't booked.'

'That's alright; we're quiet at the moment. Is it a double?'

'With an en suite if possible.'

'Yes certainly, we have one double available at the back of the house, it has a nice garden view. It's very quiet,' she added, looking at Kitty's pale and tired face.

Kitty smiled slightly at her. 'That sounds ideal.'

'If you would sign in and fill in your details while I get the key, how many nights would you like the room for?'

'Well...' said Gordon, looking at Kitty. 'I'm not too sure at the moment.' He looked at the woman. 'Would that be a problem?'

'No, not all, if you just pay for tonight and then let me know in the morning. As I said we are quiet at the moment, it's the end of the season so we're winding down.' She looked at the details on the card. 'Mr and Mrs Bishop? My name is Angela Hawes and my husband is Roger. He's out at the moment but you'll meet him in the morning, he cooks the breakfasts.'

'Right, how much is it by the way?'

'It's sixty five pounds a night; are you paying cash or card?'

'Umm...' Gordon looked through his wallet. 'Have you got any cash, Kitty?'

She stared blankly at him blankly. 'What?'

'No, it will have to be card then.'

Angela led them to a high ceilinged room on the second floor. 'Here you are,' she said, opening the door. 'Number seven, I hope you find the room comfortable.'

She crossed the room and opened a door to the side of the room. 'And this is your en suite, there are towels over there on the rack and there are complimentary shower gels and shampoo in the basket.'

Gordon looked around the room. 'This will do just fine, thank you.'

'There's tea and coffee over there, and if you need anything else just let me know, I'll be in the kitchen.' Angela started to leave the room but then thought of something. 'Would you require a meal tonight?'

'Thanks, but we're going to our daughter's tonight for a meal.'

'She lives locally?'

'Yes, in Axminster. We do as well, in Medbury.'

Angela looked at them curiously. 'That's not far away.'

'No, just a couple of miles, that's all.' He added, 'We're moving house.'

'Oh, I see.' She smiled sympathetically. 'I don't envy you that. Now the front door will be open until ten after that you will have to ring the bell when you come back.'

'We won't be that late,' Gordon reassured her. 'We're both really tired.'

'In that case, I will see you in the morning for breakfast. I start serving at eight. Just come down when you're ready.' She smiled at them and pulled the door closed behind her.

Kitty wandered across the room and peered into the bathroom. 'No bath.'

'You will have to make do with a shower tonight.' Gordon picked up the kettle. 'Tea?'

'Oh yes,' she said gratefully. 'I can't remember when I had one last.'

'It was before Sheena came.'

'Sheena!' Kitty shuddered at her name. 'Bloody stupid woman.'

'Yeah,' he replied, ruefully shaking his head. 'That was a really bad idea, wasn't it?'

'And we're still no better off; all we have is a name.'

'Yes... well, we'll forget all about that now.'

He stirred some sugar into the tea and handed Kitty the cup.

'Forget it!' she said indignantly. 'How on earth are we going to forget it?'

'We're going to forget about it for tonight,' he said sharply. 'And tomorrow I'll get an estate agent around to value the house.'

'Gordon, we have just moved in, and where are we going to live until it's sold? And that could take months.'

'I don't know,' he replied stubbornly. 'But we're not going back there.'

Kitty sat on the edge of the bed and sipped her tea. She closed her eyes against her thumping headache.

'Is your head bad?'

'Hmm,' she murmured, rubbing her cold hands over her forehead. Kitty opened her handbag and pulled out the box of aspirin. 'I'll take a couple of these; that will help.'

Gordon watched her swallow the pills. 'You don't really want to go back there, do you?'

'I don't know,' she confessed. 'But it felt right that we were there, it felt like home. We have moved so much over the years and I've never felt really settled anywhere but there I did.' She rubbed her forehead and stood up. 'Oh I don't know..,' she sighed.

Gordon pulled the duvet back.

'We don't have to be at Eve's for over an hour, there's time enough for you to have a sleep. Go on...' as she hesitated. 'I'll wake you in time for you to have a shower.'

Kitty sighed and looked longingly at the bed.

'I think I had better shower first, I'd feel a bit fresher.' She wrinkled her nose and pulled a wry face. 'Especially after being sick.' She tipped the contents of the rucksack onto the bed and found a brush and some toothpaste. 'I won't be long.'

Gordon kicked off his shoes and climbed onto the bed, stretched out and put his arms behind his head. 'At least the bed is comfortable,' he said, relaxing. 'See you in a minute.' His eyes flickered and closed, and his deep breathing showed that he was already asleep before Kitty had reached the shower.

Clouds of steam billowed into the room as she opened the door. Gordon hadn't stirred from his position on the bed.

She walked softly across to the bed so as not to wake him and slipped under the duvet.

Kitty checked the watch on his arm, it was three forty five. She sighed. Great over an hour for a snooze, she thought in relief and pulled the duvet up higher and settled down.

It was a cold miserable day in April and a heavy shower had caught Hannah on her way home to the cottage on the hill. She had been up all night with old John Trevitt, he was not long for this world and she had been doing her best to make sure that his last few hours of this earth was as pain free as possible. Sarah, his daughter had taken over from Hannah for a while, giving her the chance to go home for a rest. Already soaked to the bone she sheltered under the wide spreading branches of an oak and waited for the shower to ease off. Just out of sight around the bend in the road she heard with a sinking heart the familiar tread and thump of a walking stick.

Hannah looked around in desperation for somewhere to hide, she was too bone weary to cope with a meeting with him. There was no cover into which she could duck so she drew back into the shadow of the tree and hoped that he would be in too much of a hurry to notice her.

At first it seemed that Hannah was in luck, he had his head down against the rain and was walking quickly by. But as he drew level with the sheltering woman some instinct made him slow and glance into the shadows.

'Well, well, what are you doing skulking there?'

'Sheltering from the rain, 'tis all.'

'And how are you feeling?' he inquired with mock interest.

Hannah looked at him in contempt. 'I be very well thank 'ee, you'm wasted your money I'm afraid.'

A slow flush crept up his neck. 'And what is that supposed to mean?'

'You know,' she said, stepping out from under the sheltering tree and advancing on him. 'Finding that drunk in one of the inns of Chard and setting him up as a white witch! What were thee thinking of man? That ain't going to fool nobody.'

'Anything to get rid of you.' he said quietly, glaring at her.

'Not man enough to do yer own dirty work eh? I hope 'ee paid him well.'

He smiled coldly at her. 'Oh I did, I paid him very well to get the job done.'

Hannah snorted. 'How is this going to go down with yer intended's family eh? Good family like that; this'll give 'em second thoughts about welcoming thee into the fold.'

He stared at her with a satisfied smirk on his face. 'Oh I've seen to that, he's more than pleased to be marrying his sister off to me now.'

'So tis true then, thee have been busy.' She laughed derisively. 'And you'm thinking yer so high and mighty. Only way thee could get 'er was it? To give 'er a bellyful!'

Without a change of expression he raised his stick and struck her across the side of her head sending her staggering back onto the wet bank.
Hannah lay there dazed, the mud soaking into her gown, a purple bruise already appearing on the side of her forehead. He paced slowly forward until he was standing over her prone figure.
　'Now, now Hannah, don't lay there in all that wet. We wouldn't want you to catch a chill and get sick, now would we?'
　He leant on his stick and smiled down at her then turned and carried on walking steadily up the hill. Just as he disappeared over the brow of the hill a snatch of whistling was carried back on the wind.

Gordon gently tapped on the front door but they had already been spotted. Emily was on look out duty in the window so they didn't have long to wait before the door was flung open.

'Hello.' Their little granddaughter bobbed up and down on the doorstep with glee.

Gordon scooped her up. 'Hello, my little poppet.'

'You're having tea with us,' she told him, putting her arms around his neck.

'Yes, and what are we having for tea?'

'Chips,' said Emily firmly.

'No, we're not,' said Eve, coming into the hall and greeting her mother with a hug. 'You had chips last night, Emily. We're having roast chicken.'

'I thought I smelled something nice.' Gordon kissed her on the cheek. 'How are you?'

'I'm okay,' she said, looking intently at them both. 'Mum, you look terrible, what's been happening?'

'Everything is fine,' Gordon lied.

Kitty flicked a quick look at him and tried to keep her face blank but Eve wasn't fooled, and stared back at him in disbelief. She shut the door behind them. 'Come on in and I'll make some tea.'

Kitty followed her into the kitchen while Gordon was pulled into the front room to inspect Emily's new doll. Nero padded after the two women and snuffled hopefully around the floor looking for crumbs. Eve turned to her mother as soon as they were alone. 'Okay, what's happened?' she asked firmly.

'Well...'

'And it's no use lying and saying everything is okay, it obviously isn't otherwise you wouldn't be staying in a guest house tonight!'

'Okay.' Kitty glanced over her shoulder and shut the kitchen door. 'We held a séance.'

'What!' yelped Eve in horror. 'Are you mad?'

'Shh!' Kitty warned her, glancing at the door. 'I know, but we thought it would help and it did in a way,' she added thoughtfully.

Eve looked at her curiously. 'And?'

'It is Hannah, she has been haunting us, if that's the right word for it and it's something to do with me and somebody called Ava. We thought she meant you, you know Ava... Eve. But it wasn't.'

'Who is Ava?'

Eve put the kettle on while she listened, watching her mother intently as she moved around the kitchen.

'I don't know, I don't recognise the name at all.'

'And that was it? I didn't realise you knew how to hold a séance, mum.'

'Well, we had help if you want to call it that, Sheena from the public house in Medbury came, we thought it would be okay,' Kitty paused, remembering the fear and nausea that had overwhelmed her. She pulled out one of the kitchen chairs and sat down. 'Something or somebody came after Hannah; Sheena said it was a man and that it was being drawn to me. She said it had an evil aura or something. It threw the Ouija board across the room and smashed it.'

'You were using an Ouija board, are you insane?'

Eve banged a cup of tea down in front of her, slopping the hot liquid over the table.

'I know,' Kitty said flatly. 'It was a stupid idea, dad really freaked out when he heard
that, he wants to sell the house.'

'Good,' snapped Eve. 'I should bloody well think so!'

'We can't sell, that's our home.'

'Mum, you've only been in there a few days.'

'Yes, I know but....'

The door opened and Emily came in, pulling Gordon in behind her.

'Look at my dolly, nanna.'

Kitty picked her up and put Emily on her knee. 'Isn't she pretty, what's her name?'

'It's my new one,' she said, pulling the pink hair back from the cheerfully smiling face. 'Her name is Hannah.'

A chilled silence fell over the room.

'Emily, why don't you call her something else, something pretty like Candy, anything but that.' Eve looked appealingly at her parents.

'Yes,' said Gordon slowly. 'Who's that pop singer that you like so much? Bouncy? Call her that.'

'No, this is Hannah.' She clutched the doll to her firmly and stared stubbornly at her mother. 'She's nice.'

'Of course she is, and it's a very nice name.' Kitty gently stroked Emily's fine hair back from her forehead.

'Kitty!' He shook his head in exasperation and sat down at the table. 'Can you believe she wants to stay in that house?' he asked Eve.

'Mum's been telling me all about it, dad.'

'I thought we agreed we weren't going to say anything.' He glanced over Emily's head and gave Kitty a hard stare.

Kitty looked at him. 'It's no good lying, Eve's not stupid. She knew something had happened.'

Eve fiddled about by the stove turning down the potatoes and checking the roast in the oven. 'Mum's right, I knew just by looking at your faces,' she hesitated, staring into the pan of potatoes and gently poking them with a knife. 'Do you have any idea who the man or spirit was?'

'No,' said Kitty blankly. 'Who would be mad at me?'

'Apart from me?'

'Shut up Gordon, it's not my fault.'

'It didn't come up on the deeds then? Quarter of an acre, complete with apple trees and a ghost.'

Gordon smiled weakly at his daughter. 'Funnily enough, no!'

'Sybil is coming home tomorrow,' said Kitty.

Eve put some plates on the table. 'And who is Sybil?'

'Mrs Leavenham.'

'Ah! The oracle of the village.'

'I hope she is going to be an oracle,' said Kitty warmly. 'I'm hoping she will be able to clear this mystery up, I want to get back into my house.'

Gordon leaned forward and glared at her. 'I told you we were selling,' he said firmly.

'But Gordon...'

'No buts, I've made up my mind.' He patted her hand. 'Now don't worry, I'll sort something out in the morning.'

She sighed and gave Emily a hug before she scrambled down and climbed onto Gordon's knee.

'Gramps, give dolly a kiss,' she said, pushing it into his face. Gordon puckered up his face, making Emily squeal with laughter.

'You give me a kiss,' he said, tickling her.

Eve drained the vegetables and took the chicken out of the oven.

'Emily, can you get down? I'd like gramps to carve the chicken.' She put the roast and a serving plate on the worktop. 'You don't mind, do you dad?'

'Of course not.' He stood up and started to carve. 'This smells really good Eve, I didn't realise I was so hungry until I started doing this; we have been surviving on sandwiches the last couple of days.'

Gordon quickly carved the bird into slices and then handed the piled plate to Eve.

'Isn't Rob home for tea?' asked Kitty.
She set the cutlery on the table and was searching for the place mats in a drawer.
Eve glanced at her watch. 'He should be home soon; I thought I'd make our meal earlier tonight, I thought you would be hungry.'
Gordon nodded. 'I am.' He gave Emily a squeeze. 'Are you hungry?' he asked her.

'No,' she said firmly, making her doll dance along the table. 'I want chips.' She suddenly dropped her doll on the table and ran into the hall. 'I can hear daddy's car.'
The front door opened and Rob pushed his way in arms full of shopping bags.

'Hi,' he called through.

Emily pulled open one of the carrier bags and rummaged through the biscuits and crisps inside. 'Did you bring me some sweeties?'

'After tea, Emily.' He picked her up and carried her through into the kitchen. 'Hello all.'

'Hi Rob.'

'How's everything going?'

'You'll never guess what my crazy parents have been doing!' Eve gave him a hug and took the shopping bags and dumped them on top of the cupboards.
Rob looked at his in-laws and raised his eyebrows. 'Oh?'
Eve hesitated and glanced at Emily playing on the table. 'I'll tell you later.'

'Okay,' he said, and shrugged his shoulders.

Rob looked rather tired Kitty thought, as he pulled out a chair and sat next to her.

'What's for tea?'

'Chips.'

'No, we're not,' Eve said irritably. 'I told you we're having chicken.'

'Are you being a pest, Emmy?' asked Rob.

'Yes.' She smiled brightly at him. 'I'm being a pest.'
Kitty grinned at her cheeky smile and turned to Rob. 'Did you have a good day at work?'

'No,' he said bluntly. 'Terrible. What's going on with the house then?' he asked curiously. 'Are you staying there tonight?'

'No, we're in a guest house for tonight.'
Rob raised his eyebrows and looked inquiringly at her. 'Oh?'
Eve gave him a meaningful look that clearly said things had happened.

'I was talking to Graham at work, you remember him, don't you?' he addressed his wife. 'He got divorced last year.'

'Oh yeah, I remember.'

'He seems to think a new house would go just like that in Medbury, well sought after location he called it.'

'Well, the market is very slow at the moment,' put in Kitty.

Eve put the plates on the table. 'I was thinking there are other options if you can't sell it; you could rent it out and then rent something for yourself or perhaps part exchange.'

Gordon picked up his knife and fork and began to eat.

'We'll see,' he said, between mouthfuls. 'I'm going to see an estate agent tomorrow and see what they can suggest. I'll sort something out.'

Kitty stared at her food; she didn't feel that hungry and just listlessly pushed the chicken around the plate.

'Aren't you hungry, mum?'

'It's lovely dear, really, it's just I'm not feeling too good.'

Eve sighed. 'Well, I thought you would want a decent meal.'

'This is lovely Eve,' put in Gordon. 'Don't worry I'll eat Mum's share if she doesn't.' He cast a worried look at his wife. 'You'd feel better if you ate something.'

Kitty nodded and put a piece of chicken onto her fork. 'This is very nice Eve,' she said. 'We didn't want to put you to so much trouble.'

'It's no trouble; I picked up the chicken on the way home from work.'

'If you went shopping how come I had to get some as well?' Rob asked irritated.

'I didn't take my shopping list and I was in a rush so I forgot a load of things,' she stared across the table at him. 'It won't kill you for once, having to do some shopping.'

Emily was carried off upstairs at seven by Rob for her bath and story, while Gordon, Kitty and Eve sat in the lounge.

'Are you working tomorrow, Eve?'

'Yes I have to drop Emily off at playgroup first and then I'm working until twelve. Why?'

'I'd like mum to stay here if you don't mind, I want to go into work and check on a few things. Then I can go to the estate agents and have a word with somebody about the house.'

Kitty looked up, meaning to protest but caught Gordon's eye and kept quiet.

'Yeah, that's okay, let yourself in and then we'll see you when we get back. Perhaps we can take Emily down to the swimming pool in the afternoon?'

'That would be great, Eve,' said Gordon thankfully. 'Mum would like that.'

Rob walked quietly down the stairs. 'She's gone off already, two pages of her story and she was out cold.'

'What are you reading her, War and Peace?'

Rob smiled slightly and sat down on the sofa next to Eve.

'I wish I could sleep like that,' she said feelingly. 'It takes me ages to drop off.' She looked inquiringly at her parents. 'Well? So what else has been happening apart from your ridiculous séance?'

Rob looked at them horrified. 'What, you're not serious!'

Eve nodded at him. 'Yep they did, can you believe it?'

'Oh, you two...' He looked from one to the other. 'This is getting out of hand, I thought you would have calmed down by now, it's all nonsense.'

Kitty looked across the room at her son-in-law, and Rob stared back defiantly.

He went on, 'How could you believe in anything so ridiculous? There must be an explanation for all this. I was talking to some of my work mates; new houses move and make strange noises.' Rob turned to Eve, who was curled up next to him. 'That's all you heard I'm sure.'

She looked at him doubtfully. 'It didn't seem like that at the time.'

He patted her on the leg. 'I'm sure it was nothing, Eve.' Rob glanced across at Gordon who was glaring at him.

'It wasn't nothing, Rob, there is something in that house and it's after Kitty.'

'Who told you that?'

'It was a psychic from the village; she runs the pub with her husband.'

'And how much did you pay her?'

Gordon's face flushed with annoyance. 'We're not that stupid, we didn't give her anything.'

Rob looked cynical and glanced at Kitty. 'She probably knew you were vulnerable and was playing on your nerves, Kitty.'

'There is nothing wrong with my nerves,' she replied flatly, and gave him a level look. 'We know what we saw, Rob.'

He shook his head and stood up impatiently. 'Anybody want a drink?' he asked, picking up the half empty bottle of wine. 'Kitty? Gordon?'

Kitty shook her head.

Gordon drained his glass and held up it up. 'I'll have another.'

'Oh,' said Eve, suddenly standing up. 'I nearly forgot.' She ran out into the hall and came back with a piece of paper. 'I looked it up on the web while I was at work.'

Eve perched on the edge of the sofa and spread the piece of paper out on her knees. 'Now let's see, water on the brain. It's called Hydrocephalus; it's a build up of fluid inside the skull leading to brain swelling. Caused by injury or stroke possibly.' She looked up. 'And the symptoms are seizures, insomnia, headaches, vomiting, memory loss and the one that has the most bearing on this is poor balance and co ordination,' Eve looked up from the paper. 'Does that sound like somebody who could climb a tree?'

Rob sighed. 'Is this to do with that silly story about the witch?'

Eve nodded.

'Damn it, can't you all just drop it? Kitty imagined it all and has sucked you two in as well.'

There was an uncomfortable silence after Rob's outburst. Kitty shifted slightly in her chair under his accusing look.

'Perhaps we ought to go,' she appealed to her husband.

'No don't go,' said Rob, suddenly looking embarrassed. 'I'm sorry that wasn't fair, Kitty.'

She stared at him. 'No it wasn't, and you're not being fair to Eve and Gordon either. They know what they saw.'

'Well,' he replied shaking his head. 'It's just so ridiculous; it was the middle of the 1800's. It's not as if it was the middle ages or something. After all,' he continued. 'There was a coroner's report wasn't there? So there couldn't have been any foul play.' He looked across the room at his father- in- law. 'Well, Gordon?'

'You've got a point. No.' He gestured at Kitty to be quiet. 'The coroner's report, perhaps we should try and find out more about it and the coroner himself.' He sat forward spilling a bit of wine on the carpet in excitement. 'We might find some answers there.'

'Whatever we find out doesn't alter the fact that Hannah's spirit is present in our house,' Kitty said impatiently.

'Yes, but mum, don't you see? The more you find out the better. Perhaps it would become clearer why she is there.' Eve looked at her father. 'Maybe the report would shed some light on it, I'm sure it wouldn't be that difficult to find out about it.'

Gordon nodded in agreement. 'I could have a quick look while I'm in the office, see what I can find out on the computer. We did well with finding information about Hannah, maybe I'll have the same luck with this.'

Kitty nodded. 'I suppose it's worth a try. Eve, while I remember, can you keep Nero here tonight? It's too cold for him to sleep in the car tonight and he won't be allowed in the guest house.'

Eve nodded. 'Emily will be pleased; she loves it when the dog sleeps over.'

Gordon nodded satisfied. 'He won't be any trouble and I can walk him tomorrow afternoon so don't worry about that.'

Thursday

'Kitty, Kitty, time to get up.'
She stirred and rolled over, half opening her eyes. 'Hmmm.'
'Come on, it's seven o'clock, breakfast is at eight.'
Kitty sighed, pushed the duvet down and yawned. 'Seven already?'
'Did you sleep well?' he asked, putting a cup of tea next to her on the bedside table.
Kitty rubbed her head and sat up. 'I don't remember, so I guess I must have. Did you?'
'Yep. I slept like a log, full tummy and a few glasses of wine and I was out cold. Do you want to shower first or shall I?' he inquired.
'Oh, you go on,' said Kitty, flopping back onto the bed and pulling the quilt back up.
He twitched it down. 'Hey, don't go back to sleep, sit up and drink your tea. I won't be a minute.'
Gordon pulled a towel off the rail and vanished into the tiny bathroom. She could hear him in the shower quietly humming as he splashed water about.
'You sound cheerful.'
'What?'
'I said... Oh never mind,' she called. 'You can't hear me anyway.'
The sound of running water stopped and Gordon came out wrapping a towel around his middle.
'The water is lovely and hot Kitty.' He picked up his tea and drained the cup. 'I'm looking forward to my breakfast.'
'After all that food you ate last night? I don't know where you put it.'
Gordon stared at her still lying wrapped up in the quilt. 'Are you going to have a shower?'
Kitty sat up sleepily. 'Yes, yes I'm getting up.' She swung her legs over the side of the bed and stood up. 'It's cold,' she complained.
Gordon put his hand on the old cast iron radiator under the window.
'Well, the radiator is warm; it's just a very cold morning. A hot shower will do the trick.'
Kitty pulled a few things out of the bag. 'I don't suppose you packed any clean underwear?'
He was rubbing his hair dry with the towel. 'Go commando,' he suggested.

She gave him a withering look. 'Maybe twenty years ago. Perhaps I could borrow
some from Eve.'

'Well hurry up,' he urged her, starting to get dressed. 'I'm dropping you off at Eve's before nine so we'll have to rush breakfast,' he reminded her.

'Okay, okay,' she replied, heading for the shower.

Gordon pulled into the empty drive of the little semi-detached where their daughter lived and checked his watch.

'Damn, looks like we've missed her.'

'What's the time?'

'Five to nine.'

'Oh she's already gone. Emily starts playgroup at nine.'

'Yes,' he said impatiently. 'That's what I just said!'

'Okay, chill gramps,' she said calmly.

'Chill?' he said, starting to laugh. 'You've been listening to Emily again.' He got out of the car and leaned in the door. 'You've got the door key haven't you?'

'It's in the glove compartment.' Kitty hesitated. 'I can let myself in if you want to get off to work.'

'No, no, I'll see you in and settled, I'm sure there's something on the TV for you to watch.'

Kitty opened the car door and got out. 'I'll be fine Gordon,' she said impatiently.

He took the key out of her hand and opened the front door.

'Of course you will be but I'll try not to be too long at work.'

Nero bounded out from the kitchen delighted to see them both and pranced round Kitty looking for attention.

She bent and gave his ears a gentle tug. 'I hope you behaved yourself, Nero.'

'I'm sure he did.' He turned to her anxiously. 'Now you're going to be alright, aren't you?'

'I'll be fine,' she repeated, and followed him into the tiny hallway. There was a note propped up on the hall table.

Gordon picked it up and handed it to Kitty. 'You read it; I've left my glasses in the car.'

"Help yourself to tea etc, See you about twelvish. xxx," she read.

'There you are, I'm all sorted; tea and telly.'

'Okay.' He gave her a hug and kissed the top of her head. 'That's fine, now I can go to work and not worry.' He opened the door again and handed her the key. 'Here you had better have this back.'

'I might take the dog for a walk.'

Gordon looked at her doubtfully. 'Well okay but don't go too far, Eve and Emily will be expecting you here when they get back.'

'I know,' she said firmly, and pushed him out of the door. 'Off you go or you'll be late.'

Gordon looked at his watch. 'I am late!'

He gave Kitty a wave as he backed slowly out into the road. Kitty waited until she saw him drive off towards the town and then went inside the house and shut the door.

She wandered aimlessly around the house unwilling to put the television on and watch the usual bubblegum programmes that were on at that time of the morning.

In the kitchen the dirty breakfast things were stacked neatly in the sink, Kitty rolled up her sleeves and filled the sink with hot water and began to wash up the china. She smiled to herself as she rinsed Emily's little pink and flowery cup and dish and then left it to drain while she wiped down the worktops.

It was all dried and packed away within half an hour, the clock ticked slowly and the desire to return to the village grew and grew as she paced around the small house. The knowledge that Sybil would be returning sometime that morning made the feeling stronger. Of course she reasoned she had no idea at what time Sybil would be there so she might miss her altogether but still the urge to return to the village pulled at her.

Oh damn it! she thought, and grabbed her handbag and the front door key and opened the door. She hesitated and returned to the kitchen to leave Eve a note.

That done she called the dog and pulled the door firmly shut behind them and hurried off to the town centre to the bus stop.

The small shuttle bus drew to a halt at the end of the lane. This was the closest that Kitty could get to the village using local transport. She climbed carefully down the steps urging Nero to follow, his nails scrabbling on the stairs as he tentatively climbed down. Kitty waved to the driver as the bus pulled slowly away, leaving her standing in the deserted country lane.

She zipped up her fleece, settled her bag on her shoulder and started walking up the lane that led to Medbury. The road as usual was quiet,

there had been heavy rain the night before and the road was awash with the muddy water that had run off the surrounding fields.
The sky was looking increasingly overcast and there was low rumble of thunder in the distance. Kitty picked up her pace hoping to get to the village before the rain came on again.
She doubted that she would be welcome in the pub if it rained too hard and for a fleeting moment she thought of their front door key that was lying in the bottom of her bag.
   'Not on my own!' she said aloud.
Nero looked around at the sound of her voice and looked at her inquiringly before losing interest and resuming his exploration of the badger sett at the side of the road. The animals had dug out an extensive run through the hedge and the piles of waste from the holes spilled out onto the road. Kitty walked around the orange mud that was being washed down the road by the rain and called the dog out of the hole.
The first few spots of rain pattered on her head as she reached the top of the hill that overlooked the village. Down in the valley Kitty could just see the rooftops, the church spire rising out of the drizzling rain. She peered over the hedge to see if she could spot Priddy Cottage but the row of cottages was hidden by the roof of the village hall.

There was a crack of thunder as Kitty walked into the village and she grinned wryly hoping it wasn't an omen.
Kitty called Nero to heel slipping the lead over his head, she hesitated, glancing towards the cottages and then gazed up the hill towards their house. Then without another thought she walked up the hill towards Castle Farm and the orchard. She slowed passing the farmyard and glanced in looking for Mr Beamish but as usual the yard was deserted. Kitty walked tentatively along the side of the wall until she reached the entrance to the gravel drive.
Nero whined and tucked himself in close to her legs, Kitty's heart started to thud in her chest but even so she felt herself drawn towards the house, it still looked welcoming and peaceful. Her feet crunched on the gravel as she walked slowly towards to the front door.
A slight noise at her feet made her jump. The grey cat stood on the doorstep fixing her with a pale eyed glare.
   'Hello puss, have you been waiting for me?' Kitty reached down and ran her hand gently along the cats back. It sat down on the step and glared at her. 'Well, you look grumpy,' Kitty said, unzipping her

handbag and feeling for the key. She hesitated, staring down at it nestling in her hand. 'How silly is this,' she said to herself.
Struggling with an overwhelming urge to open the door and enter the house her hand involuntarily moved towards the handle. At her feet the cat stood up suddenly and growled menacingly. Surprised she stared down at the furious cat; its fur was standing on end and it continued to hiss and growl at her. Unnerved by the cat's behaviour Kitty moved back from the door, and tugged on Nero's lead pulling him away from the furious feline. He stared in baffled surprise at the spitting cat, pushed his nose forward to give it a curious sniff and got a clawed swipe across the snout for his troubles. Nero yelped and jerked back out of reach of the furious cat and its claws.

'Okay cat,' Kitty said slowly, looking at the door and replaced the key into her bag. 'You're probably right.' She stared up at the windows, a chill prickling ran over her skin and she shivered. 'Come on Nero, I think it's time we left.'
The cat trotted after them, staying a few paces behind all the way down to the village.
Kitty walked on unaware that the cat was following. She slowed, passing the shop and peered into the lit interior, but there was a teenage girl serving behind the counter so she moved on heading towards the cottages near the church.
The rain was falling steadily by now and Kitty and the dog were soaked by the time they reached Sybil's cottage. She noticed with relief a light on inside and tapped on the door waiting impatiently while drips ran off the eaves of the cottage soaking her even more. The door opened and Sybil stood inside, a warm smile of welcome wreathing her face.

'Kitty, how lovely to see you; oh you're so wet, come in,' she urged, standing to one side.

'Is the dog alright to come in? He's very wet as well,' Kitty apologised.

'Yes, yes, come in, don't worry about him.' She shut the door firmly against the driving rain.
The door opened straight into a small front room, a gas fire was popping in the hearth and two comfortable armchairs were pulled up in front of it.

'Come and sit down and dry out, let me have your coat. I'll hang it up in the kitchen.'

'Thanks Sybil, it's lovely and warm in here.'

Kitty shivered and moved thankfully towards the fire, struggling out of her coat. Nero pushed his way past her legs and flopped down on the hearth next to Sybil's little dog.

'Your dog's making himself comfortable already Kitty, why don't you sit down as well? Sybil turned on a small table lamp behind the armchairs. 'There that's better; it's so dark this morning...I hear you've been trying to see me... Rose,' she replied, to Kitty's inquiring look.

'Ah, the flower lady.'

Sybil looked puzzled.

'She was arranging some flowers in the church yesterday.'

'Of course, I forgot she would be doing the flowers. That's why I came back early, it's Isobel's wedding today and I want to see her go into the church.' She stared out of the small cottage window. 'But look at this weather, what a shame!' Sybil turned back to Kitty and explained. 'Isobel is Colin and Sara's daughter, they live at Forge Cottage. Have you met them yet?'

Kitty shook her head.

'Rose was quite worried about you Kitty; she said you looked so ill.' Sybil stared intently at her face.

'I wasn't feeling very well yesterday.'

'Well, you do look very pale, how would you like a nice hot cup of tea?'

'I would love one,' she said gratefully.

'I'll go and put the kettle on and I'll hang your coat over the radiator, that'll soon dry it out.'

Kitty looked at her sodden fleece hanging from Sybil's arm. 'Oh dear, it's dripping all over your carpet,' she said, feeling guilty.

'Now stop worrying Kitty, I'll get a towel for the dog and then we can dry him off as well.'

Kitty huddled closer to the fire, as she slowly warmed up she noticed in amusement that her damp clothes were starting to steam.

Sybil bustled back in with a towel over her arm and carrying two cups of tea. 'Here you are,' she said, handing Kitty a steaming mug.

She sipped it slowly, noticing gratefully that it was already sweetened. The elderly woman sat down with a sigh in the opposite chair and watched Kitty over the rim of her cup as she drank. The room was silent except for the slow ticking of the clock on the mantelpiece.

Kitty shifted slightly under her silent scrutiny; she thought curiously that she hadn't noticed before how pale Sybil's eyes were, almost colourless.

'Well?' she asked quietly, making Kitty jump. 'What did you want to see me about?'

Kitty put her empty cup down on the hearth next to the sleeping dog and clasped her hands together over her knees. 'Sybil, I really don't know how to start.'

'Start at the beginning, always the best way,' she said calmly, watching Kitty fidget in the armchair.

'Do you remember I told you I was hearing things in the house?' she paused, and watched Sybil nod. 'Well... other things started happening, strange things. I heard footsteps and there was somebody in the house with me,' she said quickly.

Kitty gazed at Sybil's blank face but pressed on. 'And Gordon saw somebody, it was a woman, in the house, but the doors were locked and she disappeared.'

'Really?'

'Yes, I know this sounds ridiculous Sybil but we think we're being haunted by

Hannah...Hannah Beamish,' she repeated, staring at Sybil's calm face. 'You don't believe me, do you?' she said flatly. 'Eve's car got damaged by her and she was so frightened. Well, we all were.'

Sybil looked at her in astonishment. 'That's ridiculous Kitty.'

'That's not all, Sybil,' Kitty continued, determined to tell all. She rubbed her hands together. 'We held a séance.'

'Oh dear, oh dear,' interjected Sybil, shaking her head. 'Why on earth would you do anything so silly? Why did Gordon let you do that?'

'Gordon was there,' she said defensively.

Sybil raised her eyebrows and put her cup down on the small table next to her.

'Well that was a very foolish thing to do. You open the door to the spirit world like that and you never know what might come through.'

Kitty looked at her stunned, a strange sense of unease sweeping over her.

'Well...'

'And what happened then? You haven't told me everything, have you?' she said, staring hard at Kitty.

'No Sybil,' she confessed. 'Sheena used her Ouija Board.'

On hearing that Sybil closed her eyes and shook her head slowly. Her eyes suddenly flicked open and she leant forward.

'Who is Sheena?'

'From the pub, she told us she had done this before.'

'And you believed her?'

'Yes.'

Sybil thought for a minute. 'Oh I know her, I've seen her around the village; all beads and black lace!' she said scornfully.

'That's the one,' Kitty smiled slightly.

Nero stirred slightly lifting his head; a faint scratching was coming from the front door.

Sybil's little dog heaved himself up from his position in front of the fire and pattered over to the door, he wagged his tail, staring at Sybil with an expectant look. She pulled herself up and walked across the room.

'Out of the way, Nigel.' She opened the door. 'Hello' she said, looking down. 'Come in.'

The cat walked slowly across the carpet to the fire and settled down next to the dog. It stared thoughtfully at Kitty then started to groom itself.

'Oh, it's your cat,' exclaimed Kitty in surprise.

'No dear, it isn't anybody cat, she belongs to herself.'

Kitty reached down and gently stroked the wet fur. 'Hello puss, it was at the house earlier.' She raised her head and caught a strange look of satisfaction on Sybil's face. She stirred uneasily. 'It must have followed me down.'

'I expect she did, well, what happened next at your séance? You didn't finish telling me.'

Kitty hesitated looking at her inscrutable face. 'We had messages, it was Hannah first and then somebody else came.'

'Ahh...' said Sybil slowly.

'Sheena said it was a man.' She stared at Sybil who was nodding thoughtfully to herself and staring at the floor.

'Go on.'

'That he had an evil aura and he was being drawn to me. We left after that. Gordon wants to sell the house,' she rushed on in distress. 'But it's my home Sybil, I don't want to leave.'

'And you shouldn't have to, my dear,' she said calmly. 'It seems to me that you have been meddling in things you don't understand.'

'But we needed answers Sybil! And who is Ava? That was one of the messages.'

'Ava?'

'Yes, Ava. I've never heard of anybody called Ava.'

'Really? Well, how strange.' Sybil looked surprised.

'It has something to do with me.'

'Yes dear.' She leant forward and put her hand on Kitty's knee, her pale eyes staring intently at Kitty's face. 'I thought you realised, I thought that was why you came back.'

Kitty sat back in her chair a sudden prickling running up her spine; she stared at the old woman. 'What do you mean?'

'Ava was your great grandmother.'

Kitty held her breath in amazement for a while then suddenly gasped with relief.

'No, no,' she exclaimed. 'You're wrong Sybil; great- gran was called Mary. Mary Marsh'

Sybil shook her head slowly and settled back in her chair, smiling slightly at the startled woman opposite.

'No dear, Ava was your great- grandmother. Mary was her second name. When she left the farm and went back to her parents at Axmouth she insisted that everybody called her Mary. She just couldn't bear the name of Ava after that.'

The clock ticked slowly over Kitty's head, on the hearth the cat had finished its grooming and stretched, then jumped nimbly into Kitty's lap. She absently stroked it while staring at Sybil with a troubled expression.

'So Ava was a relative? Are you sure? And she was Hannah's friend, wasn't she?'

Sybil nodded slowly. 'They were very close; Hannah thought the world of that little girl. You look like her you know. Same eyes, same mouth.'

'Did you know her?' Kitty asked, surprised.

'No, but somebody told me you resembled her.'

'Oh...' It suddenly dawned on Kitty. 'So Ava, my great-gran, was the servant girl? From the inquest!'

Sybil looked at her in amusement. 'You've finally got it.'

'Well, then who was the farmer?'

Sybil stared at her for a minute, a strange expression on her face. She carried on flatly, 'It was William's grandfather, Robert Beamish.'

'But Hannah was his sister- in- law, his brother's wife!' Kitty said, horrified. 'Why would he do that to her?'

Sybil sighed and stared pensively at the cat on Kitty's lap. 'He hated her and he hated his brother. Strange things families,' she sighed again. 'Both from the same parents, and yet so different. I think in the end he became so twisted with his hatred that he hated everybody, especially Ava.' She looked across at Kitty.

'He hated Ava as well?'

'Oh yes, after the fuss the inquest caused, he hated her with a vengeance. That's why she left the village, she had jobs offered to her here but it was better that she left. Safer.'

'Safer?'

Sybil looked at her with a faint grimace. 'You don't really think that Old Nick himself came and snatched Hannah away, do you?'

Kitty shook her head. 'Of course not, that's ridiculous. And the man he gave a hundred pounds to, what happened to him?'

Sybil shrugged. 'Nobody knows; he just disappeared after they found Hannah's body.'

'Do you think he did it?'

'Maybe, although he was such a drunk I'm not sure he was capable of anything.'

'How do you know so much about it?' she asked in amazement.

Sybil paused and smiled slightly. 'Family dear; and families talk. We were all related in the village, one way or another. Up to about twenty or thirty years ago I could count on one hand the people that weren't family, but not now.' She sighed. 'It's all changed but.' She stirred herself. 'That's life and perhaps it's just as well.'

Outside a few cars drove past the cottage and pulled into the car park. From her position by the fire Sybil craned her neck to peer out the window.

'Oh look, the guests are arriving already; Isobel is due at the church at twelve.'

Kitty looked up at the clock on the mantelpiece.

'It's quarter past eleven, I should be going really,' she said slowly.

'Eve will be home at twelve and she will be expecting me to be there.'

'Did you drive over?'

'No.' she smiled. 'I had to take the bus; Gordon went into work this morning so I couldn't use the car; he left me at Eve's house. I'm afraid he's not going to be pleased with me. Sybil,' she went on diffidently. 'Does William know about all this?'

'No dear.' Sybil looked aghast. 'I've never mentioned any of this to him, after all it is his family and I'm very fond of him. I wouldn't want to upset him.' She looked at Kitty and said sharply, 'And don't you say anything to him either.'

'No, no I won't,' Kitty reassured her. 'But what are we going to do Sybil? We are at our wits end.'

Sybil looked up as a shadow passed the window followed by a swift rap. She said quietly, 'Don't worry, we'll talk later.'

The door opened and William ducked his head through the low door. 'Sybil? You're back then.'

'Come on in William,' she called from her arm chair. 'We were just talking about you.'

'I wondered why my ears were burning,' he said, and closed the door behind him.

He caught sight of Kitty sitting near the fire, a slow smile spread over his face. 'Kitty, there you are.' He came forward to greet her, quickly ducking his head to avoid the low beams in the cottage. 'I've been quite worried about you.'

Kitty smiled up at him, pleased to see him but the cat on her lap growled ominously at the old man.

'Shush,' Sybil reproached the cat. 'William doesn't mean you any harm.' She stood up and motioned William to her seat. 'Sit down and I'll make some more tea.'

He sat down in her vacated armchair and stared keenly at Kitty across the hearth.

'I've been wondering where you both had got to. I called round and the lights were on and the front door was open. Is everything okay?'

'We had to leave suddenly.'

He rubbed his hands on his knees and half smiled at her. 'It's strange but I've been feeling very uneasy about you for the last couple of days, I just couldn't shake the feeling that something was wrong.'

'Oh William.' Kitty suddenly felt very guilty. 'I'm sorry we worried you.'

'Who's worried?' asked Sybil, coming back in with a tray and casting a curious look at the pair sat by the fire.

'I was, Sybil.'

'Oh. I've made a pot full, I'm sure you could do with another cup,' she said, looking at Kitty. 'No William, stay there,' she said to him as he stood up. 'And sit down before you bang your head.'

'This cottage is just too small, Sybil,' he said, stooping to avoid the low beam.

'Bijou, William, bijou,' she said firmly. 'And what are you worrying about now?'

'I was just telling Kitty that I was worried when I saw the lights on in the house and the door open.'

'Yes, I'm afraid we rushed off last night and forgot to lock up,' said Kitty, looking uncomfortable.

Sybil placed the tray on the table and pulled up a small wooden chair to the fire. She handed him a cup of tea. 'Here you are, William.'

Outside the church bells started pealing.

'Wow, that's loud.' Kitty winced. 'I suppose that is the downside of living so close to the church.'

'I'm used to it now. When we first came to this house it used to drive me mad, especially on Tuesdays when it was practice night. But I don't notice it so much now.'

William smiled slightly and winked at Kitty.

'And no, my hearing isn't going. I saw that smirk, William.'

'I didn't say anything,' he protested. 'Why don't you go outside?' He smiled slightly, watching her. 'You'll give yourself a stiff neck like that.'

Sybil had half raised herself from the chair and was craning her neck to see out of the cottage window at the cars pulling up outside.

'His parents have arrived. Oh, I like her hat,' she exclaimed. She looked at the clock and started to fidget. 'Well, it's nearly twenty to, I'll get the coats.' She hurried off into the small kitchen at the back of the house and came back shortly wearing a bright red duffle coat and carrying Kitty's jacket. 'Here you are dear.' She looked at it critically before handing it over to Kitty. 'It's dried quite well. Are you coming outside, William?' she inquired. 'Hurry up if you are, I don't want to miss anything.'

'I suppose I'd better,' he said, standing up.

'Mind your head,' reminded Kitty.

William grinned ruefully as he rapped his head one of the beams. 'Bugger!'

'William!'

'Sorry Sybil.' He took Kitty's coat from her hand. 'Here, let me help you.'

'Thanks, William,' she hesitated. 'I really am sorry that we had worried you, we just didn't think.'

'Don't apologise Kitty, it was just me being an old fusspot, I'm not used to having neighbours.'

'You *are* an old worrier, William,' said Sybil, looking at him in amusement. She opened the door. 'Come and look at this, it's stopped raining and the sun has come out. "Happy is the bride the sun shines on",' Sybil quoted happily.

Another three cars drove slowly down through the village and turned into the crowded car park.

'There are quite a few people turning up, they told me it was going to be a small wedding,' Sybil said quietly, as they walked down to join the group of onlookers gathered around the War Memorial, Kitty following reluctantly. A group of wedding guests walked across from the car park and climbed the stone steps to the church.

'The groom comes from a large family Sybil so I guess they weren't able to. Look there's Rose waving at you.'

She came hurrying over. 'Sybil,' she cried. 'You got back in time, I was watching for your daughter's car but I didn't see it drive past.'

'I got home about ten; thank goodness it's stopped raining.'

Rose turned her attention to Kitty. 'I'm glad to see you looking better; you've got a bit of colour in your cheeks today.'

'Yes, I feel much better today, thanks,' Kitty replied quietly.

'I was so worried about you yesterday and I knew Sybil would want to know, so I had to call her last night and tell her, didn't I?' she said, turning to Sybil, who absently nodded while watching more of the guests arrive.

'What's the time?' asked Sybil.

'It's five to twelve,' William said, checking his pocket watch.

'She'll be here in a minute; I'm looking forward to seeing the dress. They had to go to London to get it.' Rose fidgeted, staring up the street.

'Yes, I know Rose, I told you.'

'Did you? I thought it was Edith that told me.'

'Well, I told Edith in the first place.'

Behind them William rolled his eyes at Kitty and grinned. 'Women and weddings.'

She grinned back at him. 'You were lucky just having boys; I only had to go through it once with Eve, thank goodness.'

'She's a pretty young thing, though I think she favours Gordon more than you.'

'Yes, she's like Gordon's mum; she's got her temper as well. Little Emily looks more like my side of the family.'

'Has she got a temper as well?'

'No, she's always happy and smiling. She's going to playgroup already; it doesn't seem that long ago she was a baby.'

'She will be a teenager before you know it.'

Kitty shuddered. 'Ugh no, having suffered two teenagers of my own that was bad enough but to go through it all again with the grandchildren, yuck.'

'But look on the bright side Kitty; you won't be living in the same house!'

Kitty smiled at him and shyly acknowledged the many friendly and curious smiles and waves of Sybil's acquaintances in the waiting crowd.

'Sybil, Sybil,' William said, tugging at her arm to get her attention. 'The car is just pulling out of the drive. Is it worth hiring a car just for that short distance?' he questioned. 'She could have walked down.' The two older women gave him a scathing look.

'Isobel can't walk down the road in her wedding dress, honestly, men!' Sybil said to Rose.

The gleaming car bedecked with ribbons and flowers slowly drew to a halt by the church steps, Colin got and ran round to open the door for his daughter and helped her out.

'You look lovely, dear,' Sybil called across.

'Thanks Sybil.' The young bride blushed and gave the waiting onlookers a little wave.

William smiled and called out, 'You look lovely as well Colin, very dapper.'

Father and daughter laughed as he helped Isobel negotiate the slippery steps in her flowing lace dress.

'Do you know how uncomfortable this get up is?' Colin said to William.

'Never mind, you'll be back in your wellies tomorrow.'

Colin grinned at the crowd as he led his daughter proudly up the church path.

A car drew slowly up behind them, parking across the front of the cottages.

'Oh dear, somebody's late' said Rose, peering around William at the car.

'It's your husband, Kitty,' he said.

Kitty started guiltily as Gordon got out of the car; he looked none too pleased and replied gruffly to Sybil's cheerful greeting.

'You've just missed Isobel going into the church.'

'Really.'

'What are you doing here? I thought you were at work,' said Kitty.

'And you were supposed to be at Eve's waiting for her to get back,' he said sharply, in a low voice. 'I thought you were taking Emily to the swimming pool this afternoon, she'll be very disappointed that you've let her down.'

'It was your idea to take her, not mine. I don't remember you asking me what I thought about it,' she replied, suddenly feeling guilty.

'Well I thought you would like to, I just wanted to know that you would be okay today while I was at work.'
William looked at the couple curiously. 'Everything okay, Gordon?'
'Fine,' he replied shortly, and turned back to his wife. 'You haven't been up to the house, have you?'
'No,' she lied. 'I came to see Sybil.'
Sybil looked around at the mention of her name. 'Why don't we go back in the warm and I'll make some more tea,' she suggested calmly, looking at Gordon's annoyed face. 'I'm sure you would like a cup, wouldn't you Gordon?' Sybil looked at William and smiled. 'And you won't say no to another cup of tea, will you?'
William hesitated, aware of the tension between the couple. 'Well,' he said slowly. 'I should be going, Sybil.' He turned to Kitty. 'I'm glad you're alright.' He glanced at Gordon's stiff face and carried on, 'I'll be off now, I'm sure I'll see you soon.' He patted Sybil on the arm and turned and walked slowly away up the street.
'Why are you being so rude to everybody?' Kitty said crossly, quietly enough that nobody else could hear her except for her husband.
'I wasn't being rude.'
Sybil opened the cottage door and ushered them in, she looked at Gordon's flushed face. 'Don't look like that, Kitty was right to come and see me.' She closed the door behind them and pulled off her duffle. 'Perhaps it's just as well William didn't come in, now we'll be able to talk freely about your problem. Now who wants tea?'
Kitty shook her head and glanced at her husband.
'No thanks,' he replied stiffly.
'Well sit down Gordon, you too, Kitty.'
Kitty sat back in her recently vacated chair and pushed Nero's warm sleeping body out of the way with her foot; as soon as she had settled back into the armchair the cat jumped into her lap and curled up. Sybil pushed the tea tray out of the way and laid her address book on the table. 'I'll take your phone number, then I can ring you later.'
'Why?'
'I'm going to call my older sister Queenie; she'll know what to do.'
'We've already had 'expert help', and I'm sure Kitty told you what happened.' He frowned at Sybil and shook his head angrily at his wife.
'Yes, yes, I've heard all about it, now calm down, Gordon. Queenie will be able to help, I promise. I'll ring her and see if she can come over as soon as possible. Though I don't expect she will able to today, she lives in Dorchester now so tomorrow will be more likely.'

'I'm not sure I want any more help, I told Kitty that we're going to sell the house and that will be the end of it.' He stared at the old woman and stood up.

'But Gordon...'

'That's enough Kitty, you're not going back into that house, I won't allow her to hurt you or any of my family.'

'Gordon!' said Sybil sharply. 'Hannah would never hurt Kitty.'

'You don't know that,' he rounded on her.

'Yes I do,' she replied firmly. 'Kitty is Ava's great- granddaughter.' Gordon stared at her in amazement. 'She can't be, your great-gran was called Mary,' he addressed Kitty. 'This is nonsense.'

'Gordon! Just be quiet and listen for a minute, Mary was her second name, I didn't realise.'

He rubbed his hand wearily over his face. 'Look Kitty, let's just calmly think about this, you would have known if she was called Ava.' He turned to Sybil. 'I think you've made a mistake, it was a long time ago and things get muddled,' he said, trying to be patient with the old woman.

Sybil looked at him and smiled slightly. 'No, no mistake, Gordon and I don't get muddled,' she added firmly.

'Then how do you explain the messages?' Kitty asked him.

He shook his head in bewilderment. 'I don't know, I really don't know and why would anybody want to hurt you? Little Emily was in the house Monday night, it was awful,' he groaned. 'God, I wish I had never bought that piece of land. What the hell is going on?' Gordon rubbed his hand over his chin and stared at Sybil in frustration.

'Sit down and I'll try to explain,' she said calmly.

'Go on then, try and explain this nightmare to me.' He sat down again in front of the fire and looked at her expectantly.

Sybil pulled up the small chair and settled herself; she placed her hands on her knees and began slowly, looking intently at them.

'Right, Ava, who was Kitty's great grandmother, worked for Robert Beamish at Castle Farm, he was, of course, Hannah's brother- in- law. After Samuel, Hannah's husband, was killed, she became very ill, I think it was from the shock. She was pregnant with their first child at that time and it came too early.

'A baby?' Kitty stared across the hearth at Gordon. 'Was he called Samuel? Because we found that other Samuel Beamish on the records. Was it hers?'

'Yes, he didn't live long, the poor little thing. The shock of Samuel's death made Hannah go into labour, so,' she sighed. 'She lost her husband and her baby within a few weeks of each other. Ava used to go up with food and help nurse her and little Samuel until Robert found out.'

'How did his brother die?' he asked curiously.

'I think that's open for debate; whether it was an accident or it was something far more sinister, I don't know.'

'Would he kill his own brother? Was he that evil?' asked Gordon, shocked.

'I don't know how far he would have gone. After Samuel died he became obsessed with the land, he offered to buy the cottage back from Hannah and when she refused he started hounding her.'

'He sounds a right bastard but what has this got to do with us?' he asked, stroking Nero's ears.

'His hatred of Hannah spilled out onto Ava, he made the poor girl's life hell but she didn't give up on Hannah. She continued visiting her and taking food up to the cottage,' Sybil paused, and stared sadly into the fire.

Gordon looked puzzled. 'But what about everybody else in the village? They must have known what was going on.'

She shook her head. 'He could be so violent that they were all terrified of him and I'm sure they thought it would all blow over eventually. And as for thinking that any harm would come to Hannah it would never have crossed their minds, after all, why would it?' Sybil shook her head. 'So you see,' she continued. 'That's the problem, as far as he is concerned Ava has returned, so to speak,' she nodded at Kitty, 'and living on his land again.'

Kitty huddled in the chair clutching the purring cat close to her chest.

'So the thing that was in the house, that came after Hannah, that was Robert Beamish?'

'I don't think there's much doubt dear but as I said Queenie's the expert. She'll be able to tell you more.'

'That makes sense,' Gordon said slowly. He hesitated and looked at Kitty. 'I saw him, the night we left with Eve. Remember there was somebody stood in the lane? And I saw him before on Monday night out of the window, I know I didn't say anything but I didn't think it was William then, it looked like him but he didn't feel right. Oh I know I'm not making sense but I'm sure it must have been Robert.'

Sybil nodded slowly. 'Well it probably was, as I said Queenie will be able to tell you for sure.'

'Are you sure she will come?' asked Kitty.

'Of course she will, she'll be able to sort this out.'

'I found an old photo album on Sunday, there was picture of great-granny at the back. She was stood outside The Anchor with her family. I think it must have been a wedding, she looked so happy.'
The grey cat stretched on Kitty's lap and yawned, showing its bright red tongue and sharp little teeth.

'She was a happy little girl; it broke her heart what happened to Hannah,

'Of course,' said Gordon suddenly. 'She's the one that stood up at the inquest and accused Robert of murder.'

'Exactly.'

'I bet that went down well.'

'Luckily Ava was living at home then.'

'And the man that was supposed to be a white witch, what happened to him?' Gordon asked.

'He wasn't seen again, I believe they searched for him for weeks but it was as if he had fallen off of the face of the earth. People said that he had done it but we knew better, not that it could be proved of course.'

Gordon stood up and took the pen from her hand; he scribbled his mobile number in the book.

'There,' he said, throwing down the pen. 'And you'll ring us tonight?'

'Yes' she said firmly. 'But stay away from the house tonight, you two, just to be safe.'

Robert opened the door to the parlour and looked into the dimly lit room.
Evans was slumped in a chair near the smouldering fire, a tankard in his slack hand.

'Well?' he inquired. 'How is it all going?'

The drunk roused himself and looked blearily at the figure standing over him.

'Everything's going well sur,' he slurred, staggering up.

Robert smiled slightly. 'So the witch will soon be gone I hope?' He stared at the bubbling pot on the hearth. 'And you think that foul potion will do the trick?' he questioned.

'Oh yes sur, that'll certainly do the trick, that'll drive the evil harridan out of her cottage for good, yes sur for good.' He swayed as he spoke.

Robert smiled in satisfaction. 'Soon?' His cold eyes flicked over the man.

'Oh yes sur, any day now.'

'Yes, I think this is going to work out very well.' He opened the door and paused. 'I'll get Rose to bring you some more ale.'

'Thank 'ee sur, most kind of 'ee.'

Outside in the passage Rose was hovering; a pile of linen over her arm. She stared grimly at her master.

'How long is he going to be in there? I need to get into the parlour to clean.' Rose's lip curled in disgust. 'And it stinks in there, what is he doing?'

'That's none of your business Rose, just fetch another jug of ale for him and stay out of his way.'

Rose turned away from him and started walking towards the scullery.

'Where's that girl?'

'If you mean Ava, she is in the dairy; she's busy scouring out the butter pans.'

'Well make sure she does her work properly, I've had enough of her running off up that hill.'

He paused and stared at the plump servant. 'I'm just stepping out for a while; I've business in the village and don't forget the ale.'

He pulled out his blackthorn walking stick from the stick stand and opened the front door.

'I'm looking forward to getting into some clean clothes,' said Kitty, pulling out a long sleeved T shirt from the carrier bag. She tugged at the plastic tags. 'Have you got a pair of scissors or something? These labels won't come off.'

Gordon looked up from the bag he was opening. 'Throw it over,' he said, holding out his hand.

'I don't know why they make the tags so hard to get off,' she complained.

'That's the idea, isn't it, to deter shoplifters.' He put the label into his mouth and nipped it off with his teeth. 'There,' he said, handing it back.

'Can you do this one as well?' She pulled out a thick jumper from the bag and tossed it onto the bed next to him.

'God, how much did you spend in that shop?' he complained, looking at the price tag.

'We needed clean clothes, Gordon.' She held the jumper up to herself and looked in the mirror on the dressing table. 'I think this will fit, it looks nice, doesn't it?'

'Uhuh...' He sat quietly on the bed and watched her pull out various pieces of clothing from the store bags. 'Kitty, I've been thinking.'

She looked up and lowered the blouse she was holding. 'About what?'

'At the weekend I'd like to go to Lyme and buy a new rod and reel.'

Kitty stared at him confused. 'Why? You have loads of rods and reels, what do you want another one for?'

'For you, a small light weight one, I thought I could teach you how to fish.'

'Why?'

'It's just that I've been thinking it would be nice to spend more time together, I've been so busy lately with work and then of course getting the house sorted. We haven't had enough 'quality time' I'd think you call it.'

Gordon sat on the end of the bed, his shoulders slumped and Kitty noticed suddenly how tired he looked. He stared blankly at the shirt he was holding. 'What do you think?'

'But you like having peace and quiet when you're fishing; well, that's what you always said.'

'I know but that was when the children were smaller, it's different now.' He looked up at her. 'It would be nice, we could go fishing together or you could bring a book. I could even get you a comfy chair to sit in. Just a bit of time together...'

'Okay,' she said. 'We could take a picnic as well.'

He brightened. 'Or stop for lunch somewhere. We'll get this sorted and then we will go shopping for a rod,' Gordon said decisively.

'Alright, if that's what you would like.' Kitty dumped the rest of the clothes on the bed. 'There you are, clean undies and socks.'

'Thanks dear, I say these are jazzy,' he said, picking up a pair of red and yellow striped socks.

'I thought you could have a change from black.'

A quiet buzzing came from the pocket of his coat that was lying on the window seat.

He pulled it out and looked at the number displayed on the screen.

'I don't recognise this number, I wonder if it's Sybil. Hello? Yeah, she is great, so what time do you want us to come? Alright... no that's fine... Where? Your place? OK and you're sure she will be able to help?' There was a long pause. 'Really?' he said surprised, looking quickly at Kitty. 'Well then, we'll see you tomorrow.' Gordon flicked the phone shut and threw it down on the bed. He stared blankly out the window; the rain had started again and was beating against the glass. 'That was Sybil; she wants us to come to her cottage about six.'

'What did her sister say about it?'

Gordon rubbed the stubble on his chin and looked worried. 'Sybil said she has been expecting this and is all prepared.'

'Expecting it, why?'

'Sybil didn't say.' Gordon picked up the shirt he had dropped. 'I could do with a shower.'

'So we have to wait until tomorrow?'

'Yeah ... Look Kitty, are you sure you want to do this?'

'I think we have to,' she said quietly.

He stared at her. 'Right, one last go at this and if it doesn't work for whatever reason, that's it! Okay?'

Kitty nodded.

'It's a deal?' he asked again.

'Yes it's a deal. One last go.'

Friday

'I think,' said Gordon, pushing his plate away, 'that we should have a nose around Axminster this morning and see what we can find about the coroner.'

'Where?' asked Kitty, spreading butter on the last piece of toast.

'We'll start in the museum, then there is the library, I expect we'll be able to use the internet there. We can ask about Hannah. If she is as famous as the landlord seemed to think, I'm sure they will have some information about her.'

Kitty looked at him in surprise. 'Aren't you going into work today?'

He fixed her with a firm gaze. 'No, I think I will stay with you today.'

She half smiled at him. 'Don't you trust me, dear?'

'Not at all,' he said grimly. 'After yesterday, you're just daft enough to go back to the house on your own.'

'No I won't,' she said flatly, remembering her visit to the house the day before. 'Not on my own.' Kitty hesitated and then asked, 'Are you going into the estate agent as well?'

Gordon threw his napkin down on the table. 'No, we'll see what happens with Sybil's sister later.'

He looked up as Angela came into the dining room.

'Was everything alright with your breakfast?' she asked.

'It was lovely thank you, and give our thanks to your husband for cooking it.' Kitty half smiled at Gordon. 'We are going to get used to being waited on, aren't we?'

'That reminds me,' he said. 'Is it alright if we stay another night? I can pay you now if it would be easier.'

Angela smiled at him while collecting the dirty plates. 'No, you can settle up tomorrow that will be fine. How is the move going? she asked curiously.

'Fine,' lied Gordon. 'We're just getting everything sorted, carpets, that sort of thing.'

'Oh I see, now would you like some more tea or coffee?'

'No we're fine; we've got some things to do in the town so we'll be off in a minute.'

'Then we'll see you later, have a good day,' said Angela, carrying the tray of dirty china back to the kitchen.

****

They parked in the car park next to the supermarket and walked up the steep hill to the centre of the small market town. The church of St Marys sat square in the middle of the green, encircled by the streets and lanes of the town.

'Where is the museum?' asked Kitty, staring up and down the street, she stepped to one side to allow an elderly man to pass on the narrow pavement.

He slowed, overhearing her. 'The museum you say? It's there through the arch.' He pointed up the road. 'Through the arch, it's the door on the right and up the stairs.'

'Thank you.'

'It's only small though,' he warned.

'That's alright; we just want to do some research on Medbury.'

'Medbury; nice little village. That witch used to live there, I remember my dad telling me about her. Now what was her name?' He stared off into the distance, his rheumy old eyes blinking. 'Oh yes, Hannah Beamish, that was it.'

'That's right,' Kitty said surprised.

'Aye, my old dad used to tell me she was terrible, cursed crops, killed cattle, stuff like that.'

'How did he know her?'

'Oh you know how it is, people gossip, and I think his mother used to scare him with stories about the Witch of Medbury. Probably tried to get him to behave himself,' he chuckled and stared at them thoughtfully. 'Why are you interested in her then?'

Gordon took Kitty's hand and squeezed it. 'Well we've just moved to Medbury, curiosity really.' He started to move towards the arch. 'Thanks for the directions.'

'That's alright, pleased to help, oh,' he said, leaning on his walking stick and staring after them, 'if you don't find anything there perhaps the Tourist Information Office will be able to help.'

'Thanks,' repeated Gordon, and pulled Kitty up the street towards the museum.

'How strange that everybody remembers her as being an evil witch.'

'Well dirt sticks, Kitty, and it makes a more interesting tale than if she was just a normal woman who was good with herbs.'

'I suppose,' Kitty sounded doubtful.

They walked under the stone arch, and just as the man had directed, a doorway opened up into a set of stone stairs that led up to the museum on the second floor.

'This must be it,' she said, climbing slowly up.

At the top a door to the right led into a small room which held an exhibition about the local Axminster carpets, while the door to the left opened into a large lofty ceilinged room filled with display cabinets. There were two women volunteers inspecting the display of Victorian jelly moulds set up on the tables running the length of the room. They looked up as Gordon and Kitty entered the room.

'Morning,' said Gordon, looking around the room. 'Hey, look at this,' he pointed to a piece of paper pinned to the side of one of the cabinets. It was a list of 'Notable Ghosts' and halfway down was Hannah's name.

Kitty read it. 'Is that it?' she whispered. 'Anything else?'

They wandered along the cabinets, peering in through the glass at the displays of First World War memorabilia and an eclectic mix of items of 'local significance'.

'Do you have any information on Hannah Beamish?' Gordon asked one of the elderly volunteers.

'Who?'

'The Witch of Medbury.'

She looked doubtful. 'I'm not sure that we do.' She moved towards a pile of books in the window. 'There might be something in one of these; there is lots of information on Devon villages but whether there is anything on the witch, I'm not sure.' She looked up from the book she was flicking through. 'What year would it have been?'

'Well, she died in 1841.'

'It's a shame Chris isn't in today, he's the expert on local history. Of course you could try the library.'

'That's where we're going next,' commented Gordon. 'But thanks for the suggestion.'

'Do you know where they would have held inquests in Axminster during the 1800's? We found a report of the inquest but it wasn't clear where it was held,' asked Kitty.

The woman looked around the room. 'This is the old Court House so any inquests would have been held in this room.'

Kitty suppressed a shudder. 'Fancy being a fly on the wall that day.'

Gordon agreed, 'Yes.' He turned to the woman and asked, 'Do you know anything about the coroner for that inquest?'

'Sorry.' She shook her head. 'I don't know anything about that, as I said your best bet is the library.'

Kitty put a few coins in the collection box on the way out and walked carefully down the worn steps to the street. Outside the early morning mist had gone and the sun had just broken through and was shining just enough to raise Kitty's spirits. There were still a few holiday makers wandering around the narrow streets of the town enjoying the last few warm days of the year.

'Right, we'll go to the library first and then a coffee.' Gordon looked up the street past the museum. 'I think it's up this way. Where's that old man when you need him.'

Kitty tucked her hand under his arm and fell into step next to him. 'What a coincidence though,' she said. 'Bumping into somebody who knew about her, people have long memories around here. I wonder if it's something to do with the slower pace of life?'

'I think it's more likely that generations of family are still living in the same area, and the family talk and gossip gets handed down, or talked down I should say.' He looked at her as they walked slowly up the street. 'Your mum's just the same, she still talks about all your old family members as though they are still alive and kicking. What she did in the war and what her father used to say and do, she goes on for hours.'

'Do you know she still has letters from her grandmother, she keeps them under the bed in the spare room. It's strange isn't it,' Kitty went on. 'We're probably the first generation that doesn't write letters anymore, we just pick up the phone and talk, and now of course it's all e-mails. It's a shame really all that, I don't know, personal information, knowledge all just lost somewhere in internet heaven.'

'Does it matter?'

'Yes,' she said surprised. 'It does matter, when I read those letters and can see great grandmother's handwriting it brings her closer, it also gives a feel of what her life was like.'

Gordon opened the door to the library and stood back to allow Kitty to go in. 'Well there are other things to make up for it, like film, photographs, that sort of thing.'

'But it's not the same,' she said firmly. 'A letter is so personal; I don't think I've ever written a letter to the children. I've sent birthday cards and Christmas cards of course, and they always go in the bin within a few days. Don't you think that's a shame?' she persisted.

'No, not really,' he replied. 'Come on let's go and use some of this modern technology to find out about our coroner. Do you know,' he said, staring at her fondly. 'I think you must have been a Luddite in a previous life.'

'I think I was born too late,' she replied feelingly. 'And he's not our coroner and I don't think I'm going to like him.'

The librarian looked up from her desk and smiled. 'Good Morning.'

'Morning, can we use one of your computers?'

'Are you a member of the library?' she asked. 'If you are, the first half an hour is free otherwise I'm afraid its two pounds eighty.'

Gordon took out his wallet from his jacket. 'Well we are, but I think we're going to need longer than half an hour.'

Kitty nodded. 'After all we don't know what we're looking for yet. Do you,' she asked the librarian. 'Have a local section? We're looking for information on Medbury.'

The woman pointed to a small section of books opposite the desk. 'That's the Local Interest section and if you look there.' She pointed to the floor under the shelves where there were a pile of blue box files. 'All that is the Domesday Project, it has information collected from all around the area. Medbury will be in one of those.'

Kitty left Gordon at the desk paying for the computer use and hurried over to the stack of files. She knelt on the floor in front of the shelves, pulled out the box marked Medbury and opened it. Inside it was crammed with brown manila folders. The top one was the Medbury folder. Inside was full of photocopied records and a few black and white photographs of the village.

Kitty looked up at Gordon, who had followed her. 'It's going to take ages to wade through all of it.'

Gordon pulled up a chair to the nearby table and sat down. 'Well, we've got until six so bring it over and we'll start looking through it.' He looked at the folder she placed on the table.

'What's in there?'

'Well,' she hesitated. 'I'm not sure; it's just copies of different articles about the village, lists of the inhabitants, forms, and reports from the Vicar, anything that ever happened in the village. And it's all muddled,' she complained. 'This bit is from the 1860's and this is 1920.'

Gordon emptied the folder and spread it out on the table. 'Let's be methodical and work our way through it bit by bit.' He put on his glasses and peered at the blurred photocopies. 'A lot of this isn't going to be of any help,' he said, after a few minutes of reading. He leafed through a few more pages and put them to one side. 'These pages are the right date, but nothing of any interest in them.' He put them on the discarded pile and pulled another sheet towards him. Gordon paused, 'Well, this looks more interesting.'

Kitty leaned forward in excitement. 'What?'

'It's a copy from a book.' He turned the sheet over. 'But it doesn't say which, look, Hannah Beamish,' he read. 'Was a well known figure in the village, very neat and clean about her appearance and kept her house in good order. She was also well known for the excellence of her cooking. Her dumplings were renowned for being the best and whitest made in the village. Hannah was also called upon regularly for her knowledge of healing and was a frequent visitor to the homes of the sick.'

'What book did it come from?' interrupted Kitty, pulling the piece of paper from Gordon's hand and peering at it excitedly.

'It doesn't say, I told you.'

She laid it back on the table and they both bent over it again.

'Look,' said Gordon, pointing to a paragraph on the second page. 'The first inquest held the day after her death had to be abandoned.' He sat back in his chair and stared at the ceiling. 'I wonder why?' he said slowly, and then reread the paragraph. 'It also says that there is no record of her death anywhere.'

'Well that explains why we couldn't find it on that Family Search site,' said Kitty, turning to look at her husband.

'How strange,' he mused. 'It's looking more like somebody hushed it up very quickly.'

'Who would have or could have done that?' questioned Kitty. She continued to read until the end of the article. 'Well there's nothing more about it, just a mention of her being buried at the crossroads.' Kitty pulled the pile of papers towards her and leafed through the remaining copies. 'Damn,' she said despairingly. 'There's nothing else about it in here.'

'Well that was worth finding anyway, it shows that not everybody considered her to be an evil woman.' He gathered up the pieces of paper and pushed them back into the folder. 'Put this back and let's get on one of the computers.'

Kitty tucked the box file back under the shelves and followed Gordon down the room to the row of pc's.

He called over to the librarian at the desk. 'Is it alright to use this one?'

She nodded. 'Come and see me if you need more than an hour.'

Gordon nodded and sat down at the desk. 'Kitty, pull up that other chair and let's see what we can find.'

'Where are we going to start?'

'What was his name? The coroner? I can't remember.' asked Gordon.

'Edward Foulstone,' replied Kitty. 'That's a name you can't forget.'

'I can,' he joked. 'Now what shall we look for? Coroner's reports perhaps.' He typed it into Google and scanned the results that came up.

'This doesn't look very helpful,' he grumbled, opening a few of the links and scanning through the contents of the sites. 'It says here that Coroners reports weren't kept and the reports put into the newspapers were only summaries and not the full proceedings. Damn! I can't believe that,' he added, sounding puzzled. 'There must be copies somewhere, I bet if we visited the County Record Office we would find them, but I don't think we have time to do that and get back in time for six.'

'How about trying coroners for the 1840's, Axminster?' suggested Kitty.

'That will throw up loads of rubbish.'

'Try anyway,' she urged, looking at her watch. 'Our hour will soon be up.'

Gordon glanced at the time. 'What already? Doesn't time fly...'

'When you're having fun,' she finished.

'No, I was going to say when you're trying to find something on the internet.' He sighed, after reading the results of his next search. 'No, nothing.'

'Try Edward Foulstone, and then add coroner.' She leant forward and peered at the results coming up onto the screen.

'Nope, no good. We could try the 1841 census records again.'

'Yes, but we don't know where he lived or what year he was born or anything.' Gordon was beginning to get irritated, he ran his hand over his face and sighed in frustration. 'There must be some information out there somewhere.'

'But his name is quite unusual and he must be local, don't you think?'

'Okay, let's try it, I can't think of anything else to try,' he paused. 'What was the site called?'

'I think it was called Family Search or something like that.'

Gordon found the site and as soon as he had clicked onto it recognised it as the one that Eve had recommended. He typed in the coroner's name. 'It wants his date of birth, what shall we do?'

Kitty stared at the screen. 'Well, we left that box blank when we were looking for Hannah, so do the same for him.'

'Okay, and I will put in Devon for place of birth and see what happens.'

The site found details for five Edward Foulstones in Devon, three of which were not the right age to be the man they were after.

'Well that counts those three out and we're left with just these two,' Gordon sighed. 'At least I have enough credit left to look at both of these, which shall we look at first? So,' he looked at Kitty. 'Pick one, dear, which Edward do you choose?'

Kitty smiled. 'You're making it sound like a game show, what do I win if I pick the right one?'

'A house,' he replied half seriously.

Kitty squeezed his arm. 'I'm sure this is going to work out you know, I have faith.'

'In what?' he asked.

'Everything,' she said firmly. 'Let's try the younger one.'

'Now are you picking him for any logical reason or is it just a wild guess?'

'No, I just think as he is the younger of the two then he might be inclined to be involved in any funny business.'

'Funny business? Is that the technical term for tampering with evidence, etcetera, etcetera?'

'Yes, now just get on with it Gordon, we're running out of time.'

'Well here goes.' He clicked on the 'view more' box and the younger Edward Foulstone's details popped up. 'Now let's see,' and he started to read out the details. 'He's living at Castle Hill House, Axminster, 31 years old, born Exeter, occupation Doctor, married. His wife is called Belinda, 27 years old born in Honiton. Arthur, son, 5 years old, born Axminster. Harold, son, 3 years old, born Axminster. Mary, daughter, 1 year old, born Axminster. Rachel, sister, 27 years old, born Exeter. Bethan Cox, servant, 35 years old, single, born Axminster. God! He had a houseful, though if he was a doctor I suppose he could afford it,' he remarked in astonishment.

Kitty stared blankly at the screen. 'Doesn't prove anything, does it?'

'Do you want to look at the other Edward?' he asked. 'Or shall we just go for a coffee?'

'No, let's carry on now we are here.'

'Right.'

The next details popped up onto the screen.

'This one was 52 years old, a widower, born in Southampton, occupation journeyman. What the hell is a journeyman?'

'Travel agent?' suggested Kitty.

Gordon shook his head. 'Not in 1841 Kitty! Well, he lived in Seaton, with a housekeeper and two lodgers. This doesn't sound like a coroner to me.'

'So the Doctor is the most likely candidate.'

'I think so, so arriving at a verdict of water on the brain and there to be no records of her death makes it even stranger, hmmm,' he said, stroking his chin and looked sideways at Kitty.

'So,' she replied thoughtfully. 'I think the Doctor is our man.'

'I'm not sure this is going to help us at all but I don't think there is anything else we can do.' Gordon sat back in his chair and looked across at his wife. 'It's all up to Sybil's sister now.'

Kitty stared blankly at the screen and said, 'We're out of time anyway. And ideas,' she added.

Gordon stood up and slipped his jacket on, he stared down at his wife sitting huddled in the chair. 'Come on dear, nothing else we can do here. Let's get a coffee.'

****

The evening was just drawing in as they drove slowly down the hill into Medbury, a faint mist hung just inches above the road, swirling and breaking away as they drove through.

Kitty shivered slightly when she saw the village lights below.

'What was her name?' Gordon asked suddenly, breaking the silence.

'Queenie, Queenie Beresford,' replied Kitty.

'Sounds like something out of an Agatha Christie novel. I wonder if she'll be wearing tweeds and flat sensible shoes.'

'Tuppence.'

'What?'

'It was Tuppence Beresford I think, I can't remember what her husband was called.'

Gordon cast a puzzled look at her.

'Agatha Christies' characters in a book,' she explained.

'Did she murder her husband or something?'

'No, they were amateur detectives. I don't remember much about the story. It's a long time since I read one of her novels.'

They pulled up outside the row of cottages; a small yellow car was already parked rather haphazardly across the front of Sybil's.

'Do you think that's her car?'

'Probably,' he replied. 'Come on let's see if she's wearing tweed and looks like Miss Marple.'

The door opened before Gordon could knock.

'Hello, I thought I heard a car, come in.'

'Hi Sybil,' said Kitty quietly, walking into the small front room. Sybil's little dog Nigel pottered over to greet her. 'Sorry, Nero couldn't come,' she said, bending and stroking his head.

'Oh where is he?' queried Sybil. 'You could have brought him, you know.'

'We left him with Eve,' explained Gordon. 'As we weren't too sure what was going to happen tonight. Is your sister here?' he questioned, glancing around the tiny cottage.

Sybil bustled about taking their coats and pulling chairs up to the fire. 'Oh yes, she's just arrived. Queenie is upstairs in the bathroom, it's a long journey for her now, bladder problems,' she whispered.

'Oh.'

'Are you talking about me Sybil?' a voice queried from the staircase.

'Kitty and Gordon have arrived.' Sybil moved to the bottom of the stairs and called up.

'I can hear them.'

'Well are you coming down then?'

'Yes,' the voice said impatiently. Heavy footsteps started slowly down the narrow wooden staircase. 'God, these stairs are so steep Sybil, I wonder you don't break your neck on them.'

The resemblance between an Agatha Christie character and Sybil's sister ended with the tweed skirt she was wearing. Queenie Beresford was definitely not a Miss Marple. But her resemblance to Sybil was uncanny, including the pale coloured eyes. But while Sybil had neat greying hair, Queenie's curls were bright pink and fluffy. Kitty instantly thought of fairground candy floss. A half smoked cigarette hung from her mouth.

'Queenie, I'd rather you didn't smoke inside,' Sybil complained. 'You know I don't like it and it isn't good for you.'

'It's okay Sybil, I'm not running the marathon this year,' she grinned and winked at Kitty. 'Hi, you two.'

'Hello Queenie,' said Gordon politely, holding out his hand.

'Yep, that's me,' she said, ignoring his hand and greeting him with a hug. 'Kitty,' she said, staring at her in surprise before giving her a hug. 'You're the spitting image of your great- grandmother.'

'Sybil said I looked like her.'

'Yes you do; peas in a pod.' She took a deep drag on her cigarette and stared at them. 'Are you ready for this?'

'I would like to discuss this first,' Gordon said firmly. 'Do you know what you're doing?'

'Relax Gordon, I'm an expert in all things spooky,' she joked, moving towards the fire. 'Move dog.' Queenie pushed Nigel out of the way and plumped down rather heavily into the armchair. 'Are you going to make some tea Sybil? We're dying of thirst you know.'

'Yes. I'm just going to make some.' She rolled her eyes at Kitty. 'Sisters! Sit down and make yourselves comfortable.'

Sybil disappeared into the kitchen at the rear of the cottage. Kitty could hear the chink of the china cups as she prepared the tea.

'Sybil has been telling me all about your adventures, Kitty.'

'Some adventure!' said Gordon. 'I've already told Kitty that this is it, if this doesn't work then that will be the end of it. The house will be sold and we'll move somewhere else.'

'And what does Kitty think of that?' She stared at him through the cigarette smoke while Kitty stared at both of them and shrugged doubtfully.

'I don't know,' she confessed.

'It won't be the end of anything Gordon, it will go on and who knows it might affect Emily in the future or even her children. You can't just walk away from this,' said Queenie.

'Yes we can,' he replied sternly.

'No,' interrupted Kitty. 'I feel that I owe it to great-gran and to Hannah to end this.'

'Good for you girl, you've got Ava's spirit as well as her looks.' Queenie smiled at her, looking pleased.

'I don't know about that,' said Kitty faintly.

'Nonsense; there's more to you than you know.'

'What have I missed?' enquired Sybil, coming back in with a loaded tray.

Gordon stood up and took it from her hands. 'I think I'm being out voted,' he said crossly. 'Sybil, sit here.' and pulled up a wooden chair for her next to Queenie. 'I think I made it quite clear to Kitty earlier that we would have one more go. We had a deal remember?' he said, turning to his wife.

'Yes, yes, Gordon but what if this all goes wrong again, how are we going to walk away from it? And where are we going to live?'

'Queenie will sort it, I have faith in my sister's ability,' Sybil said calmly.

Gordon shook his head in exasperation and then looked across at the old woman.

'Why Queenie?' he asked suddenly.

'Excuse me?'

'Well, it's rather an unusual name.'

'It's Maud really,' said Sybil.

'Terrible isn't it? I mean, do I look like a Maud?' she said dramatically, waving her arms about.

Kitty smiled at her. 'No definitely not, Queenie suits you.'

'I've always been Queenie; mother said it was because I used to order everybody about, like a Queen Bee, you see.'

'I'm sure she said bossy.'

'Whatever, so I was always Queenie. Oldest girl of ten, so I had a lot of ordering to do.'

'Bossing, more like.'

'So,' said Gordon, interrupting the two elderly sisters' good natured bickering. 'What are we going to do?'

'Right,' said Queenie. 'First we will finish our tea and then we will go up to the house.'

'Do we have to? Can't we do it here?' Kitty looked nervously at the group sat around the fire. 'And what are we going to do anyway?'

'Sorry dear, but yes. We are going to get his spirit out of the house.' She smiled confidently at them all and stubbed her cigarette out on the hearth.

'Are you sure it is Beamish?' queried Gordon.

She sighed and drained her cup. 'Yes, it can't be anybody but Robert Beamish. If anybody's soul was going to walk this earth it would be his, he was an evil man. Totally driven by his hatred, but,' she looked up cheerfully. 'I'll sort him out.'

Gordon looked at her soberly. 'And if you can't?'

'Don't be so negative.' She stood up and straightened her tweed skirt. 'Come on, let's get at it.'

'Do you need anything Queenie?' Sybil inquired. 'Do we need to take anything with us?'

'I've got everything I need in my handbag, which is where?' she asked, distractedly looking around the room.

Gordon picked up a big tote bag from the floor. 'Is this it?'

'Yep,' she rummaged through it. 'Oh, the only thing I haven't got is a jam jar. Sybil have you got one we can use?'

'A jam jar! What are you going to catch him in it?' he said in amusement.

'That's right; I'm going to trap his spirit in the jar.' Queenie looked at Gordon and Kitty's horrified faces. 'Don't look so worried you two.'

'Tell me you're joking, please.' he groaned, looking even more unsure about the whole idea.

'Now, do I tell you how to do your job?' she replied irritated. 'No! I know what I'm doing. A jam jar is the perfect thing. Some people use boxes or bottles, but I prefer a jam jar, with a nice easy screw lid.' Queenie looked at them. Kitty was looking increasingly worried while Gordon's face was flushed with irritation.

'What exactly did you expect me to do? Wave my hands about and say begone foul one? There are certain ways laid down to deal with these situations. If we stick to the correct method then we will be fine,' she said sternly. 'And using a secure container for his spirit is essential.'

Sybil put an arm around Kitty and gave her a reassuring hug. 'Don't worry, we'll look after you.'

'I don't know if I can do this,' she confessed. Kitty stared into the fire with her hands clenched between her knees. 'I'm sorry,' she said, looking up at them.

Queenie grasped her shoulder and gently shook it. 'If you don't, Robert will win again. Do it for Hannah, Ava would want you to help.' She stared up at the old woman and nodded slowly. 'Yes you're right, okay.' She gave herself a mental shake. 'Yes, I can do this.'

Queenie nodded in satisfaction. 'Good, right let's get going.'

Sybil pulled the door shut behind them and stared up and down the village street.

'Quiet tonight, just as well,' she remarked. 'Are we going to walk or shall we take the car?'

'I'm not going to walk all the way up to William's,' Queenie said firmly, and looked at Gordon's car parked behind hers. 'We'll take yours; we won't all fit in mine.'

He opened the doors and helped the two elderly women into the back seats.

'I say this is rather nice Gordon, very posh,' Queenie said admiringly, running her hands over the brown leather.

'Thanks,' he replied drily. 'I'm glad you like it.'

He closed the doors and got in behind the wheel. He glanced across at Kitty. 'Are you alright?' he asked quietly. 'Are you sure about this?' Kitty smiled nervously at him. 'No, I'm scared stiff, what are we getting ourselves into?'

Gordon reached across and squeezed her cold hands. 'Don't worry, I'll look after you. I promise.'

Hannah had pulled the bolts across on the door early that night. Michael had been up to visit her in the morning and had fitted the two new sturdy bolts onto the front door. He had been very concerned to see how edgy Hannah had become and had done his best to persuade her to return with him to the village. But Hannah had resisted his pleas and stayed firm in her desire to remain in her cottage. But she had become increasingly uneasy after Michael had disappeared down the path. Dusk was falling, the birds were still singing in the trees but as she stood on the doorway watching him leave she could not shake the feeling that she was being watched. A small finch suddenly burst out of the brambles trilling in alarm and she jumped. Stepping back quickly she slammed the door and pushed the bolts home.

Her supper that night was a dreary affair, a dry heel of a loaf and some pottage was all that she could scrape together, not that she was bothered. Hannah's appetite had been poor for several weeks. Ava had tried to coax her to eat and she had eaten a little of the mutton pie that Ava had brought just to keep the little girl happy but when she left scurrying quickly back to the farm Hannah's spirits had plummeted again.
Hannah ate her meagre supper huddled near the fire, her single candle burning low in the holder. The wax was winding to one side in the draught from the chimney. Hannah shuddered. Tis a sign of death she thought to herself. She put down her plate on the hearth and raked the embers of the fire together in a bid to coax a few last flames before she went to bed.
The kettle hanging over the fire was still steaming gently, and there was just enough water left in the bottom for Hannah to make herself a last cup of tea. As the tea steeped in the old brown teapot, she began her preparations for bed. She slipped on her nightdress and then carefully unpinned her hair, placing the pins in a dish on the mantelpiece. Hannah began to slowly brush her hair, her hand slowing as she heard the familiar footsteps approaching up the path and her heart sank as the latch on the garden gate clicked.

   Beamish smiled grimly satisfied with his nights work. The light breeze blowing around the hill caught the edge of Hannah's nightdress fluttering it above his head and he stared up at the figure lying across the branch of the tree. Robert gathered up the length of rope and coiled it carefully and then slung it over his shoulder. His blackthorn stick was lying in the damp grass at his feet; he picked it up and grunted with displeasure at the sticky liquid on the handle. He was about to wipe it clean on the grass when he had a sudden thought; smiling slightly to himself, he rubbed the coil of rope over the end of the bloodied stick. Satisfied, he settled the rope back onto his shoulder, grasped his stick and gave a last look at the still figure in the tree. Robert picked his way down the dark path to the lane and walked on tiptoe into the deserted farmyard. The farm dogs remained silent and hidden in their kennels, recognising their master's footsteps on the cobbles. He stole into the house, letting the latch on the front door click gently back into place and walked silently along the passageway to the parlour door and pushed it open. The fire had burned low in the hearth and Evans was sprawled across the hearth, drunk and clasping an empty tankard to his chest.

The soiled rope was dropped next to his pack of belongings and Robert smiled grimly to himself as he backed slowly out of the room leaving Evans still sleeping, unaware that his employer had entered the room.

Beamish had left the house early the next morning and was inspecting his flock of sheep and their new lambs in the fields by the river, by the time he reached home a few hours later the alarm had already been raised. He met Rosie hurrying out of the front door of the farmhouse; she was wrapping a shawl around her shoulders against the early morning chill and started to speak as soon as she spotted him.

'Mr Beamish,' she gasped. 'Tis terrible news, Guppy has just been here, it's Hannah sir. He says she's dead. He found her, sir, hanging in a tree.' Rosie started to cry. 'Oh sir, what could have happened?' She wiped a shaking hand across her face and stared at her employer in surprise at his continued silence.

His face showed no emotion and he just stared at her. 'Well?' Beamish said flatly. 'What do you expect me to do about it?'

'But Mr Beamish, she's your brother's wife.'

'My brother is dead, and,' he said with a strange expression. 'Now it seems my sister-in-law is as well. What an unfortunate pair.'

He pushed past her into the house leaving Rosie staring after him with a look of growing unease upon on her face. 'You'll not go up then?'

'I'm sure Guppy can manage,' Beamish replied shortly. He walked swiftly down the passage to the parlour and opened the door to the now empty room. 'Where is Evans?' he shouted after Rosie, who was hurrying across the yard to the gate.

She paused and glared back at him. 'He's gone, he heard Guppy telling me that Hannah was dead and he snatched up all his things and scarpered.' Rosie stared at him triumphantly. 'He won't get far though, Guppy is rounding up some men to go and find him.'

'Really,' he said flatly. 'Mr Guppy is taking quite an interest in this, very public spirited of him I'm sure. And where is the body?'

'Still up there where he found it, he's going for the magistrate as well.' She wrapped the shawl tighter round her and turned her back on him.

'And where do you think you're going, Rose?'

She whirled round and shouted at him, her voice echoing off the walls of the buildings. The pigeons flew out from their nests in the barn and flapped up and over their heads in panic at the sudden noise. 'I'm going up there, to her cottage. What do you think!'

Beamish strode across the yard and grabbed her arm pulling her away from the entrance.

'Get back to the dairy and your chores, woman. This is none of your business. Leave it to the proper authorities.'

'Oh yes,' she sneered. 'That would suit you down to the ground, wouldn't it?' Rose pulled her arm from his grip and walked quickly out into the lane. 'The less people see what has happened up there the better, as far as you are concerned.'

'What do you mean by that?' He glared at her, the colour rising in his face. Beamish grasped his stick in a shaking hand and slammed it down on the paved yard. 'You watch your mouth,' he shouted at her. Rose pointed an accusing finger at him. 'I've been wondering what was going on in the parlour, with that drunk and his stinking mess over the fire. Now I know,' her voice trembled as she stared at him. 'Well he won't get away with it, he'll get caught and then we'll see what happens!' Rose stared out into the lane, her attention caught by the sound of hurrying footsteps approaching up the hill.

'Rose,' called Donald Trevitt, arriving out of breath at the farm entrance. Followed by his wife and two stout sons. 'Any sign of him?'

'If you mean Evans, no.' She glanced back into the farmyard where Beamish was still standing sardonically watching the group clustered around her. 'I've told him though,' Rose jerked her head towards Beamish. 'Not that he gives a damn.'

'Well, well, look at all this,' Beamish drawled. 'The circus has come to town.' He laughed slightly before turning on his heel and heading back towards the house.

He shut the door firmly in the face of their disapproving looks and they plainly heard the bolt being drawn across.

'Well,' said Mrs Trevitt slowly. 'Perhaps Michael was right after all.' She glanced at her husband in shock.

'Aye,' muttered her husband. 'Maybe so.'

As one they walked on past the orchard to the path that Ava used every day and climbed the hill to Hannah's cottage. The sound of crying reached their ears as they neared the garden.

They found Ava huddled under the large beech tree from which Hannah's body was still hanging, she had her face buried in her pinafore and was rocking backwards and forwards as she wept.

Rose hurried over the damp grass to the child. 'Ava, Ava what are you doing here? I thought you were down in the village.' She folded the girl in her arms and helped her up from the ground. 'Come away child.' Rose held Ava's face pressed to her chest as she led her way from the dreadful sight above her.

'I heard Michael tell Sarah, I thought he was fibbing, so I came up here,' she sobbed.

Ava pulled away from Rose's close embrace and stared back at the body hanging over the branch. 'Oh Rose, poor Hannah!' she started to wail hysterically, clutching at Rose's arm.

Rose wiped the hair back from her streaming face. 'Come on, my dear,' she said gently. 'Let's get you down to the village; this is no place for you.'

'I can't leave her,' she cried. 'She's my friend.'

'Shush child,' Mrs Trevitt gently took her arm and spoke to her earnestly. 'We'll look after her, and do everything that is needful for her now. You go with Rose.' She looked at the other woman. 'Take her to our cottage Rose, Ida is there with the younger children.'

Rose nodded and wrapped a plump arm around the little girl. 'Come on dear; let's get you away from here. There's nothing that you can do for her now.'

On the way down the steep path that led to the village, they met Michael Guppy with three men from the village.

He paused, while he caught his breath. 'Any sign of Evans?' he asked. She shook her head and glanced warningly at Ava.

'Damn him.'

'You think he did it? Beamish got right upset when he found Evans gone.'

Michael shrugged his shoulders and wiped his sweating face with his sleeve.

'I dunno, maybe, I do know Hannah was worried though. I saw her yesterday morning and she was right spooked. Reckoned Beamish was out to get her.'

'Beamish?' said one of the other men. 'But he's family.'

'Shush,' warned Rose. 'Not in front of Ava, please.' She pulled her close and carried on walking down the path. 'I'm taking her down to the Trevitts' cottage; let me know if you hear anything, Michael.'

He nodded and said to the others, 'Come on, let's get up there and see what we can do,' he paused for a minute and stared at the little girl. Michael hesitated not knowing what to say to her and satisfied himself with just patting her roughly on the shoulder. 'Go on the,' he said and jerked his head in the direction of the village.

Trevitt and his sons were standing at the base of the tree and staring up at the branch, they looked round on hearing the men's approach up the stony path.

'There you are Guppy, we were just wondering how we're going to get Hannah down, we could do with a rope,' he jerked his head at his oldest son. 'Peter here thinks he can climb up and lower her down.'

Michael shook his head and pushed the three men out of the way. 'No, I'll do it,' he said roughly. He took off his jacket and laid it on the grass, and stared at the smooth trunk of the tree. 'Can you give me a leg up and I'll see if I can grab that smaller branch, I should be able to pull myself up from there.'

They linked hands and bent so that Michael could use their hands as a step, he reached up for the branch while from underneath helping hands propelled him farther up the trunk until he had both hands firmly on the branch.

Michael climbed carefully up the remaining few feet to the large branch over which Hannah's body was lying. He inched slowly forward, feeling the branch giving beneath his feet.

'Careful up there lad! That branch is going to break.'

Michael hesitated and eased his weight farther along the branch and leant forward to grasp a limp arm. 'I've got her,' he said panting, and looked down at the waiting men. 'I'll try and lower her down and then you'll have to catch her.'

He gripped her wrist and held firmly onto the branch with his other hand and tugged the body free of the branch. The sudden shift of *weight made the branch creak alarmingly and as he leant forward to lower her down, the wood began to split just in front of him. There was nothing he could do as the branch slowly broke away taking the body of Hannah with it as it fell to the ground. Michael just had enough time to shout a warning to the men below before the branch landed. Hannah's body hit the ground and rolled down the hill into the ditch bordering her garden.*

Queenie stared into the farm yard as they drove past.

'How's William these days? I haven't seen him for months.'

'He's fine, I saw him yesterday. I haven't told him about this of course,' replied Sybil.

'Good, least said I think.'

'Oh definitely.' They nodded their heads and Sybil pursed her lips. 'He's getting on a bit now, I don't think he would be able to cope with this, you know.'

'Hmm.' They both nodded again.

'Is this it?' Queenie leant forward and gazed at Orchard Cottage. 'It looks nice, not too big and not too small.' She turned to Sybil. 'Something like this would suit you.'

'Of course we remember this when it was still an orchard,' said Sybil ignoring her sister. 'It used to be full of apple trees.'

Queenie started grinning. 'Remember how we used to climb over the wall and steal the apples?' They both started laughing. 'William's father used to get so mad with us!'

Kitty smiled back through the gap in the seats. 'Sounds like you two used to have fun.'

'Oh we did,' said Sybil. 'There was a whole gang of us running about the village getting up to mischief. Of course William was part of it as well but he used to scarper when he saw his father coming. And he thought his son was so well behaved, butter wouldn't melt in his mouth!'

Even Gordon smiled in response to the women's laughter coming from the back seat.

'I can't imagine William misbehaving,' he said.

'Oh don't you believe it, we used to get up to some pranks I can tell you.'

Gordon slowed the car to a halt and switched off the engine. Outside it was already dark.

They sat in silence looking at the house until Queenie stirred. 'Come on everybody, let's go in.'

'Did we have to come in the dark?'

'Well Kitty at least most people will be inside and won't notice what we're doing. That's the idea any way,' Queenie said practically. 'The less they see the better.'

Kitty huddled deeper into the front seat, the cold knot in her stomach tightening even more.

'Come on,' Queenie repeated, opening the car door. 'The sooner we start, the sooner we'll finish.'

Gordon pushed open the front door and flicked on the hall light, a cold fusty smell filled the house.

'It smells damp, Gordon.'

He led the way into the front room and switched on the light. 'Come in here and I'll go and put the heating on; warm the place through for a while.'

He disappeared into the kitchen while the three women waited, staring around the quiet room.

'Ahh.' Queenie spotted the Ouija board lying in the hearth and picked it up. 'Well that's not going to work very well now is it?' she said, examining the broken pieces and then threw the bits into the empty fireplace. 'There, best place for that.' She ran her hand over the wood of the fireplace. 'How strange that you ended up with this, fate perhaps?' she asked, gazing intently at Kitty who had walked slowly over to join her.

'It was Gordon that picked the fireplace out, he found it at the local reclamation yard and fell in love with it. I didn't like it at first,' she confessed 'I thought it was too big.' Kitty gently touched the wood. 'Strange isn't it? How things are meant to be.'

Sybil had perched on the sofa while they waited for Gordon. 'Is this the photo album you were telling us about?' She picked up the old brown book and started flicking through the pages.

'Yes, great-gran's picture is in the back.' Kitty moved away from Queenie and sat down next to her. 'There she is.' And pointed to the child stood at the front of the group.

Sybil peered closely at the faded photograph and started to gently laugh. 'Well, look at that,' she said wryly.

'What?' asked Queenie.

Sybil pointed to a figure in the crowd and looked up at her sister. 'Look who's there.'

Kitty looked from one to the other puzzled. 'Who?'

'It's Hannah. There, just standing to the right of Ava.'

Queenie leaned on the back of the sofa and peered at the book. 'So it is.' She twitched the book out of her sister's hand and stared at the picture. 'I wonder who's wedding it was?' she pondered, looking at the back of the page and then pulled the picture out of the album.

'Queenie, be careful with it!' said Sybil, in protest.

'I want to see if there is anything written on the back,' she replied briskly. She scanned the back. 'What a shame, nothing.' Queenie turned it back and stared at the group. 'It might have been one of Ava's older brothers.' She handed the photo to Kitty. 'You'll have to do some research and find out who was married about 1839ish.' She looked at Sybil, lifting her eyebrows. 'That would be about the right year wouldn't it?'

'Right year for what?' queried Gordon, coming back in. He looked keenly at Kitty who was sitting speechless on the sofa.

She held up the photo. 'Hannah is in the picture as well as great-gran, look.'

Kitty handed it to Gordon who stared at the blurred picture. 'Which is Hannah?'

'She is standing to the right of Ava.' Sybil came over to his side and pointed at the blurred figure.

'Are you sure? It's not very clear.'

Sybil smiled slightly. 'That's her.'

Gordon dropped the photo onto the coffee table and sat down next to Kitty.

'Okay?' he asked, putting an arm around her.

She nodded and stared up at Queenie. 'What do we do now?'

'Yes, well we'd better get organised. I'm sure he will be here soon.'

Kitty flinched. 'What about Hannah? She's not here.'

'Yes, she is dear, 'replied Queenie calmly.

'But I always smell lavender when she is around.'

'And we have been finding the stuff as well, scattered everywhere,' put in Gordon.

'Lavender? Oh! I know what she's been doing. Lavender repels evil spirits; I suppose she's been putting it across the thresholds?'

'Yes.'

'It was a traditional protection, everybody used it, Mother's used to pin it to the clothes of their children as well for protection against evil spirits.'

'Really? Perhaps that is why she gave some to Emily,' said Gordon quietly. 'That really freaked us out.'

'Oh dear, she was only trying to protect you all.'

'It didn't work when Sheena was here, he got in then.' said Kitty.

'When she used that board she opened a door and invited him in and I don't suppose that woman bothered to say a prayer for protection did she?'

They both shook their heads.

'You were lucky nothing else came through, believe it or not there are worse things than Robert Beamish crawling about in the shadows.'

Kitty shivered and held Gordon's hand tightly. 'We didn't realise.' Queenie stared around the room. 'Well... I suppose we had better get started, come along,' she said firmly to Gordon, who was looking very reluctant

'What's going to happen, do you know?' he asked, casting a worried look at his wife.

Queenie sighed and pulled him out of earshot of Kitty, she looked at him earnestly.

'You do love your wife, don't you?'

'Of course,' he answered indignantly. 'How could you ask that? And why I'm letting her do this I don't know!'

'Because she has to, that's what brought you both back home. Justice for Hannah.'

'Hannah is dead,' he said fiercely. 'We can't bring her back and what this is going to do Kitty, I dread to think. This is looking more and more like a bad idea Queenie.' He shrugged his shoulders helplessly. 'I don't think we can do anything about this situation at all, what's done is done and if he's as evil as you say, what can we do about it?'

'We can do this, and Kitty can do this,' she said firmly. 'This is her home, she belongs here and she needs to claim this soil for her own. And Robert will be sent back to where he belongs. But she will need your help as well. I know it sounds corny but love is the strongest power there is and here Kitty is surrounded by people who love her. On this plane, and in the spirit world. They will help you to protect her but they want justice Gordon.' She waited for a while, staring at him but Gordon refused to meet her eye.

He stared nervously at Kitty, chewing his lip. 'I don't know. I really don't.'

Queenie shrugged her shoulders and turning her back on him called the others over.

'Come on, let's get prepared. You too, Gordon,' she said firmly, staring at him. 'It's time.' She took out from her pocket a bundle of dried leaves and twigs and lit them.

'This is sage,' she explained. 'This will purify the room.'

She wafted the burning twigs around them filling the air with an aromatic smoke. The bundle of sage slowly burnt down until the smouldering twigs reached her finger tips, she threw the remains into the fireplace on top of the broken board where it gently glowed, still releasing its scent into the room. From her tote bag she pulled out four candles and placed them about the room, one on the fireplace, one on the book shelf, the other two she put on the table. She lit them one by one.

'You're not going to turn the lights out, are you?' Kitty sounded worried.

'No,' she replied calmly 'we want to be able to see what we're doing.' She gestured to Kitty. 'Right, I want you here in the middle. Gordon, here on the left of Kitty. Sybil on the right and clasp your hands around Kitty and I will stand in front. Now.' She looked at each of them in turn. 'We will be alright as long as you do exactly as I say, do you understand?'

Kitty and Gordon nodded.

'Right, first I want you all to imagine yourself surrounded by a bright blue light; try to keep this fixed in your mind all the time, especially you Kitty. Sybil's aura is very strong so she will be able to help you.' Sybil looked at Kitty and smiled reassuringly. 'You'll be fine dear. We know what we're doing.'

Kitty looked doubtfully at Gordon, who smiled slightly and nodded at her.

'I'll be right next to you all the time,' he reassured her.

Queenie gazed at them all intently. 'Good,' she said. She put the empty jam jar onto the table and pulled a bottle of water out of her bag along with several small plastic bags. She held out the jar to Kitty. 'Now, I want you to hold this in both hands, straight out in front of you.'

Kitty took the jar from her and held it while Queenie unscrewed the lid and poured the water from the bottle into it, filling it up half way then added a handful of salt.

'What's that?'

'Water from the church font. Remember to hold it firmly Kitty and don't drop it.'

Queenie hesitated and smiled grimly to herself. 'Well, we didn't have long to wait, he's coming.' As soon as the words had left her mouth, the temperature in the room plummeted. Their breath billowed out in front of them and Kitty began to shiver uncontrollably.

The lights started to flicker.

'Oh no,' whimpered Kitty.

'It's okay, keep calm.'

The candle flames began to flicker in a sudden icy draught that came from nowhere and sank lower and lower into the wax. As the room grew dimmer dark shadows appeared in all the corners of the room moving and swaying in the half light.

'Stand close to Kitty. Gordon, Sybil, hold hands around her and keep the image of the blue light fixed in your mind.'
Kitty suddenly felt a crushing weight on her shoulders and she cried out in panic.
Gordon released his grip of Sybil's hands.

'No,' said Queenie sternly. 'Stay in your place Gordon. Think of the blue light Kitty, be strong. His evil spirit is powerless against the love and light that surrounds you.'
Kitty tried to concentrate on a blue light enveloping her and filling the room. To her side she could hear Gordon's heavy breathing and on her other side she became aware of a strength emanating from Sybil. Kitty glanced at her, Sybil stared fixedly back at her, small points of light flickering in her pale coloured eyes. She looked away quickly and shivered again. The lights were dimming fast and she could only just make out Queenie's face in the dark.
Strange shadows flickered across her face changing it into someone she barely recognised. Queenie's voice came from the darkness.

'Saint Michael the Archangel, defend us in battle. Be our protection against the wickedness and snares of the devil. May God rebuke him, we humbly pray.
And do thou O Prince of the heavenly hosts thrust into hell Satan and all the evil spirits who prowl through the world seeking the ruin of souls... Amen,' she finished solemnly.
For a while there was silence and then a strange acrid smell rose up around them.

'Angels of protection, guard us, help us, remove all unwelcome spirits from this place,' she called out firmly.
There was a brush against Kitty's hand making her jump.

'It's alright it's just me.' A little splash came from the jar that Kitty was holding. 'Hold it tightly,' ordered Queenie. 'And repeat after me, what is dark be filled with light, remove this spirit from my sight.'
Kitty repeated it haltingly at first but gaining strength towards the end. Her hands were shaking so much that the water from the jar splashed onto the floor.
The odour of damp and rot grew stronger and dark shadows slowly rose up from the floor and swirled around her, engulfing her so that she could no longer see the other three in the room.

'Close your eyes Kitty; imagine you're surrounded by the light,' Sybil urged her.

'Be strong all of you, he will fight this,' as Queenie spoke, a strong wind blew up out of nowhere and swirled around the room, rattling

the furniture and sending the lighted candles to the floor. What little light there was in the room was slowly being extinguished.
Queenie placed her hand over Kitty's on the jar and dropped something into the water.

'What is dark be filled with light, remove this spirit from my sight,' she shouted above the noise of the wind howling around the room. The force of the wind made Kitty stagger, her hair whipping into her eyes but she carried on repeating after Queenie.

'Good Kitty, keep going,' she urged her.

On either side Gordon and Sybil were joining in. Gordon's voice was shaking and Kitty could feel his arms trembling around her.
Queenie dropped another rose thorn into the water.

'Thou demon presence be no more. Guardians of the spirit realm hear us and aid us. Protect us and hinder those who bring harm to this door,' she shouted.
A wave of nausea swept over Kitty and she began to retch.

'Kitty,' shouted Gordon. He dropped Sybil's hands and grabbed his wife by the shoulders. 'This isn't working,' he shouted at the old woman in panic.

'Yes it is Gordon, stand firm.'

Kitty opened her eyes and stared up at him, Gordon's fingers were digging into her arms and his face was contorted with terror.

'Kitty, let's get out of here,' he shouted, and pulled at her arm.
'That's it, we can't do this.'

Her eyes flickered away from his gaze and became fixed on something behind him; the dark swirling shadows were flowing together and had concentrated itself into one dark pillar that grew upwards to the ceiling. And before her terrified eyes it formed into the indistinct figure of a man.

She found herself staring into the eyes of Robert Beamish.
Kitty screamed and dropped the jar.

'Kitty!' wailed Queenie.

There was silence just for a second, the wind seemed to pause and then with a sudden explosion the windows blew in, shattering the glass over the room and the cowering figures.

They huddled together on the floor, Gordon holding on firmly to Kitty and protecting her head with his arms.

Within just a few seconds of the window breaking, the wind suddenly dropped and the dark shadows disappeared into the corners of the room. They held their breath, waiting.

'What's happening? Has he gone?' Kitty asked, her voice wobbling.

'No' said Queenie, struggling to get up off the floor. 'Something happened, I don't know what though.'

There was a sudden hammering on the front door.

Kitty screamed again and buried her head into Gordon's chest. The front door slowly opened, and in the dim light the four of them could see the figure of a man.

William stood in the doorway.

'I heard a scream, what's going on?' He paused, staring at the two sisters and then around the room, his gaze lingering on the smoking candles. 'What are you doing, Queenie?' he demanded, advancing across the glass strewn carpet towards them.

She paused before answering and stared at him curiously. 'So that's what happened, well, well, I wasn't expecting this.'

Sybil looked at her puzzled. 'What do you mean dear?'

'William, we needed William.' They both stared at their elderly friend who was gazing at them perplexed.

'It doesn't matter now.' Gordon put his arm around Kitty who was shivering uncontrollably and led her towards the door. 'We're leaving and this time we're not coming back.'

'You can't go now!'

'Queenie!' He turned on her. 'Look at my wife!' he shouted. 'Look what you've done to her.'

'Wait a minute,' said William anxiously. 'What do you mean you're not coming back?' He followed them to the door and laid a restraining hand on Gordon's shoulder. 'What's going on here?'

Gordon looked across the room at Queenie. 'She can explain.'

Queenie nodded. 'I will explain but not here, let's find some neutral ground to have a chat. Come on Sybil.' She gathered up the fallen jar and put it back into her bag. 'We need to have a talk with William.'

The two sisters followed him out into the hall where Gordon and Kitty were waiting impatiently for them.

Gordon hesitated before opening the door. 'Do you think it's safe?' he asked anxiously.

Sybil nodded slowly and took William's arm. 'What are you doing here?'

'I heard an awful noise and then I heard screaming, was that you Kitty?'

William peered into Kitty's tear streaked face; she stared blankly at him before managing a weak smile. 'Are you alright?' He took her hand in his work roughened one and squeezed it gently. 'What's been happening here?' he asked anxiously.

Her face crumpled and she sobbed out, 'It's Robert, he's here.'

'I don't understand, Robert who?'

'Your grandfather.'

He looked at her blankly and then looked at Sybil. 'What's she talking about?'

Sybil gently pushed the three out of the door. 'In a minute William, we'll explain outside.' She turned to her sister who was following close behind. 'Shall we go back to my cottage? I think that would be best, don't you?'

Queenie nodded in agreement and banged the door shut behind her. They walked slowly along the drive to the lane; time had passed since they had driven up to Orchard Cottage and it was now dark. The night sky was filled with winking stars and high up on Castle Hill a fox barked.

'Right, down to Sybil's Gordon,' Queenie said firmly.

'No,' he replied sharply. 'That's it! We're out of here; we're not getting involved in any more of this.'

'Now... let's calm down a minute, I want to know what's going on and what my grandfather has to do with this.' The old man had stopped and stood in front of them determined to get an answer.

'This is a story that shouldn't be told in a dark lane, William,' said Sybil, taking hold of his arm and pulling him towards the village.

'Well let's go into the farmhouse then,' he said impatiently. 'It's closer.'

'No,' Kitty put in weakly. 'Not in there, sorry,' she apologised to the old man. 'But you see it's his house.'

'Kitty is right, we shouldn't set foot in there,' Queenie warned. 'Sybil's cottage will do. Come along.'

She led the way along the darkened lane until they came close to the entrance of the farmyard. She slowed to a halt. From across the paved yard came the sound of approaching footsteps. Footsteps that Kitty immediately recognised.

'Who's that?' bristled William. 'Hi,' he shouted, striding forward, pushing past Queenie who put out a restraining hand. But he brushed impatiently it aside. 'Who's there? You're trespassing.'

His voice echoed around the buildings but the footsteps did not slow, they drew closer and closer to the group huddled in the lane.

'It's him,' whispered Kitty, trying to pull away from Gordon's tightening grip. 'It's him, Queenie,' she hissed again.

Queenie nodded in recognition. 'Yes Kitty, it is,' she said quietly. She raised her voice

'Well Robert? What are you going to do now, eh?'

William glanced at her quickly before returning his gaze to the entrance of the yard.

A dark shape slid into the shadows of the wall, and as they watched it gathered itself together pulling in the darkness of the night and becoming more solid.

A figure walked slowly out from the shelter of the wall and stood in the middle of the lane and raised his head. Dark sunken eyes stared across the intervening space between him and his grandson.

'Oh my God!' whispered William in horror. 'It *is* him.'

The old man staggered back and would have fallen if Gordon hadn't grabbed his arm to steady him.

'William, are you alright?' Sybil whispered to him urgently, gripping his other arm to support him.

'What in God's name is this? He's dead!' William's voice echoed around the lane making the apparitions face wince.

Queenie took a few paces forward and peered at the shade of Robert Beamish.

'So that's it! William is the key,' she said triumphantly. She turned back quickly to the others. 'Back to the house; all of you.'

'Are you mad woman? We're not going back in there,' Gordon shouted at her.

He stared at the figure in the lane and watched in horror as it approached slowly towards them.

Queenie pulled Kitty back towards the house. 'You have no choice now; he's not going to stop. He'll come after Kitty, where ever she is.'

'You don't know that,' he shot at her.

'Look at him!' Queenie shouted at him. 'He is on the road! This road doesn't belong to the Beamish family, it never has done. He's not on his own soil!'

They backed slowly away down the lane to the entrance of the drive, William last of all. He stood frozen to the spot staring at his grandfather's form approaching along the road.

Sybil pulled at his arm. 'Come on William,' she shouted at him.

'I thought I had forgotten him,' he whispered. 'But one look at his face and it has all come back.'

Clouds drifted across the night sky casting even darker shadows onto the road but the shadow of Robert Beamish was darker still as he paced slowly forward; the regular thump of the stick hitting the tarmac echoing off the buildings.

Gordon slammed and locked the door once they were all inside. 'What the hell are we going to do?'

'Keep calm Gordon,' Queenie urged him. Taking Kitty's arm she pulled her back into the sitting room. 'We'll start again and this time we have William and we won't fail.'

'What difference is he going to make?'

Sybil pulled him and William into place around Kitty.

'Don't you see? This time one of his own blood will be casting him out.'

He looked at William's shocked face. 'Will he be alright to do that?'

'Well, are you going to help Kitty?' she asked William.

He shook himself and looked back at her.

'That man was the devil incarnate, I will stop him,' he said firmly. 'He made my father's life hell and I thought I was rid of him,' he paused and added, 'And this time I will be rid of him.' He leant forward and gave Kitty an awkward hug. 'I don't know what the hell is happening but if Sybil and Queenie say that I have to do this then I will. They've been giving me orders since I was a child and it's a habit hard to break.'

Queenie refilled the jar and placed three red berries in the salted water.

'Rowan berries,' she explained, then gave the half filled jar to Kitty. 'Good for you William. Now hold onto it this time Kitty and we'll start again.'

'What about the candles?'

'No time for that now.' She pushed her damp hair away from her face. 'Surround Kitty, you three.'

Kitty shivered slightly and held the jar tightly to her chest. Gordon was breathing deeply as he stared around the room. The lights were still high and bright and no shadows had appeared in the corners.

'Perhaps he won't come back,' he said hopefully, looking at Queenie. She cocked her head listening to the noises outside; the sound of the fox barking on the hill was carried by the breeze that blew in through the broken window.

Slow footsteps approached the house.

'He's coming,' she said calmly.

Sybil reached out and grasped Gordon's hand and took William's hand to form a circle around Kitty.

'Remember to imagine yourself surrounded by the blue light.'

They nodded in response and gripped each other's hands. Gordon looked at his wife's face, it was very pale but she looked determined. She caught him looking at her and smiled slightly in response.

'I'm fine.'

'Okay, it begins,' said Queenie.
The breeze blowing in through the shattered windows became colder and stronger, whirling around the figures in the centre of the room, whipping their clothes and hair around them. But their hands held firm and they stayed in place, surrounding Kitty.

Her breath plumed out in front of her face and out the corner of her eye she could see a dark shadow rising in the corner of the room. As it grew, the lights dipped lower and lower until Kitty could only just make out Queenies face in front of her. Kitty gripped the jar firmly.

'Now after me, Saint Michael the Archangel, defend us in battle. Be our protection against the wickedness and snares of the Devil. May God rebuke him, we humbly pray. And do thou, O Prince of the heavenly hosts thrust into Hell Satan and all the evil spirits who prowl through the world seeking the ruin of souls...Amen.'

The shadow wavered and flowed around the walls of the room as they repeated the prayer after Queenie. William's voice rang out with each word and each word making the shadow tremble and shudder.

She reached into her pocket and pulled out the bag of thorns.

'Thou demon presence, be no more,' she called out against the buffeting wind and dropped a thorn into the water. As it hit the holy water a low groan rose from the ground beneath the house and grew in strength until it shrieked and raged around the room, homing in on Kitty, swirling around and around her until she could hardly breathe. The jar jerked in her hand and she clutched at it desperately.

'Hold it tight Kitty,' Gordon shouted at her.

Queenie reached across the linked hands and dropped another thorn into the water.

'Thou demon presence, be no more.'

The groaning and shrieking grew and Kitty's shoulders slumped under a huge weight that began pressing on her and she fell to her knees.

'Guardians of the spirit realm, hear us and guide us, remove all evil from our path and let your presence protect us, we beg you,' Queenie shouted. She reached forward and tried to pull Kitty to her feet. 'Stand up, come on,' Queenie urged, but the wind continued to buffet her kneeling figure.

Kitty cried out, 'Help me I can't do this.'

They stared in consternation at Kitty kneeling on the floor.

'Get up,' they urged her. 'Come on, you can do it.'

She shook her head weeping, terrified of the black shadows that were whirling and shrieking around her. Kitty closed her eyes in anguish and then felt a gentle touch on her hand. Her eyelids flickered opened and she could see a pair of child's hands over hers on the jar. The child smiled encouragingly at her and tightened her grip pulling Kitty to her feet. The tiny figure stood in front of her, insubstantial but yet she could feel her touch and feel the child's breath on her face. The little girl smiled at her and nodded encouragingly, shadows moved across her face changing it subtly, aging it until Kitty recognised the lined face.

One that she knew so well.

Her face changed again reverting to her younger self. Ava smiled again and pressed Kitty's hands tightly over the jar.

Queenie reached over their joined hands and dropped in the final thorn.

'What is dark be filled with light, remove this evil from our sight, I bless this house in the name of God and banish all evil from this place, in the name of God.'

The shadows wavered; a shrieking groan echoed around the room and then faded sinking into silence.

The room was still dark apart from the shaft of light that was Ava. The rainbow colours that made up her form danced and flickered in front of Kitty. Her face came in and out of focus with just her eyes remaining steady, fixed on her great grand-daughter.

'It's great- granny,' Kitty whispered, her eyes spilling over with tears. Without thinking she relaxed her grip on the jar and it began to tilt, the precious holy water draining out of the top. Ava's spirit shook her head in warning and she realised with a start that he had not gone. If her great- grandmother was still with her and then so must Robert. Kitty looked away from Ava and stared at the others. 'Careful,' she whispered.

Queenie nodded, looking around the room.

'Is he gone, is that it?' Gordon looked across at Kitty. 'Are you alright?' he asked anxiously.

She nodded. The breeze had dropped but the room was still freezing, they were all shivering from the shock and cold.

William released his grip on Sybil's hand and wiped a shaking hand over his face.

'Thank goodness it's stopped.' He touched Sybil gently on the shoulder. 'Are you alright?'

She nodded. 'It's okay William, we're doing fine but,' she said, glancing across at her sister. 'I don't think it's over yet, is it?'

Queenie shook her head. 'No. Look at the jar,' she said quietly.

The water in the jar was still clear and empty apart from the rose thorns and the red rowan berries.

'He's proving to be a bit more difficult than I had thought,' she muttered.

'What are you saying?' blurted out Gordon. 'Can't you deal with him?'

'Yes, yes,' she rushed to reassure him. 'But we must be on our guard, he's not finished yet.'

'You're right,' hissed Sybil. 'Look behind you!'

Just behind Queenie a black spot appeared hovering just inches above the floor, the stink of rotting flesh grew stronger and a low moaning and scratching noise came from the centre of the expanding shadow. A low guttural voice whispered, *'Bitch...bitch...not on my soil....not here...slut of a child.'*

Kitty gagged and began to retch as the foul stink grew stronger around her.

Queenie jumped at the first sound of the voice and turned to face it. The shadow coiled and writhed growing in size until it reached the ceiling and then began to sink back down condensing into a cloudy figure.

'Robert, you have no business here,' she commanded him.

'Witch....' it muttered. *'Witch...not on my soil.....slut...child'*

She reached into her pocket and pulled out a jar of salt and scattered a handful across the carpet in front of him.

'I bless this house in the name of God, I banish all evil spirits from this house, in the name of God.'

She raised her hand and threw the rest of the salt into the whispering shadow. It parted as the salt hit and then flowed back together; a hissing noise came from inside the mass of shadows and then the sound of chill laughter.

They all froze and Queenie staggered back as though hit by an invisible hand.

'Bitch....old woman....stupid bitch....my soil.'

She backed slowly to the group behind her.

Sybil whispered to her 'Are you okay?'

Queenie shook her head; sweat stood out on her forehead and her whole body was quivering.

'Queenie,' wavered Kitty. 'What are we going to do?'

There was a second blow and Queenie fell to her knees holding up her hands to protect her face as she gasped out, 'I adjure thee, most evil spirit, by almighty God, begone!'

The shadowy figure did not halt; it slid slowly forward and flowed around her, engulfing her shaking body until she was almost hidden from sight.

'No!' wailed Sybil, releasing her grip of the two men's hands, she threw herself towards her sister on the ground.

'Sybil!' William shouted, as the two sisters were lost in the shadow. A scream was heard from inside as they were thrown violently to the side of the room. 'Sybil, no!' He pulled Gordon forward and thrust him towards Kitty. 'Look after her,' he said and staggered forward to the two still figures lying on the carpet.

Looming over them stood Robert Beamish, fully formed and visible. William faced the spectre of his grandfather.

To one side the spirit of Ava appeared and slowly on the other side of the old man another flickering shape appeared. He was hardly aware of the two figures flanking him. William stared into Robert's face, a mirror image of his own but so different in nature.

'No,' William said firmly. 'I can't allow you to do this. Go! You're not wanted here.'

The form of Robert writhed in the face of his accusing stare and mouthed silently at him. 'No I won't listen to you,' William shouted. 'You were an evil old bastard, and damn it, you still are! Go away and leave us in peace.'

'*Mine...*' he whispered, glaring malevolently at William.

'*Mine....mine,*' it got louder with each word until it was shrieking, '*Mine... mine...*'

'You stupid old man, this isn't your land, it's mine! Mine! Do you hear me?' William shouted into his grandfather's face. 'You do not belong here, you are not welcome. These are my friends; I will not allow you to hurt them.' William paused as Robert's shade writhed under the hail of his words. 'Now go!' he commanded.

Robert's body shook and trembled, the cloud forming his body began to dissipate into a fine mist that floated slowly up getting thinner and thinner before descending rapidly back to the floor.

Kitty pushed Gordon off and threw herself and the jar under the falling stream of mist before it disappeared back into the soil from where it came. The essence of Robert's spirit was sucked inside by the age old magic of the thorns and the rowan berries and was imprisoned in the Holy water.

Gordon grabbed the lid from the table, slammed it on and screwed it down.

Inside the black shadows writhed and twisted against the glass, in constant motion searching for a way out of its prison.

'Did you get him?' a shaky voice asked from the floor.

Queenie and Sybil were sprawled across each other in a tangle of arms and legs. Sybil half rolled off of her sister and sat up groaning, she pushed a curl out of her eyes and stared shakily up at them. 'Has he gone?'

Kitty held up the jar. 'Look,' she said triumphantly.

Queenie lay back on the floor. 'Oh thank God,' she said weakly. 'What a bugger!'

'Queenie! Language,' said Sybil primly, struggling to get up.

William hurried over and helped her up. 'Sybil,' he said 'What can I say? All this trouble from him.' He blinked back a tear. 'I thought you had been hurt.' He looked at Queenie who was still lying on the carpet. 'Are you hurt?' he asked suddenly worried.

She grinned at him. 'No dear, just getting my breath.' She extended her hand. 'Wouldn't mind a bit of help, though.'

He smiled and pulled her to her feet.

Queenie looked at him and gently patted him on the arm. 'You shouldn't feel guilty, this isn't your fault; you don't have to carry his guilt you know.'

He nodded and pulled a handkerchief from his trouser pocket and blew his nose.

'But he was family Queenie; I do feel responsible for all this.'

'Well, you shouldn't dear.' Sybil put her arms around him and kissed his cheek. 'You're a good man William, you've nothing to feel guilty about,' she added firmly. She looked down at Kitty who was still knelt on the floor with the jar held in front of her; she was staring fixedly at the writhing black shadow trapped inside. 'Umm, Queenie?' She nodded at Kitty and raised an eyebrow.

'Oh yes,' she replied, and quickly took the jar from Kitty's hands. 'I'll have that, dear.' Queenie walked away from her and put the jar carefully on the table. 'It can sit there for a minute while we catch our breath.'

Gordon picked up the chairs and pushed Kitty into one. He knelt down in front of her and stared into her glazed eyes. 'Kitty? Are you okay?' He lifted a hand and smoothed her tousled hair back from her face. 'Kitty?' he repeated.

She blinked and looked at him blankly for a minute before smiling faintly. 'I'm fine Gordon.'

'Thank goodness, I was getting worried,' he said relieved. 'Sit here and I'll get something for us to drink; I need one after all this!' Queenie and Sybil joined her around the table.

'What a good idea, Gordon. Whiskey if you have some.'

'Sherry?' asked Sybil.

'I'll have a look Sybil, it's not something we usually drink but there may be some in the cupboard.' He looked nervously at the black shadow in the jar. 'He will stay in there?'

Sybil nodded and looked at William who was still hovering over her.

'Come and sit down.' She pulled out a chair for him and patted the seat. 'Come on, dear.'

He sat down slowly, still looking very shocked. He stared across the table at Kitty who was sitting hunched over, with her arms wrapped tightly around her waist. She was still staring blankly at the jar. He looked at the swirling mass inside.

'Will somebody please explain now?'

The two sisters looked at each other. 'You or me?' said Sybil.

'I'll do it, I'll be more succinct. You tend to waffle, dear. Well,' she started. 'I suppose you've heard about Hannah?' She looked at him raising an eyebrow. William nodded. 'Hannah was accused of being a witch by a local farmer.'

He nodded impatiently. 'Yes, yes. I know that, Kitty told me.'

'It was Robert who paid the white witch to get rid of her.'

William stared at Queenie. 'That was my grandfather?' He looked across at Kitty. 'You didn't tell me it was him.'

'We didn't know then, Sybil told us yesterday.'

William rubbed his chin. 'Go on,' he said.

'Robert spread a lot of nasty tales about her, killing animals, blighting crops that sort of thing. Now whether he killed her or the white witch did, nobody really knows for certain but for myself I think he did it. But the man, Evans I think his name was, was paid one hundred pounds, which was a lot of money in those days. Anyway, to cut a long story short, Kitty's great grandmother Ava worked for Robert when she was young girl and she was friends with Hannah. At the inquest Ava testified that she had seen Robert threatening to kill Hannah but her evidence was discounted. It seems the whole matter was hushed up; Hannah's death was put down as water on the brain. Robert never forgot or forgave Ava for standing up in court and denouncing him and Robert's spirit took exception to Ava's descendant returning to live on his land.' Queenie looked at him calmly. 'And you saw for yourself how he felt about it.'

William still looked confused. 'Is this why you were asking all those questions about Hannah and Samuel?'

Kitty nodded.

'Oh.' He stared at his hands clenched on the table. 'And you think Hannah was murdered?' he asked the three women.

'I know this has been a shock William.' Sybil leant towards him in concern. 'But the circumstances surrounding her death were very strange.'

'Yes,' interrupted Kitty. 'Her body was found hanging over a branch of a tree, and there was blood inside the cottage. In the account we found it was believed that she was killed by the devil himself.'

'By the devil himself,' he repeated quietly to himself, looking blankly at the wall.

Sybil gently took his hand. 'Now, nobody is saying that Robert was the devil. Ah Gordon,' she said, looking towards the door. 'That's well timed; I think that William could do with a stiff drink.'

Gordon came in with a tray of glasses and a full bottle of whiskey. He looked at William's pale face and poured a tumbler full of whiskey and put in front of him.

'There you go. Now,' he said, turning to Sybil. 'No sherry, I'm afraid. It's going to have to be this.' He filled four glasses and handed them out. He lifted his glass. 'And thank goodness that's over with.'

'Indeed,' agreed William, sipping his whiskey. He coughed slightly. 'I'm not used to drinking whiskey.' He took another gulp. 'But this is going down well.'

Queenie drained her glass in one gulp and waved the empty glass at Gordon.

'Nice, could do with a bit more though, Gordon.'

Kitty was nursing her glass in clasped hands and staring blankly at the wall. Gordon looked across at her anxiously and put his hand on her shoulder. He squeezed it, 'Are you feeling okay?'

She didn't answer but suddenly leant forward and chinked her glass against the jar.

'Up yours, Robert!' she said firmly. She looked up and met Queenies quizzical gaze. 'Well?' she asked defiantly.

There was a stunned silence for a while until the two sisters started laughing.

'I'll agree with that,' said Gordon grinning slightly. They started laughing and all raised their glasses in the toast.

Gordon knelt down next to her and put his arms around her. 'Thank God that's all over; I've been so worried about you.'

She didn't answer, just put her arms around his neck and rested her head against his shoulder.

'A witch though! How ridiculous,' said William, after awhile.

Gordon straightened up and gave Kitty a kiss on the top of her head. 'Yes and apparently she could turn herself into a hare!' he said with smile.

'Now that is ridiculous,' agreed Queenie, taking another sip of her whiskey. 'A hare of all things, in the country as well. Is it jugged hare or jugged rabbit that they are so fond of around here?' she asked her sister.

Sybil thought for a while. 'Both, I think,' she said rather muzzily. Her cheeks had gone a delicate shade of pink.

'Are you alright Sybil?' asked Queenie, grinning.

'I'm not used to whiskey you know. Nice bit of meat on a hare,' she continued. 'Makes a good pie. She wouldn't turn herself in to a hare.' Her eyes were slightly out of focus and Queenie prudently took the glass away from her.

'I think you've had enough, Sybil.'

Gordon thoughtfully stared at Queenie while toying with his glass.

'Why didn't he just arrange an 'accident' instead of trumping up anything as ridiculous as that, accusing her of witchcraft of all things!' Queenie glanced across the table at Sybil who was staring blearily at him.

'Well... what do *you* call a witch? Black pointy hat and broomstick?' He stared at her and smiled but his smile faded when he saw the serious expression on Queenie's face.

'What?' he asked flatly.

'It's difficult to explain but Hannah had certain abilities, shall we say, and she used this power to heal and her knowledge of herbs was well, amazing. Some people would view this as witchcraft I suppose.' Queenie looked Gordon sternly in the eye. 'She was a good woman and never harmed anybody and until Robert started all this fuss it was never a problem, they were grateful enough when they needed her.'

'I think they just turned a blind eye. I say Gordon do you think I could have a coffee, that whiskey has gone straight to my head,' asked Sybil.

'Yes of course.' He seemed confused for a minute, gathered his thoughts and got up slowly from the table. 'So you mean after all this,' he said indignantly. 'She *was* a bloody witch?'

'Gordon!' exclaimed Sybil in distress. 'She looked after so many people in the village and beyond, they used to come from miles around to get her advice. It was a black day when the village lost Hannah, in more ways than one.'

He looked apologetic. 'I'm sorry, I didn't mean that, Sybil. Look I'll just go and make some coffee; I'm having problems thinking straight.' He hesitated and tried to speak calmly, 'I think the milk has gone off so it will have to be black.'

'That will be fine.' She turned to William who had been unusually silent while they talked. 'Do you need a coffee?'

'Oh yes. I think I had better, I'm having problems thinking straight as well.' He frowned to himself and went on slowly, 'Kitty, do you remember you were talking about Samuel's death? How he drowned?' He stared across the table at Queenie. 'Did Robert have a hand in that as well?'

She looked uncomfortable and took another sip of her drink before answering.

'Oh dear, I'm sorry William, but yes I think he probably did.'

He sat back in his chair and closed his eyes for a minute. 'No wonder father never said anything about his death, mother never mentioned it either, the bastard,' he added feelingly. 'His own brother. What a monster.'

'I wonder why he was like that?' mused Kitty. 'What made him become so ...well,' she hesitated.

'Evil?' added William.

'Sorry, but yes.'

He shook his head. 'Bad blood, but there was nobody else in the family like that, so why he would turn out like it... strange,' he mused sadly.

Gordon returned with a tray of coffee. 'I've made coffee for everybody,' he said. 'And I found some biscuits as well.' He placed the tray on the table and glanced around the table. 'You're all looking very glum, what have I missed?'

'We were discussing Samuel,' said Kitty.

'Oh,' he said thoughtfully, and looked across at William. 'I'm sorry.'

He looked up. 'That's alright Gordon, but I just never knew about any of this.' He stared at the jar on the table. 'And what are we going to do with that?'

Queenie stirred a couple of spoonfuls of sugar into her coffee.

'Well,' she said, staring about the rubbish strewn room. 'I need my bag for that.'

Kitty eventually found it behind the sofa, she handed it over after giving it a vigorous shake.

'Be careful it's covered in little shards of glass.'

Queenie took it carefully and opened it, a shower of window glass scattered over the table. 'Oh dear, look at all this.' She looked around the room. 'I'm afraid your front room is in a bit of a mess.'
The window frame had splintered and was hanging half way into the room, the curtain rail had come down and there were strange scorch marks on the carpet. Gordon looked around at the debris.

'Never mind,' he said slowly. 'It's nothing that can't be fixed, and,' he added brightly 'I didn't like the carpet anyway.' Gordon looked apologetically at Kitty. 'Sorry dear.'

Kitty shrugged. 'Doesn't matter.' She was more interested in watching Queenie pull a bundle of small sticks from her bag. 'What are those for?'

She separated the bundle and pulled out one of the sticks. 'Well.' She held it up. 'This is rowan.' She found another. 'This is holly and this.' She held up one covered in thorns. 'This is bramble.'

'And?'

'They are all very effective in holding evil at bay.' Queenie started spacing the sticks around the jar and tying them on with red thread. 'This will hold him inside the jar.'

Gordon sipped his coffee and watched.

'Don't look like that, Gordon,' she said, without looking up.

'I didn't say anything!' he protested, but carried on. 'What happens if the jar breaks?'

'We're going to put it somewhere really safe.'

'Where exactly?'

'We're going to put him where he should be,' she said firmly, with a wicked glint in her eye.

Sybil nodded. 'I hope the village will be quiet, we don't want anybody watching us.'

Gordon looked at them and winced slightly. 'Oh dear, what have you got in mind?'

'We're going to put the jar into his grave,' Queenie said firmly. She looked at William. 'Any objections?'

'Not from me,' he said quietly.

Kitty sipped her coffee thoughtfully. 'And he'll stay in the jar?'

She nodded. 'Oh yes, he'll stay trapped in there.'

'For all eternity,' added Sybil. 'It doesn't seem like a very nice thing to do to him but...' She looked around. 'I don't think we want to go through this again, do we?'

They nodded in agreement and Gordon reached across the table and squeezed Kitty's hand.

'I wouldn't want you or the girls to have to experience this again.'

'You'll be able to move back into the house and know that everything will be okay,' Queenie smiled at them both and nodded in satisfaction. 'Although you will have to do a few repairs.'

'I can help with that, Gordon.' William held up his hand when he started to protest. 'No, no, I insist, it's the least I can do for you both.' Kitty smiled at him. 'That is so kind of you, and we would be happy for you to help, wouldn't we?' She looked at her husband for confirmation.

'I wouldn't want to lose you as a neighbour, either of you.' William smiled at Kitty as he spoke.

She impulsively got up and went round the table to give him a hug. 'William, if it hadn't been for me moving back in you wouldn't have known about any of this. It must be so upsetting for you.'

William patted her on the back. 'That's alright Kitty, this isn't your fault.'

Queenie looked at her watch 'It's getting late, let's get on with it shall we?' She picked up the twig covered jar and put in her bag. She slung it over her shoulder and helped Sybil to her feet. 'Okay Sybil, sobered up yet?'

'I'm fine,' she protested, straightening her clothes and smoothing her hair carefully. 'I'm just not used to strong alcohol.'

'Me neither,' said William taking her arm. 'Come on dear, we can hold each other up.'

Gordon helped Kitty put her jacket on then patted his pockets.

'Where did I put the keys?'

'The kitchen?'

He headed back into the kitchen and called through a few minutes later. 'Found them, next to the boiler.' He took his coat off the end of the banister and shrugged it on. 'Right, so it's down to the graveyard?' Queenie nodded and opened the front door.

'Do you remember where his grave is?' asked Sybil suddenly. 'Because I can't and I don't fancy wandering around there all night trying to find it.'

Gordon paused in the doorway, looking out into the dark night.

'I have a torch in the garage.' He looked outside. 'And it's pitch black out here now so I think we're going to need it. A dark graveyard isn't my idea of fun you know.' He looked at his wife. 'Does Kitty need to come? Perhaps it would be better if she waited in the car.'

Queenie walked over to his car and opened the back door.

'Stop fussing Gordon, and yes I do know where it is, Sybil, and yes, a torch would be a good idea and a spade if you have one. There,' she sighed. 'Did I answer everybody's question?' She looked around enquiringly. 'Yes? Good. Let's go.'

'Silence!' the Coroner Edward Foulstone shouted, banging his hand on the desk. 'Any more noise and this room will be cleared.'
The angry muttering of the crowd subsided.
'Now I'll ask you again, what did you see on the night of April 9th?'
'Nothing,' said Ava. 'But I knowed he did it.' She stared at the rigid form of Robert Beamish sat on the benches near the front of the room.
Ava pointed at him, trembling, and shouted, 'He murdered her! I know he did. I saw him threatening Hannah before. Sir,' she pleaded.' You've got to believe me.' Ava turned to look appealingly at the people in the room, picking out the familiar faces in the crowd. 'We all know he did it, he's a bad man, Sir.' She wiped the tears that were trickling down her face with her sleeve and stared at the Coroner.
He was staring at the papers on his desk and fiddling nervously with his watch chain, he cast a desperate look at Beamish sitting just in front of him, who stared quietly back at him, a slight smile on his lips.
'Sir,' he said quietly, stroking the head of his walking stick. 'If I may point out that she is just an ignorant farm girl, young and foolish. I tried to discourage her friendship with the woman, who I believed to be a bad influence.' He paused and glanced across at Ava. 'And it seems that I was right. She is naturally upset that the woman died in this way and has become overwrought and judging by this outburst, hysterical.'
'Indeed,' said the Coroner. He stared first at his paperwork and then glanced back at Ava. 'You are very young and your emotions have made you lose any sense that you, I hope, previously had. Mr Beamish is a respected member of the community and to suggest that he would have had anything to do with this is ridiculous, and,' he carried on warming to his theme. 'You are fortunate that Mr Beamish has decided not to sue you for slander. Now...' he went on, staring at Ava's parents. But Ava jumped to her feet interrupting any further comments that he was about to make and shouted across the courtroom. 'He murdered Hannah and he murdered his brother as well, we all know it.' And she pointed at the Coroner. 'And you know it as well.'
'That's enough!' Foulstone's face flushed and he glared at the young girl and then around the room, quelling the mutterings with his stare. 'Your testimony will be discounted; any more outbursts and you will be taken downstairs to the cells. It is clear to me, with my medical experience,' he continued, glancing quickly at Beamish, 'that the woman Hannah Beamish died of water on the brain....'

The rest of his words were drowned by the groans and shouts from the onlookers. Beamish smiled slightly and stood up from the bench and walked quietly through the hostile crowd to the door. Ava could hear, even over the noise from the court room, the sound of his footsteps descending the stone steps to the street below.

****

'Beamish wait!' Edward Foulstone hurried after the figure striding up the street. 'Wait,' he repeated.
He turned around. 'Well Edward, a good result don't you think?'
Edward stared at him in dislike. 'This is the last favour I will do for you. I cannot and will not be a party to any more of this; I have my reputation to think of.' His face twitched as he said this, hardly able to meet Beamish's eye.
Beamish stared at him coldly.
 'Keep your voice down Edward; we wouldn't want any of this to come out would we? And you should think of your poor sister, an unmarried woman with a baby, that wouldn't do your family's reputation any good either, would it?' He looked him up and down 'So protesting now is a bit late isn't it?' He pushed his face into Edward's and said softly, 'So I think you had just better keep quiet and we'll just jog along as we have been doing. After all we're nearly family now.' Beamish slapped the man on the arm and left him standing on the pavement outside the court house.
He strode up the street ignoring the hard looks directed his way from the people milling about in the market square and headed back towards the Inn where he had left his horse.
Just in front of him and walking slowly surrounded by her family was the young girl Ava. She heard his footsteps close behind and moved closer to her father.
 'You, Ava!'
The family turned to meet his furious gaze.
 'You brat, how dare you tell such lies in court, showing me up in front of the town and Foulstone,' he raged at her.
 'Twas the truth,' she said boldly. 'And you know it, we all know it.' Beamish's face became mottled with rage. 'She was an evil old harridan and you're just as bad, you little bitch,' he shouted at her.
 'Now that's enough,' put in her father, stepping in front of Ava. 'You've no right to talk to her like that.'

'Right! Right! I'll tell you what rights I've got, you and your blasted family.' He pointed his stick at Ava. *'I'm warning you now, Ava Marsh, if you or yours ever set foot on my soil again, the devil take you! And that's a promise. It will be the worse for you! Do you hear me girl?'*

Gordon switched on the torch and led the way up the church path, past the porch and round behind the church where the majority of the graves were. It was very dark behind the building, a dog barked in one of the houses and they could just hear the sound of music coming from the pub.
Kitty shivered and stayed close to Gordon. 'I don't know why I'm worried, after all what could be worse than Robert?' she whispered.
　'Not a lot. Where is it?' he asked Queenie.
　'It's over there,' she said, gesturing towards the hedge.
They wound their way through the gravestones following the wavering light from Gordon's torch and stumbling over half sunken kerb stones hidden in the grass. The dog barked again and in the distance a door slammed.
　'I hope nobody's going to see us,' said Kitty, glancing nervously towards the village.
　'Nobody will notice us up here,' reassured Sybil.
　William was walking closely by her side with a hand on her shoulder.
　'I hope not,' he added. 'I haven't been up here for years,' he said quietly.
　'Don't you have anybody buried here?' whispered Kitty.
　'My wife is buried in Colyton; that was where she was born.'
Queenie slowed and tugged at Gordon's jacket. 'Stop,' she whispered, and pointed to the right. 'Over here,' she added, 'and be careful you don't trip on the stones.'
They followed single file after Queenie who had stopped by a neglected grave near the hedge. The headstone had toppled over to one side and the writing was nearly illegible from weathering and the grey lichen that had grown on the stone. 'Here he is,' she said quietly. Gordon knelt down on the grass and read the inscription.
　'Robert Beamish Died October 31st 1910. Is that all?' he asked surprised. 'It's not much of an epitaph, is it?'
William snorted. 'What else could we have said about him?'
Gordon stood up, wiping the damp grass from his knees. 'Sorry William, I didn't mean to be rude.'
Kitty glanced around the graves nearby. 'Where is his wife buried?'
　'His first wife was buried in Axminster and his second, my grandmother, is buried over there.' William pointed back to the path. 'Father didn't want them together.'
　'I didn't know he was married twice,' Kitty said curiously.
The sound of a zip opening behind her made her jump.

Queenie pulled out the jam jar from her bag. 'Now who's got the spade?'

'I have,' said William. 'Where do you want me to dig?'

'Just in front of the headstone will do, I expect the ground is going to be really hard but get as deep as you can.'

There was grunt as William put the spade into the turf.

'You're right, it's as hard as rock.'

Gordon handed the torch to Kitty. 'William, let me try,' he said and held out his hand for the spade.

'Okay,' he said ruefully. 'You have a go; you're a bit younger than I am.'

He stepped back and watched as Gordon began to dig a small hole in front of the headstone.

Kitty kept the torch trained on the hole. The sound of the spade hitting the ground seemed to travel far in the night air and she glanced back towards the village, expecting at any moment to see a curious person coming to investigate the noise.

'Kitty, keep the torch still,' hissed Gordon. 'I can't see what I'm doing.'

'Sorry.' She gripped it firmly and pointed it towards Gordon struggling to dig into the hard packed soil.

He straightened after a few minutes, panting and wiping the sweat off of his forehead.

'Is this deep enough?'

Queenie peered forward in the dark. 'I can't see, how far have you gone down?'

He knelt on the grass and pushed his hand into the hole. 'It's about ten inches deep.' Gordon looked up at her. 'That's about as far as I can get, it's too hard and rocky here.'

She patted him on the shoulder. 'That should do.' Queenie held out the jar to William. 'I think you should be the one to put it in.'

He nodded and took it carefully from her hand and bent stiffly over the hole. She held his arm to steady him as he placed it in.

'Do we need to say anything?' William asked.

'Let Gordon put the soil back first.'

William straightened, moved back to Sybil's side and watched as Gordon refilled the hole.

'It's going to show where I've disturbed the soil,' Gordon sounded worried and glanced up at the two sisters. 'Somebody is going to notice all this fresh earth.'

'Nobody comes over this side of the graveyard, so don't worry.'

'I'll come up tomorrow and disguise it,' added Sybil. 'I'll put some flowers on top of it or something, and Arnold isn't due to cut the grass for another week.'

Gordon carried on reassured. 'Okay if you're sure, now what?' he asked Queenie, who was opening her bag again.

She handed him a bundle of short sticks. 'I want you to push these in around the hole and get them in as far as possible.'

Kitty peered over her husband's arm and directed the torch beam at his hands.

'What are they?'

'Rowan, holly, bramble, the same as the sticks I put around the jar. They are all magical protective trees which will hold his spirit in the grave and prevent it from wandering.'

'Couldn't his spirit have just been sent on to where he should be?' Kitty hesitated. 'It just seems a bit cruel to trap him in there forever.'

'Are you feeling sorry for him?' asked Sybil acidly. 'Because we don't, he deserves this.'

Queenie put her hand on her sister's arm. 'Now Sybil, don't be like that,' she said calmly and looked across the grave at Kitty in the dim light. 'You see, I'm afraid our sympathies lie with Hannah, not Robert. Kitty nodded. 'I know but,' she hesitated and stared at them, their faces were unusually grim. 'I'm sure you know best,' she finished lamely.

'Well, I for one agree with the girls,' Gordon said firmly, hefting the spade in his hand. 'Is that it? I've pushed the sticks in.'

Queenie peered at the filled hole. 'Push them down a bit farther, until they are level with the ground. I don't want anybody spotting them and pulling them all up,' she instructed.

Gordon tapped them down gently with the flat of the spade.

'That's better, now.' Queenie stood over the grave of Robert Beamish and breathed deeply and extended her hands slowly over the grave. All around the grave yard the sounds of the night grew still, even the soft breeze dropped, it became so quiet that Kitty could hear the blood pounding in her ears.

Queenie began to quietly speak, the torch light casting strange shadows across her face. 'When the witching hour rings true, and the moon is burning bright above,

Let mine will be done this night. Answer now my Pagan spell. Lend thy power to these words, Protect us and banish his spirit, and let evil be no more.'

Kitty watched, a chill in her heart as Queenie imprisoned the spirit of Robert in his grave forever.

Her words hung in the breeze for a while and then slowly all around them the usual night time noises started in the hedges and fields and an owl hooted in the trees. They all shifted and looked at Queenie.

She sighed. 'Well that should do it,' and stared down at the grave for a minute, only turning away when Sybil spoke.

'A cup of tea now, don't you think?' Sybil put her hand on William's arm making him jump.

He dragged his eyes away from Queenie. 'What? Oh yes, a cup of tea, that would be nice.' He glanced doubtfully across the grave at her sister. 'I think it's time we got out of here.'

'Yes, let's go,' Gordon said shakily, and took Kitty's arm. They walked carefully back to the path skirting around the gravestones. A light autumnal mist had risen and swirled around their feet.

'Careful where you're walking,' warned Gordon. He paused and stared back at Queenie who was still staring down at the grave. 'Coming?'

She looked up blankly before replying, 'Yes, yes, I'm right behind you.' Giving the grave one last look she turned and followed her sister back to the path.

To their left the church still stood dark and quiet, a light wind whistling around the tower, rattling the rope on the flag pole. A slight noise came from the front porch and they paused, looking nervously into the dark space in front of the church. Out from the shadows strolled the grey cat.

Kitty sighed in relief, bent down and picked it up, welcoming the warmth of its fur.

'Hello puss,' she said. 'What are you doing wandering around a dark churchyard?'

'It's probably thinking the same about you Kitty,' whispered Gordon. 'Come on let's go, I have had enough fun for one night.'

Behind them they could hear the voices of the two women close behind.

'Have you got any cake Sybil? I am feeling a bit peckish.'

'Rose brought me a fruitcake yesterday, so we can have that.'

'Oh dear, well I hope it's better than her sponges,' she said acidly.

****

Sybil unlocked her front door and pushed it open.

'Come in, William can you put the fire on? My feet are so cold and wet from that grass.' She bustled about switching on the lamps around the room and pulling out chairs for everybody. 'Now, tea everybody?' she asked.

'Tea would be great, Sybil.'

'Would you like some help?' offered Kitty, putting the cat down near the hearth.

'No, no, dear. You sit down and relax for a while, you've had a long night,' she replied before disappearing into the small kitchen at the back of the house.

William knelt in front of the gas fire and fiddled with the ignition switch. 'Now, let's see if I can get this thing to work.' There were a few clicks and the flames flared up and started to leap up over the false coals. 'There, lovely,' he said, and looked sideways at the grey cat who had sat down next to him. 'Well, well, I'm not getting hissed at,' he said and struggled stiffly to his feet. He rested his hand on the mantelpiece and smiled at Kitty. 'Come and sit here Kitty, you look quite done in.' He shifted one of the armchairs closer to the fire, 'There, you'll soon warm up.'

'Thanks William.' She stepped carefully over Nigel and the cat and settled into the chair.

Queenie sat down in the chair opposite and felt in her pockets.

'Anybody seen my cigarettes?' she complained, staring around the room.

William pulled up a chair and sat down next to her, he looked at her questioningly.

'I thought you had given up?'

'Bad night to quit smoking,' she said seriously, and leant back in the chair and sighed. She closed her eyes and a slight frown appeared on her face.

'Are you feeling alright?' asked Kitty.

Queenie was looking very pale and tired and there was big bruise which was turning purple on the side of her face. She opened her eyes and looked over at Kitty and gave a rueful grin.

'Not as young as I used to be, and boy did I feel it tonight!' She sighed and rubbed her forehead. 'Well, that's over with anyway.'

Gordon had sat down at the small dining table and found Queenie's cigarettes hidden beneath a church magazine.

He passed them over and said, 'Here you are, I think you deserve one of these. Just finish it before Sybil gets back otherwise you'll be in trouble again.'

Queenie pulled one out of the packet and lit it, taking a deep pull; she sighed and blew out a puff of smoke. 'That's better.' She offered the packet around. 'Anybody else? No? What about you William, have you given up?'

He looked sheepish. 'I caved into the nagging I'm afraid.'

She grinned and winked at him. 'She's half your size, you know.'

William laughed. 'It doesn't make any difference, she still bullies me.' He shrugged his shoulders at Kitty as she laughed.

'I'm sure Sybil wouldn't call it bullying, it's all for your own good you know,' she said mockingly.

The cat opened her eyes on hearing Kitty laugh, stretched and delicately stepped over the sleeping dog and jumped up into her lap. She gently scratched behind its ears feeling the deep throbbing purr reverberating through her legs.

Sybil tottered in bearing a loaded tray.

'Here, let me take that for you, Sybil.' Gordon stood up and put the tea tray onto the table.

In the middle of the tray sat a very pale flaccid looking fruit cake.

'Well, I have brought in the cake but don't blame me if you get a stomach ache tomorrow, I didn't make it,' she said firmly handing out cups of tea.

William looked at the cake. 'Did Rose make that?' he asked. 'Well,' hesitating for a second, 'I'm sure it's fine.' He took a slice from Sybil and bit into it, ignoring the snort from Queenie and chewed slowly. 'Um, yes I see what you mean,' he said grimacing.

Sybil handed him a plate of biscuits 'Have one of these instead, dear.' Sybil grinned and offered the sliced cake around. 'Cake anybody?'

Her sister grunted in disgust. 'What do you think she does to her cakes to make them taste like that?'

Sybil shrugged and put it back on the table. 'I have no idea. I'll throw it out in the morning, she'll never know.'

Gordon passed over the plate of biscuits to Kitty. 'Would you like one?'

She shook her head. 'No thanks, I'm just thirsty.'

'How are you feeling now dear?' asked Sybil, reaching over and refilling her cup.

Kitty sipped her tea and nodded slowly. 'Okay, considering.' She smiled slightly. 'It's been an interesting night, hasn't it?' Kitty looked across the room at her husband. 'Are you okay?' she asked.

He nodded and smiled reassuringly.

Queenie drained her cup and sighed. 'Well, that was a good night's work.'

'Do you think Hannah will be satisfied with this? I mean is she going to feel that justice has been done, or will she still be haunting us?' asked Gordon, he still looked worried. 'I would like to think that was it.'

Queenie looked up from her contemplation of the cat that was still curled up and purring contentedly on his wife's lap.

'Oh, I think so.'

The two sisters exchanged a strange look and Sybil smiled. 'Definitely happy now.' Her smile became broader as the cat jumped down from Kitty's lap and walked across to William. It fixed him with a stare from its pale coloured eyes then sprang up onto his knee.

'Well I am honoured!' he said quietly, and put out a tentative hand to stroke it.

'I think it's all settled now, don't you think sis?' said Sybil.

'William, if you don't think I'm being nosey,' asked Kitty quietly. 'What happened to his first wife?'

Gordon snorted. 'That is being nosey Kitty.'

'No, no it's okay Kitty, after tonight I don't think I have any secrets from you.' William smiled slightly. 'Rachel, his first wife died trying to give birth to his third child.'

'Third? Oh... of course,' she exclaimed. 'He had two other sons' didn't he?' She turned to Gordon. 'We saw that on the census form. What happened to those two boys?'

'I'm not too sure, all I know is that they left home as soon as they could and nobody heard from them again. Although I'm sure my mother knew something, she kept it very quiet but I think she used to get letters from one of them. She never told grandfather about it, of course,' he said thoughtfully. 'Mother did let it slip once that one of them had gone into the army.'

'And his second wife?' prompted Kitty.

William smiled at the protest that came from Gordon.

'I'm sorry William, you'll have to excuse my wife, she never knows when to stop.'

Queenie laughed. 'Don't take any notice of him Kitty; ask away, I think you have earned the right.'

He sat back and raised his hands. 'Okay,' he laughed. 'Just don't give her your bank account number William, she loves shopping.'

William grinned at Kitty's indignant face. 'Well if you want to know, my gran was born in Medbury, she was the daughter of Rose who

used to work in the dairy at the farm.' He sighed and looked thoughtful. 'Why she married him I'll never know, well actually I do,' he admitted, looking uncomfortable. 'Let's just say that my father was a seven month baby.'
Kitty looked baffled and glanced at Queenie.
 'What?'
Queenie started laughing. 'He used his charms on her, Kitty, and got her into trouble!'
She winked at Kitty as it slowly dawned on her what Queenie meant.
 'Oh, you mean...?'
 'Yes, that's right Kitty,' William said, and gently stroked his hand along the cat's back. 'I suppose he wanted an heir as the two boys had gone. Sad really, two sons and he drove them away.'
Kitty looked at the old man. 'What a way to live, hating everybody and everybody hating you.' She shivered and looked around the room. 'He should be pitied really.'
 'Kitty!' said Sybil.
William turned and looked at his friend sat at the table. 'No Sybil, she's right, my grandfather had everything that he could want, a family, a good farm, a lovely home and he wasn't happy. There's many a man that would have given his right arm to have all that, so what went wrong with him?'
Sybil banged down her cup and glared at the back of his head. 'Huh,' she snorted. 'He was a horrible evil man and I for one am glad that he got his just deserts.'
 'You won't convince my sister that he deserves any pity, you know!' Queenie grimaced. 'I think the worst thing is that if Hannah had been still alive she would have been able to save Rachel and his third son, I wonder if that ever crossed his mind?'
 'Ah but,' said Sybil firmly, 'if she had saved Rachel then he wouldn't have married William's gran and William wouldn't have been born. So there!' she finished triumphantly.
Queenie nodded. 'You are right Sybil, but I think you're getting off the point a bit though.' And she lit another cigarette, staring at her through the smoke.
 'Queenie, not in the house!'

*****

The night air was quite cool, the mist had gone and the sky was clear and full of twinkling stars. Kitty shivered as she waited by the car outside Sybil's cottage. They gathered around her talking in hushed tones, their voices carrying on the night air.

'Are you going to spend the night at the house?' William asked. Gordon hugged Sybil and looked across at the old man. 'No,' he said. 'We'll go back to the guest house tonight and come back in the morning. We will start clearing up then and I'll have to board that window up.' He looked up at the cloudless night sky. 'Doesn't look like rain, thank goodness, so I'm sure it will be okay for tonight.'

William nodded. 'Well make sure you come and get me in the morning and I'll give you a hand,' he added thoughtfully, 'I'm sure there is some wood in one of the sheds that we can use.'

Kitty smiled at him and gave him a hug. 'Thanks William.'

He gave her a kiss on the top of her head and said seriously, 'You're welcome, my dear.' He turned to Sybil. 'I'd better be off, it's getting late. Queenie, will I see you in the morning before you go home?'

She nodded, finishing another cigarette and flicked the glowing butt into the road.

'I'll be off in the afternoon so we will drop in on you sometime in the morning, just to see how you are getting on with the cleaning, not that we are going to help of course.' She grinned as Gordon reached forward and hugged her.

'Thanks for all your help Queenie, and you too, Sybil. I don't know what we would have done without you.'

Queenie gave him a kiss on his cheek. 'We should thank you, especially Kitty.' She reached across and squeezed her hand. 'It gave us a chance to finish this business and put it right, and without you we wouldn't have been able to.' She moved over to William's side and patted him on his arm. 'Sorry that you had to find out about it like this, we tried to keep you out of it, but I'm glad you were there, William. You have been a good friend to us over the years and we appreciate everything that you have ever done for us.' She looked around at her sister. 'Oh dear, this is getting very mawkish, isn't it? I'll shut up now,' she laughed.

Kitty moved slowly over to stand next to Sybil. 'Sybil,' she started diffidently. 'Tomorrow, do you think you could come up to the cross roads with me?'

She looked at Kitty and raised her eyebrows. 'The cross roads? What do you want to go up there for?'

Queenie heard the surprise in her sister's voice and turned away from her conversation with William.

'What was that?' she asked.

'I would like to take some flowers up there and put them on Hannah's grave and I don't know where it is,' she went on quietly. 'It just seems awful that she's up there on her own.'

Kitty felt embarrassed that everybody was staring at her and cast an appealing look at Gordon. 'Don't you think that it would be nice to put some flowers up there for her?'

The two sisters started laughing.

'Oh bless you, Kitty,' said Queenie, putting an arm around her and giving her a hug.

'Hannah's not at the crossroads.'

'But Beamish had her buried up there,' protested Gordon, looking from one sister to the other.

'Yes, and the Vicar helped him do it. But they weren't going to leave her up there. That night, Michael Guppy and the Trevitt boys dug Hannah up and took her body down to the graveyard.'

Kitty sighed and closed her eyes. 'Thank you,' she said, blinking back a few tears. 'Do you know where?'

'Of course we know, dear.' She smiled softly at Kitty. 'They buried her with Samuel and her little baby boy.' She patted Kitty on the arm.

'We'll show you where their grave is tomorrow.'

Kitty wiped her eyes and smiled in relief at her husband who had moved closer to her.

Gordon sighed. 'Nowhere near Robert I hope?'

They both shook their heads.

'Good.' He put an arm around Kitty's shoulder. 'We'll come down tomorrow and visit the grave,' he reassured her. 'And now I think it's time we went, Kitty. I think you have had enough excitement for one day, I know I have.'

He opened the car door for her and helped her into the passenger seat. Gordon paused, his hand on the car door and stared at the two old women standing in the dim light in front of the cottage.

'Would I be right in assuming that you both have the same abilities, as you call it, that Hannah had?'

Queenie looked at him; a strange light flickered for an instant in the depths of her pale coloured eyes and she smiled slightly.

'It runs in the family dear,' they said in unison.

Authors Note

The Lavender Witch is based on the true story of Hannah Henley who lived in the small remote village of Membury in Devon during the early 1800's. She is now the most famous witch in Devon and was rumoured to have killed several people in the surrounding area. Hannah was believed to have been able to change form at will and would regularly be hunted by the local hounds. She angered several of the local farmers in Membury by constantly begging for food and money, when they refused and ill luck came their way Hannah was blamed. One of the wealthier farmers hired a white witch from Chard who spent a month living in the farmhouse trying to get rid of her. At four in the morning on Good Friday 1841 he went to Hannah's cottage and found her body lying over the branch of a tree wound in a sheet. There was blood and glass inside the cottage and her body was also covered in bruises and cuts, looking as though she had been dragged through a window. It was widely rumoured in the village that she had been taken by the devil. Villagers had met her several days previously and noted that she had seemed frightened, stating 'that he was going to come for her'. They assumed in hindsight that she had meant the devil but did she?

One hundred pounds at that time was a lot of money; was it enough to kill for?

The young servant girl who was friends with Hannah would often visit her before her death and the so called witch would give her food; the excellence of her cooking was well known in the village while in another account it stated that despite being poor she was known for keeping a clean and tidy house and was often seen around the village wearing a silk bonnet and clean white pinafore.

Despite the strange manner of her death the inquest found that she had died of water on the brain. There are no full records of the inquest as no coroners records have survived from before 1940 and there is no record of her death.

I would like to thank Prof. Mark Brayshay Hon. Editor of the Devonshire Association for allowing me to quote from the Transactions Volume 14 concerning Hannah, however I have edited it slightly, for the full account visit their website www.devonassoc.org.uk

Other books by Elizabeth Andrews

Illustrated
Faeries and Folklore of the British Isles
Faerie Flora

Fiction

The Psychic Sisters series:
The Lavender Witch
The Cunning Man
The Haunting of Stoke Water
The Doll

Children's Illustrated

The Faeries Tea Party
The Mice of Horsehill Farm series:
Teasel's Present
The Great Storm
The Whale's Tooth

To keep updated with news and future books in the Psychic Sisters Series subscribe to my newsletter. *www.magic-myth-legend.co.uk*
(Scroll to bottom of Home page and you will find the subscribe button)

If you have enjoyed reading this book and would like to share your thoughts with other readers please leave a review.
https://www.amazon.co.uk/dp/B0843QVJFG

Printed in Great Britain
by Amazon